There is an intruder in the woods near King Robert Bruce's camp, but when Sir Thomas MacKelloch comes face-to-face with the interloper, he is shocked to discover his assailant is a *woman*. The fair lady is skilled with a bow and arrow and defiant in her responses. The wary Knight Templar dare not allow her beauty to lower his guard. Irritated by his attraction, he hauls her before his sovereign to expose her nefarious intent.

Outraged Sir Thomas dismissed her claim, Mistress Alesone MacNiven awaits the shock on the arrogant knight's face when he learns that she has told the truth. But it is she who is shocked, and then horrified, as it is revealed that her father, the king's mortal enemy, has betrothed her to a powerful noble, a deal that could jeopardize the king's efforts to unite Scotland. Robert Bruce orders Sir Thomas to escort Alesone to safety. As they embark on a harrowing journey through the Highlands, Alesone tries to ignore her attraction to the intimidating warrior, but as she burns beneath Thomas's kiss she realizes this fearless knight could steal her heart.

Also by Diana Cosby

The Forbidden Series
Forbidden Legacy

The Oath Trilogy
An Oath Sworn
An Oath Broken
An Oath Taken

MacGruder Brothers Series
His Enchantment
His Seduction
His Destiny
His Conquest
His Woman
His Captive

*When I first began writing, while collecting research books on medieval Scotland, I was blessed to "meet" Donella Mackenzie, who owned a bookstore in Scotland. Over the years our friendship has grown, and I thank her for being a part of this amazing journey. You're truly a blessing in my life. *Hugs**

Acknowledgments

My sincere thanks to Cameron John Morrison and Jody Allen, for answering numerous questions about medieval Scotland and England. I would also like to thank The National Trust for Scotland, which acts as guardian of Scotland's magnificent heritage of architectural, scenic and historic treasures. In addition, I am thankful for the immense support from my husband, parents, family, and friends. My deepest wish is that everyone is as blessed when they pursue their dreams.

My sincere thanks to my editor, Esi Sogah; my agent, Holly Root; my production editor, Rebecca Cremonese; and my critique partner, Cindy Nord for helping Thomas and Alesone's story come to life. A huge thanks to the Roving Lunatics (Mary Beth Shortt and Sandra Hughes), Nancy Bessler, and The Wild Writers for their friendship and support over the years!

A very special thanks to Sulay Hernandez for believing in me from the start.

Chapter One

Scotland, late fall, 1307

Wind sharp with the edge of winter battered Alesone MacNiven as she ducked beneath the thick limb of an oak. She scanned the surrounding trees, her body aching with exhaustion after two days of hard travel.

Withered brown leaves scraped across the snow-smeared ground like harbingers of death. She shuddered, damned the images haunting her. Though she hadna seen Comyn's men since last night, his knights hadna given up their search for her.

Fingers trembling, she withdrew the ring from a hidden pocket inside her cape. A snowflake settled upon the ruby embraced by the gold filigree carving of a lion.

"*Give this to King Robert,*" Grisel Bucahn rasped. "*Tell him—*" *A cough wracked her body.*

"*Dinna try to talk,*" *Alesone pleaded to the woman who'd raised her.*

Her beloved mentor placed the ring in Alesone's palm, curled her fingers over the circlet. "Lo-long ago I saved Robert Bruce's life. He said if ever I had need of his assistance, to bring him this ring. 'Tis too late for me, but he will protect you."

"*Grisel—*"

"*Our enemy returns any moment. Go!*"

Tears burning her eyes, Alesone hugged Grisel, slipped the ring into her pocket, and fled.

Sunlight shimmered off the ruby as if to mock her heartbreak. Fingers trembling, Alesone stowed the ring. Aye, the bastards would pay!

After taking a drink, she secured her water pouch, shifted the bow hung on her shoulder, and continued on. Beyond the stand of fir and oak, a field came into view. She kept to the woods. As much as she needed to put distance between herself and her pursuers, 'twas safest to travel beneath cover.

A pain-filled scream sounded nearby.

She ducked behind a clump of bushes.

"Tell us where King Robert is!" a man's rough voice demanded.

Dread ripped through her. *Sir Huwe!*

Another agony-laden scream.

Pulse racing, Alesone looked where the voices had come from, in search of the knights. A distance away stood another stand of fir trees.

Go! 'Twas death to linger.

And if she fled, whoever suffered Sir Huwe's brand of twisted brutality would die like Grisel.

With quiet steps she crept to the trees. Between the breaks in the needled boughs, she caught sight of the burly knight's back.

From her limited view, she couldna see if his detestable friend aided him with whomever he tortured. Little doubt the vermin was near. Like wolves, bad blood traveled in packs.

She withdrew her bow, nocked an arrow, then edged closer.

Another knight, ill-kempt, walked into view.

Her skin crawled with disgust.

With a curse, Sir Huwe hauled the man who lay sprawled on the ground to his feet. "The king is camped nearby; tell us where!"

Blood streaked the prisoner's swollen face. He remained silent.

"Let me kill him," the scrawny man spat. "He is naught but a traitor to Lord Comyn."

Their captor struggled to break free. "King Robert is Scotland's rightful sovereign."

"Rightful sovereign." Sir Huwe grunted. "The Bruce murdered his rival at the church of the Greyfriars to ensure he received the crown." His fingers tightened on the man's garb. "Tell us where he is or die!"

Alesone straightened, stepped into the opening, drew back the bowstring, and aimed. "Leave him."

Sir Huwe's gaze shifted to her. Surprise darkened to recognition. Thick brows narrowed. "You are a fool to dare threaten me."

"Move back," she ordered, praying he didna see her trembling, "and I will allow you to walk away, which is more mercy than you showed Grisel."

With a cold smile, he shoved the wounded man to the ground, strode toward her. "Like you, she deserved none."

Bastard! She released the shaft.

The arrow drove through the knight's heart. On a gasp, Sir Huwe collapsed.

Outrage reddened his accomplice's face. He withdrew his sword, charged.

Her second arrow plunged deep into his chest.

Face ashen, he stumbled back, dropping to the ground with a thud.

After ensuring nay others were in sight, Alesone secured her bow, then hurried to the injured man. "I am a healer." She knelt by his side, tore a strip from her garb, and pressed the cloth against the large gash across his shoulder.

Pain-filled eyes held hers. "You must leave! A contingent of Comyn's troops wait beyond the corrie. I was on my way back to warn..." The stranger's face paled.

"King Robert. I heard you. Dinna worry," she said as she secured his broken arm. "I am loyal to the Bruce."

His body sagged with relief. "The king must be informed of the threat."

"Aye." She assisted him to his feet. "Can you walk?"

He nodded. "My name is Sir Deargh."

"I am called Alesone." With one last look around, she helped him into the shield of trees.

* * *

Firelight illuminated the powerful sovereign's face, that of a warrior, a man renowned for his tactical expertise. Fighting to steady her nerves, Alesone curtsied before Scotland's king. "'Tis an honor to meet you, Your Grace."

"Rise, Mistress Alesone," Robert Bruce said.

Exhausted, she stood, relieved they'd arrived before the last rays of sunlight faded.

The crackle of the campfire melded with the murmurs of men outside the tent as the king settled in a sturdy but unadorned wooden chair. He motioned for her to sit on a bench paces away. "You saved the life of one of my knights. For that I thank you."

She clenched the ring in her palm. "I am a healer. I did naught but come to the aid of a wounded warrior."

"Which explains your actions in part." He paused. "My knight could have been a criminal."

"A worry I would have considered, Your Grace, had I not heard his attackers demand that he reveal your camp's location. Both men serve Lord Comyn."

Surprise flickered in his eyes, and then his gaze narrowed. "How would you know their allegiance?"

"My loyalties lie with you, Your Grace," she rushed out, aware that with but a word he could name her a traitor and order her hanged.

"From my man's account, I believe your claim." The Bruce rubbed his chin. "You are brave to have faced down two knights alone."

Brave? Nay, furious.

"Tell me, why are you in the forest without protection when Scotland is at war?"

She drew an unsteady breath. "'Tis complicated."

A frown worked his brow, and he leaned back. "I have time."

Against the crackle of the fire, Alesone met the king's eyes, found sincerity, patience, and intellect. Grisel's dying words rolled through her. Though the healer had saved the Bruce, would his pledge given to her those many years ago override Alesone's blood tie to his enemy?

As smoke curled from the flames, she explained how Grisel had taken her in as a child, gave a brief history over the years, and told him how two days earlier she'd returned to her home and found the woman who'd raised her beaten and dying. And how, with her last breath, Grisel had revealed those behind her attack.

Face solemn, the Bruce held her gaze. "What did she do to incite their outrage?"

Tears burned in Alesone's throat as she struggled with the loss, with the knowledge that she'd never again see Grisel. "I found one of your knights wounded and hid him in our hut. Until Comyn's men demanded entry, neither she nor I believed anyone was aware of his presence. Before they broke into her home, she helped your knight slip out through a secret passage. Loyal to you, she stalled the men while your knight escaped." She paused, angled her chin. "Neither will I apologize for killing any of Comyn's men."

"Nor should you." A frown deepened on his brow. "You are alone and on the run?"

"I am."

"You travel to relations?"

"Nay." Alesone damned the waver in her voice.

He arched a brow. "Friends?"

She shook her head. Hand trembling, she held out the ring. "Grisel Bucahn said to bring you this and you would offer me protection."

Recognition flared in the king's eyes, and his hands tightened on the arms of the chair. "God's teeth."

At the emotion in his voice, her own throat tightened. "I will never forget her."

"Nor I," he rasped. "She was a fine woman, one to whom I owed my life." For a moment he studied her, and then gave a curt nod. "I will honor my promise to Grisel and offer you my protection. And your arrival is fortuitous. I am in need of a healer to care for me as well as my men, a position I offer you."

Overwhelmed by his generosity, she nodded. "I thank you. 'Twould please me to serve you, Your Grace."

"'Twill nae be easy," the king cautioned. "Life on campaign is difficult at best."

"I am well aware of the demands necessary and more than prepared for the task. In addition to my knowledge in the use of herbs, I am proficient with a bow and a dagger," she said, proud of her skills, a proficiency that'd saved her life many times.

Satisfaction filled the king's eyes. "Mistress Alesone, 'twould seem we have a bargain."

Dread eroded her happiness. Though he'd offered her a position along with his protection, neither did he know of her own circumstance. Terrified of admitting her bond to his enemy, she refused to allow the truth to be unearthed later and be labeled a spy. "There is one more issue, Sire. I fear when you know of my lineage, you will withdraw your offer."

Shrewd eyes narrowed. "Go on."

"I am...or rather, my mother was..." Bedamned! "Lord Comyn is my father," she breathed, nae wanting the guard at the entrance to hear.

A gust of wind battered the tent.

His mouth tightened, and a tremor slid through her. *Please let him look past my heritage.*

"You said as a newborn you were left with Grisel?"

Shame warmed her cheeks. "Aye. My mother was Lady MacNiven. While her husband was on Crusade, she went to Comyn's bed. Upon learning she was with child, she went to Lord Comyn, admitted that she carried his child, and begged him to aid her. Instead, he cast her out. After she gave birth, she had her personal maid, Burunild MacCheine, bring me to Grisel. Then"—Alesone paused and inhaled, lifting her chin—"preferring death over a lifetime of shame, my mother threw herself from the cliffs. As I grew, my father, along with those in the castle, shunned me. Though I hold a blood tie to Comyn, I swear to you I loathe the very name."

A cinder snapped within the dance of flames.

Face taut, the king exhaled. "My offer for you to serve as my healer remains. But"—the Bruce glanced toward the guard at the door, lowering his voice to a whisper as he turned back to her—"you must swear fealty to me, and never shall you disclose to those loyal to me your father's identity. Nae all who serve me will be so tolerant."

Thankful, she dropped to her knees. "Until my death, Your Grace, I swear my fealty, and I shall keep my blood tie a secret."

The king laid his hand upon her shoulder. "Mistress Alesone, I welcome you."

* * *

The rush of water filled the crisp morning air and a light mist clung above the land as Sir Thomas MacKelloch glanced toward his knights at the river's edge. "While you finish watering your mounts, I will climb the knoll and ensure nay one is about."

His men nodded.

Unless King Robert had moved, they should reach the sovereign's camp by midday. Thomas tugged his fur-lined cape closer and led his bay up the steep incline.

The frozen ground crunched beneath his steps as he searched the shadows where an enemy could hide.

Overhead, gray clouds moving east slowly smothered the sun.

Snow was coming, a storm paltry to the tempest raging within France.

Two months had passed since the Grand Master had secretly dissolved the Knights Templar, a decree Thomas still struggled to accept. In but a breath, the Order—a way of life he loved—had ceased to exist. Few Templars still in France knew of the decision. For the sake of ensuring their treasures were safely removed and hidden, the Templars' dissolution was a secret he and the others within the Brotherhood who had sailed from France must keep.

Thomas clenched the reins as he cursed the arrests of the Knights Templar in France. Charges included claims of heresy, idol worship, sacrilegious acts, and more.

Lies.

Falsehoods spewed by malcontents who'd been cast from the Order.

However despicable the allegations, all within the Brotherhood who'd escaped knew their nefarious origin.

King Philip IV.

Plummeting toward financial disaster, in his desperation to replenish his coffers, France's king had sacrificed the elite warriors who'd protected him over the years.

Thomas jammed his boot into the hard ground and continued up. Naught could change the king's heinous act. Thank God the Grand Master had received warning of the charges, allowing Thomas and many of his fellow Templars to flee.

Still, too many knights remained in France, including the Grand Master. Honorable men falsely defamed. Thomas swallowed hard. Mere weeks had passed since the arrests had begun, and many Templars had been killed. Before 'twas over, many more would die.

A branch cracked beneath his boot.

He cursed, tugged the reins, and pushed on, ready to reach Scotland's king, to wield his blade once again for right.

Fragments of sunlight slipped through the clouds, illuminated the few stubborn leaves clinging to their branches overhead. For a moment, the ice-laden shells danced within the current, the fragile brown shimmers warming to amber. The gust abated, and the leaves hung limp like forgotten promises.

Watching a bloody leaf. With the enemy about, a fine way to get oneself killed.

Thomas tugged his mount forward. As he rounded the next tree, the clouds thickened. Gloom settled upon the forest. With a wary eye, he scanned the ridge above. Once he reached the top, he could—

An arrow hissed past, a finger's width before his heart.

The shaft lodged in a tree to his left.

God's teeth! Thomas clasped the hilt of his sword.

"Withdraw your blade and die!" a lass's voice warned.

Furious, he glared at the slip of a woman emerging from the tree line a short distance away. With her skill, neither had she wanted him dead.

A bird's cry sounded from behind him.

Relief slid through Thomas. His men had heard her, understood trouble was about. Now to keep the lass talking until his warriors seized her. Then, by God, he would have answers. "I am nae a threat."

"Remove your hand from your weapon, state your name and your loyalty."

Bloody damn. Unsure if her fealty was to Comyn or the Bruce, a wrong answer could hold a fatal consequence. "Sir Thomas MacKelloch."

"Release your sword and state your loyalty!"

A hand flashed to his far right, alerting him that his knights had surrounded her and were closing in. "Lass, I am but passing through." Another arrow whipped past, sliced the first straight down the center. He stared at the severed shaft in disbelief. An expert archer, he was proud of his ability and could match her skill, a level of proficiency held by few. Who was this lass? More important, why was she so close to King Robert's encampment? God's teeth, if her intention was to kill the Bruce, with her accuracy she would need but one attempt.

With quiet steps, his knights crept behind her.

"I would be asking for your loyalty as well," Thomas said.

With a panther's grace, the slender archer drew back her bowstring.

His knights lunged.

The woman screamed as Rónán caught her hands and jerked them behind her back. "Release me," she demanded, her legs kicking out with dangerous accuracy.

Rónán held tight.

Aiden retrieved her bow while Cailin made a quick search.

Cailin removed several weapons hidden within her garb, then held up the dagger she'd hidden in her boot. "A *sgian dubh*." He scowled. "The lass is well armed."

Furious at placing himself and potentially his men in danger, Thomas stormed over.

Blond hair tugged free from her braid and whipped against her comely face.

"Who are you?" Thomas demanded.

Bewitching moss-green eyes narrowed.

Though impressed by her daring, he wouldna have his question go unanswered. "Your name."

The woman twisted to free her arm; Rónán held firm.

"Alesone MacNiven."

"Why did you threaten me?"

"I only sought your name and loyalty, 'twas far from a threat."

Thomas grunted. "You have an intriguing way of *asking*. Whom are you loyal to?"

Fear edged her eyes.

A dose of nerves would serve him well. "Tell me, by God, or I will haul you before King Robert and expose your plans to assassinate him."

At his words, her face paled. "Never would I harm Scotland's king."

"You are loyal to the Bruce?"

She nodded. "I am his personal healer and under his protection."

An untruth. He'd received a detailed account on those of importance who traveled with the king. Never was a woman mentioned, certainly not one who was a healer. "Indeed?" Thomas said, his voice ripe with suspicion. "With Scotland at war, I find it odd for the Bruce to allow a lass under his protection to leave camp without a proper guard."

"He doesna know I left," she said, her tone unapologetic. "I needed a few herbs. I was returning when I heard you tramping up the knoll."

Tramping? Bedamned the woman's daring! "'Twould seem a fortuitous day," he drawled. "My men and I are en route to meet with the king. 'Twill be interesting to hear our sovereign's response to your *claim*." Thomas glanced at his friend. "Cailin, how many weapons does she carry?"

"Counting the bow and arrows, eight."

Thomas arched a brow. "Well-armed for a healer gathering herbs."

"'Tis dangerous away from the encampment," she stated, temper sliding into her voice.

"Aye, but nae for a mercenary intent on killing the king."

Her eyes narrowed. "I told you my reason for being in the forest."

"You did, a claim I find of great interest." Thomas caught her wrist, stunned by the shock of desire he felt at the touch. He nodded to Rónán. "I will escort Mistress Alesone, if indeed 'tis her name, to the encampment."

His friend released her and stepped back.

Alesone struggled against Thomas's hold. "I dinna need an escort!"

"What you need is yet to be determined," Thomas warned, nae pleased by the delay, nor by being saddled with this mule-headed woman whom he couldna trust. "If you continue to fight me, you will be tied and carried to camp. How you meet the king is your choice."

Outrage flashed in her eyes. "How dare you treat me with such disrespect, you ill-bred lout! I am nae a criminal."

"A decision I will allow King Robert to make." Though beautiful, this woman promised to be naught but trouble. With a muttered curse, Thomas tugged her with him and headed toward the king's encampment.

Chapter Two

With a muttered curse, Thomas pulled the reckless woman past the camp's outlying tents, her blistering scowl trying his patience.

"Release me!" she hissed.

Thomas shot the lass a warning glare. "Mistress Alesone." He kept his voice level as he strode toward the king's tent. "One doesna shoot arrows at a warrior and then make demands."

Alesone tugged hard to break free from his hold.

Enough. He halted, jerked a thin hemp rope from his pack, and secured her wrists.

She gasped. "W-what are you doing?"

"I believe," he said, his voice dry, "'tis obvious."

Lavender eyes narrowed. "I told you I wouldna try to escape."

"A promise broken by your action moments ago."

"This is ridiculous! One woman surrounded by several knights. I hardly think I present any threat."

He scoffed. "Your skill with the bow, along with the wide array of arms you had concealed upon your person, tends to undermine that argument."

"Your men seized all of my weapons," she said. "And I do not appreciate being brought before the king restrained like a common criminal."

"Continue to argue and you will find yourself tossed over my shoulder with a gag in your mouth."

"An action you would sorely regret."

Thomas resumed walking. "The only thing I regret is that I didna tie you from the start. As for your being freed, once the king has confirmed that you are indeed his healer, you will be released."

Defiance flashed in her eyes. "A moment I shall relish."

Thomas forced a smile. However much she irritated him, the lass was a fighter. She clung to her declaration with the tenacity of a beggar fighting over crumbs.

When they'd entered the encampment, he'd expected her to panic, petition for her release, and admit her claim of being the king's healer a lie spoken out of desperation. Given Scotland's turmoil, reasoning he'd understand.

With the Highlanders' loyalty torn between King Robert and Comyn, the king wouldna be amused by the woman's false claim; less so once he learned of her impressive ability with a bow. The precision of her shots, her confidence, and her daring bespoke highly specific training. Well he knew the time and dedication necessary to gain such skill.

Regardless of her insistence, she was more than just a lass trained in the healing arts. Whoever had sent her believed that with her beauty, none would perceive her as a threat. If nae for her warning shot, he might have made that error himself. It was a blunder he'd make sure she would come to regret.

As they passed several knights training with their blades, her steps slowed. "We are drawing notice."

A hint of nerves tinged her voice, pleasing Thomas. Confident of an impending confession, he glanced over. "Nay doubt roused by your being a stranger."

She leveled her gaze on him. "They know who I am."

"Yet nay one comes to your rescue?" Thomas nodded at several knights he'd recently met at Avalon Castle before turning back to her. "A fact I find odd."

Red crept up her face. "In truth, I arrived but days ago. I have met only a handful of those in accompaniment with the king."

"Indeed?" he said with mock surprise. "Earlier you led me to believe otherwise."

"As if with your treating me as a threat to the king's life you would have believed anything I said?"

Bedamned, her spirit would impress the stoutest man. However, with the danger about, there was naught laudable about her presence or untruths. Somber, he resumed his stride, tugging her along.

"Enough! I came with you to camp with minor resistance. Release me now, and I willna tell our king of your reprehensible behavior."

A slow pounding built in Thomas's head. "Mistress Alesone, you are nae in a position to state conditions."

She set her jaw. "We shall see how smug you are once we meet with the king."

They would. Robert Bruce wouldna allow a woman to join him while on campaign. Except for Lady Katherine Calbraith: a woman so desperate for vengeance that less than two weeks ago she'd made demands of the king. That twisted tale had hurled Thomas's friend and fellow Templar, Stephan MacQuistan, into a forced marriage where in the end, Stephan and Katherine had both found love.

After years of personal torment, Stephan had found happiness, which pleased Thomas.

He glanced at the woman. Regardless of her beauty, intelligence, or the way she made a man ponder more than a lingering glance, he didna seek a lass. Nor did he trust her. She was a fine example of how well treachery could be disguised.

However dangerous, life served wielding his blade for the king and the country held great appeal. Though he'd enjoyed Katherine's wit and daring while he'd stayed at Avalon Castle, neither did he envy Stephan's being sentenced to a wife.

Irritated his thoughts had strayed beyond those of duty, he stopped before the guard, more than ready to relinquish his unwanted prisoner. "Inform the king that Sir Thomas and his men have arrived from Avalon Castle."

"Aye." The fabric making up the entry scraped against the tent as the man disappeared inside.

Thomas glanced over impressed by her steely glare, halfway between outraged queen and one of the fae. "'Tis a surprise you didna plead your case to the guard."

She stared straight ahead with cool disregard. "My words are reserved for our king."

"The lass seems adamant," Aiden stated, his voice edged with concern.

"Or desperate." Thomas dismissed a trickle of unease. "It matters little. In a moment we will have the truth."

The canvas flap opened, and the guard stepped back. "The king will see you."

"I thank you." Thomas hauled her inside. The rich tang of smoke filled the air as he halted several paces before the king. He bowed, the soft thud of his men's boots in his wake. "Your Grace."

The formal greetings to the Bruce sounded behind him.

A frown furrowed the king's brow as his gaze shifted to the woman. "Why is she with you?"

"Sire," Thomas replied, "en route, my men and I captured this assassin near camp."

The king's surprised expression shifted to fury. "Assassin?"

"Aye, Sire." Thomas slanted her a cool look. "She stated her name is Mistress Alesone, and dared claim that she is your healer."

His men dumped the well-made bow, arrows, and quiver, and lethal knives onto the ground before the king.

"Weaponry we relived her of," Thomas said.

He shot to his feet. Face taut, the Bruce stormed over. "Where did you find her?"

"A league from your camp, Your Grace," Thomas replied, astonished that with the king towering over her, Alesone didna flinch.

At her defiance, the king's face reddened.

Neither could Thomas blame the sovereign for his anger. There comes a time when even the finest warrior has the wisdom to show deference.

"What say you, lass, for your daring?" the king growled.

Her mouth tightened.

God's blade, she didna have a whit of sense. Or, more chilling, was she this hardhearted? A good judge of character, Thomas could believe her highly trained from her confidence and skill, but naught about her comportment during the journey had suggested the cold, ruthless woman before him.

Unsure if he was more disgusted with himself for missing the depth of her callousness or ashamed he'd been drawn to her spirit, Thomas glared at her. Under most circumstances, he would feel sorry for the woman receiving the king's wrath. In this case, she deserved whatever punishment the Bruce served.

The sovereign's fierce expression fell upon her wrists, and the anger on his face faded to surprise. "You tied her?"

Confused, Thomas nodded. Had he known the depth of her treachery, he would have run a blade through her and left her for the wolves. "Foolishly, the woman tried to kill me. Much to her regret, she failed. Once caught, Sire, she ignored my warning to nae try to escape and left me little choice."

"Which tells me," King Robert said, his each word weighted, "that she is either foolhardy or very brave." A twinkle flickered in the sovereign's eyes. "Mistress Alesone, is what Sir Thomas states true?"

Stunned by the king's teasing, Thomas stared at the monarch in disbelief. Did he nae understand the gravity of the situation? "Your Grace—"

The Bruce held up his hand. "She will answer me."

The brazen expression on her face melted to a smile. "Sire," she replied with complete innocence, "I sent but a warning shot."

As if accepting her words as truth, the king withdrew his dagger, pressed the blade against the rope at her wrists, slashed.

God's teeth! Thomas caught her freed hands. "Sire, she isna to be trusted."

Without warning, Alesone laughed.

The Bruce joined in, his eyes twinkling with mirth. "Sir Thomas, forgive me. With the demands on campaign, little time exists to have a bit of fun."

Thomas struggled with the king's assertion.

"Furthermore," Robert Bruce continued, "having met you several weeks ago at Avalon Castle and knowing of your penchant for a jest, even if you were the subject of the teasing, I knew you would find amusement in the situation once you learned the truth." Beaming, he nodded to the woman. "She is indeed my healer, whom I trust with my life."

The king's explanation roared through Thomas's mind, but it eroded down to two words. *A jest?* The entire time she'd stated naught but the truth? However stunned to be caught off guard, he wouldna apologize. With the dangerous state of the Highlands, the weapons she carried, her skill as an archer, and Comyn's ruthless determination to kill the Bruce and claim the crown, his conclusions had been logical.

Laughter danced in her eyes. "You can release me."

Thomas let go as if he touched a hot coal.

"And Sir Thomas, had I meant to kill you," she said, "my arrows would have lodged in your heart."

With the accuracy of her shots, the truth. Far from pleased with the situation, neither did he miss the smiles of his men. Why wouldna they find amusement in his being the object of a bit of fun? As the king had pointed out, his enjoyment of antics were well known, along with his ability to take as good as he gave.

Under normal circumstance, he'd laugh at the ruse. Except something about this woman left him on edge. With the limited time he and his men would remain in camp, nor would he ponder thoughts of her further. "Regardless the confusion, Sire, she is safe."

"For that I thank you." The last wisps of humor in King Robert's eyes faded as he faced her. "You willna again take such risks."

"Sire, I needed but a few herbs to restock my supplies, and I am more than able to—"

"Enough!" The king's jaw tightened. "With Comyn's forces in search of us, whatever your weaponry skills, 'tis too dangerous to be outside the encampment alone. You willna do such again. I forbid it!"

Her face paled. "Aye, Your Grace."

Submissive? That Thomas doubted. The hint of frustration in her eyes betrayed her calm, her words offered to defuse the king's ire. Neither was she a fool. However much the lass chafed at the restrictions, she'd obey.

"Mistress Alesone," the Bruce continued as he returned to his chair, "if you need to leave camp in the future, 'twill be under proper guard."

God's teeth, after her foolish risk, how could their sovereign allow her to remain with their force? Thomas cleared his throat. "Sire, within a fortnight we head into battle. A situation far from fostering a safe haven for a *willful* lass."

"I explained the dangers to her upon our initial meeting." The Bruce frowned. "She wouldna be swayed."

Why had the sovereign allowed her a blasted choice? After today's fiasco, he could order her to leave, under escort if necessary, or confine her within one of his recently seized castles. To Thomas, the latter held great appeal. "I beseech you to reconsider, Your Grace. For *her* safety."

Alesone scoffed, "I am far from helpless, and as I explained to our king, neither am I afraid of war."

Furious she'd ignore the risk, or believe herself immune to the danger, Thomas's well-cultivated reply shattered. "Only a fool has no fear."

Her lavender eyes flared with annoyance, inciting him further.

The senseless chit. "You think you understand, but a bard's stories of combat told around the hearth hardly paint the truth. In the haze of battle," Thomas said with cold precision, "the air is wrought with screams of death, the earth stained with blood, and mercy nonexistent." His ire mounting, he stepped closer, determined to sever her belief that she would be unaffected. "Brave men lay mutilated, each breath filled with agony, pleading for an end to their suffering. You are so caught up in your own struggle to live as you wield your blade, you ignore them." He fisted his hands at his sides as the horrific images stained his mind. "Only if you dinna fall victim to an attacker's sword, and once the fighting is over, can you grant those mortally wounded their lethal wish."

Despair flickered on her face, but her eyes remained defiant.

Blast her for pushing him to this point, that she'd dare. "Your words are noble, but—" Thomas noticed the king's interest in their tense interaction. Stunned by his outburst, he bit back the storm of words yearning to burst free. Few could unleash his emotions to such an extreme.

Men, he trusted.

Never a woman.

As their sovereign continued to study him, Thomas silently cursed, too aware of Robert Bruce's affinity for women who defied the norms of society, proven by his dealings with Lady Katherine months before. Regardless of his own belief that this lass should be carted off and left in one of his holdings for her own safety, 'twould seem her boldness had earned the king's favor.

"Mistress Alesone," the king said, "Sir Thomas raises valid concerns about the dangers we face. If you have changed your mind and wish to leave, I will ensure you are escorted to a safe holding."

She shook her head. "Sire, I want to remain."

With a sigh, he nodded. "As you wish."

Outrage burned in Thomas's gut. 'Twas her choice, her life. Her presence here wouldna affect him. Once they'd defeated Comyn he would move on, and this exasperating woman would be forgotten.

The king lifted a goblet on a side table and took a sip. "Sir Thomas, I didna expect your arrival so soon."

"We took a shorter route along the cliffs, Your Grace, and were able to slip past the enemy." He shot Alesone a hard look, wanting her to understand her antics had neither won him over nor earned his praise. "I admit my surprise to learn you have a woman healer." The king must have sent for her, 'twould explain his protectiveness and their familiarity to the point where they could jest. "'Tis always welcome to have those alongside us whom we know."

Tenderness touched the king's expression. "'Tis, but until her arrival a few days before, we had never met. We have a mutual friend, one who saved my life."

A debt paid, a logical explanation for why the Bruce had taken in a stranger versed in the art of healing. Clearly in the short time, a close bond had formed between them. Nae that he approved of the king's offering his trust to her so quickly. With Scotland at war, spies lurked everywhere.

Time would reveal which cloak she wore.

Sir Thomas nodded his acquiescence to the king, but Alesone caught the doubt in his eyes, misgivings she'd expected. Loyal to the Bruce, the knight would ensure his sovereign was safe. A stranger gaining a position close to the king would invite his suspicion.

She appreciated the fierce warrior's concern for their king, but with the knight's tenacity, Alesone dreaded their upcoming confrontation.

There would be one.

From the short time she'd known Sir Thomas she'd discovered he was a man who did naught by halves. Until he and his knights departed, 'twas best to keep her distance.

"You and your men will be tired after your journey," Robert Bruce said, his voice breaking into her thoughts. "We depart at first light. Once we have made camp on the morrow, we will begin discussions of the upcoming attack. Mistress Alesone, take the knights to the tent by the rowan tree."

'Twould seem she would have little reprieve from the daunting knight.

"When you are done," he continued, "return."

"Aye, Your Grace." She turned to Thomas and his men. "Follow me."

Several steps away from their sovereign's tent, Sir Thomas glanced over. "You are fortunate to have the king's protection."

"He is a generous man," she replied, refusing to be baited by the suspicion coating his words.

"Generous, aye, to those he trusts. *Rarely* with strangers."

"Our king explained the reason."

"He explained naught except you have a mutual friend. I find myself curious to learn more."

Alesone nodded to several men as they walked past. "Sir Thomas, I would think a knight would have better things to do than conjure misgivings, however subtly woven, about a woman he has never met."

"Know this," he said in a cold voice. "If I learn that you have deceived our sovereign in any manner, I will deal with you personally."

Alesone tamped down her frustration and glanced at his warriors, noted each watched her with unfeigned interest. With her emotions in turmoil, the loss of Grisel too fresh, the last thing she wished was to argue. "As you, I am loyal to the Bruce. If necessary, I will give my life to protect him."

Thomas studied her for a long moment and then nodded.

Thankful to arrive at their tent, she halted. "Extra blankets to make your pallets are inside. I will ensure food is sent to you posthaste."

"I thank you," Thomas said.

Exhaustion washed over her as she watched the lean, muscled knight, his sandy hair framing intense green eyes that left her unnerved. After being chased several days prior, why wouldna she feel threatened by a man who stared at her as if he could see straight into her soul?

For an unexplainable reason, she found making him understand her and gaining his trust, if only a degree, important. "Throughout my life I have been forced to deal with unforgiving, arrogant men. If you are looking for treachery from me, you willna find it. If you seek a reason to deem me disloyal, you shall fail."

She started toward King Robert's tent, half expecting the intimidating warrior to confront her. When the men's voices of the encampment filled the air, she eased out a relieved breath.

Alesone didna turn, refused to tempt fate, understanding that he watched her and pondered her words. A man like him did naught without reason.

And with his suspicions, God forbid he learned the truth about her father.

Chapter Three

"Sir Thomas?"

The unfamiliar male voice had Thomas reaching for his dagger, then he remembered that he and his men slept in the king's camp. Loosening his grip, he sat. Moonlight spilling through the tent's opening outlined one of the Bruce's guards. "Speak."

"The king requests your presence. He says 'tis urgent."

What in Hades had occurred? Thomas shoved to his feet.

Aiden, his faithful friend and fellow Templar, moved from his bed as the others began to rise. "I will go with you."

"Nay," the runner stated. "His Grace requested Sir Thomas come alone."

Troubled by the possibilities raised by the summons at this late hour, Thomas tugged on his cape then faced his men. "I will brief you upon my return." Preparing for the worst, he stepped into the night.

A gust tossed snowflakes falling within the waxing moon's silvery glow into a shimmering whirl. A wolf's howl echoed in the distance, a lonesome sound against the silence filling the camp.

That the Bruce's warriors still slept ruled out concerns of an imminent attack. Still, with his sovereign's command to speak to him at this late hour, he suspected the reason involved the Brotherhood. God's teeth, what twisted mayhem had King Philip wrought now? Thomas damned France's ruler, and prayed he was mistaken.

At his approach, the king's guard moved back.

With a silent prayer, Thomas shoved aside the flap, stepped inside, then halted.

Paces away Mistress Alesone stood rigid before their sovereign. The thick fabric scraped closed, and she turned. Her face grew ashen.

What in God's name was going on? With her presence, whatever had occurred didna concern the Templars. Relived, Thomas stepped forward, bowed. "I am here as you requested, Sire."

Within the firelight, the king's troubled gaze met his. He waved him closer, then, glanced toward a stocky, blond nobleman at his side. "Lord Kinlock, I thank you for your haste. We will speak further in the morning."

"Aye, Your Grace." Lord Kinlock bowed. He glanced at Alesone, his gaze lingering a moment before shifting to Thomas. Then he departed.

Confused by the stranger's presence, Thomas moved beside Alesone. A spark popped to the frozen ground, flared, and then blackened.

Robert the Bruce clenched the arms of his chair. "Sir Thomas, the Earl of Kinlock has brought troubling news this eve. I informed Mistress Alesone of this prior to your arrival."

That explained her upset appearance as well as the earl's presence.

"Your Grace," she said on a shaky whisper, "I beg of you. There are other alternatives to—"

"'Twill be done as I explained. However much I wish otherwise, we dinna have the luxury of time."

She gave a curt nod.

The monarch's eyes shifted to him. "Sir Thomas, I sent for you and your men to train my knights and support my cause. Now an issue of grave importance has arisen, one I entrust to you."

By the way Alesone had begun to tremble, the reason involved her.

"Time is crucial. I will share essential details, nay more." The Bruce paused. "What I tell you is in the strictest of confidence."

He nodded. "Aye, Your Grace."

"This night I have learned that Mistress Alesone's father has posted an offer of gold for her capture."

Her hands fisted at her side.

Gold? God's teeth, to warrant such ransom, she was far from the common lass he'd believed. More perplexing, with a camp full of trained knights, why would King Robert require the skills of a Templar for the task?

"Your Grace," she rasped. "The details of the situation are irrelevant."

Robert the Bruce scowled. "With the amount of coin your father has offered for your return, my concern is the amount may sway the allegiance of one within my ranks, which I canna allow. Few men are as loyal as Sir Thomas. As he will provide your escort, he must know the truth." The king's gaze shifted to him. "Sir Thomas, Mistress Alesone's father is Lord Comyn."

Through sheer will he kept his face void of shock, but the disclosure reverberated through him with brutal force. The paleness of her skin and the fear in her expression all now made sense. And why wouldna she be shaken? Her father was the Bruce's enemy, the man their forces were preparing to battle.

More unsettling, the king's anger wasna at the blood tie, but at Comyn's offer of ransom, which meant that the Bruce had known her father's identity from the start. Yet he'd allowed her within camp and offered her protection. Unsure if he was more confused or upset, Thomas focused on their sovereign.

"In secret," Bruce continued, "Lord Comyn and King Philip have made an alliance. Upon the marriage of Mistress Alesone to one of France's powerful nobles, King Philip will send gold, men, and arms to support Comyn. A union I canna allow."

"Why does King Philip care about Scotland?" Thomas asked, damning France's ruler with his every breath.

"'Twould seem with his coffers refilled," the Bruce said with disgust, "France's king has decided to expand his power. The marriage of King Philip's daughter to King Edward II gives Phillip a powerful ally to our south. With Scotland's loyalties torn, King Philip intends to take advantage of our weakened state to claim our country as his own."

The merciless bastard. 'Twould seem his destroying the Knights Templar and the treasure stolen from their temple in Paris had nae sated his hunger for wealth and power. However greedy, France's monarch had an elemental problem.

"Sire," Thomas said, "regardless of the marital tie, Edward of Caernarfon holds little interest in seizing Scotland. Any actions that suggest otherwise are due to pressure from his nobles rather than his own desire."

The king nodded. "On that we agree, but caught up in his own provincial agenda, once the wedding is done, with a pledge of unity forged between King Philip and Lord Comyn, I fear there will be little Edward of Caernarfon can do to stop France's king. Further, unless the aggressions affect the young sovereign or his soil, I doubt England's king will care little about Scotland's plight." Grave eyes held his. "Now you understand why I canna allow this match to occur."

Indeed. However much he and the lass didna see eye to eye, he regretted the circumstance that had placed her as a pawn of nobility. Like the Knights Templar, a sacrifice by those in power.

Any concerns of Alesone's loyalty faded. The Bruce having accepted her within his camp, more so in the position as his healer meant she'd earned his trust, a difficult feat to achieve.

"Your Grace..." Her cheeks grew red. "Given my...heritage, 'tis unfathomable France's ruler could possibly accept such an arrangement."

Robert grunted. "Nobles are fickle, more so when gold and power are cast about. With my forces closing in on Comyn's stronghold, your father understands his castle is in danger. He views the alliance as more than a way to keep his home. With a tie to King Philip, the opportunity exists for him to become Scotland's king."

Thomas scoffed. "If Comyn believes King Philip will allow him to rule any portion of Scotland, then he is a fool."

"Aye," Robert Bruce agreed, "but Comyn is desperate. And well we know of the acts of desperate men."

Indeed, 'twas desperation that had King Philip turning on the Knights Templar, men who'd protected him for decades. Earlier this year he'd debased France's currency to a fraction of its worth to increase his revenue, a move that had incited riots.

For his safety, the Brotherhood had offered him safe haven in the Paris Temple. Instead of gratitude, the valuables within had enticed the king to devise a nefarious plan to destroy the Templars and claim their wealth.

A horrendous act that King Robert despised.

Thomas studied his sovereign, still amazed by the fact that Robert the Bruce was a Knight Templar. However unexpected, he was thankful. King Robert's religious exclusion, and the Scottish clergy's refusal to acknowledge his excommunication, had allowed him to offer all Knights Templar entry into his realm with impunity.

These were facts Alesone didna understand, nor ever would.

"Sir Thomas."

He dragged his mind from the smothering outrage of the French king's dealings. He couldna change the past, but by God he would do whatever he must to stop King Philip from claiming Scotland. "Aye, Your Grace."

"You will escort Mistress Alesone to Avalon Castle. Upon your arrival, brief the Earl of Dunsmore on what I explained this night. Inform him that until I send word otherwise, she will remain within his protection." He paused. "Any questions?"

"Nay, Sire."

"Mistress Alesone?" the Bruce asked.

"Nay, Your Grace," she whispered, her eyes filled with a mix of hurt and disbelief.

Thomas fisted his hands. The lass was in shock—nae that he, too, wasna staggered by the news of the past few moments.

With a weary sigh, the king leaned back in his chair. "You will depart immediately. Sir Thomas, your mount is ready along with another for Mistress Alesone." He paused. "Scotland's freedom lies in your hands."

Humbled by the king's trust, Thomas bowed. "Mistress Alesone will be kept safe, that I swear on my life."

* * *

The thrum of hooves filled the late morning air as Alesone galloped beside Sir Thomas. She understood Robert Bruce's decision nae to send a large contingent of knights to protect her. The last thing they needed was to draw the enemy's notice, but she prayed he'd chosen well in giving his trust to this knight. Though fierce, he was but one man.

Her father was a seasoned warrior and a worthy adversary to the Bruce, and now, shamefully, a desperate noble who conspired with France's king.

They rounded another copse of trees, and she searched the breaks in the woods and dense brush for any sign of men hidden in wait.

Naught.

Guilt festered that her presence brought complications to King Robert as he battled to reunite a torn kingdom. Damn her father, a man who hadna recognized her throughout her life, now acknowledged he had a daughter, however illegitimate. And for what, to trade her like cattle for his own gain.

"Halt!" Thomas called.

She reined her mount beside him. "What is it?"

A grimace furrowed his brow as he scoured the thick line of pine, elm, and ash ahead. "Something feels wrong."

A tremor rippled through her as she scanned the forest, and then the cliffs slashed by sunlight in the distance. "I see naught."

"Nor I. Still, we will ride south. By dusk we should come across a burn, which we will follow until we lose daylight. We will continue riding south for several hours, then we will head seaward. If anyone is trying to track us, we should lose them."

She nodded, impressed by his knowledge of the Highlands. "Earlier I caught a touch of a French accent in your voice. Did you grow up here?"

Caution darkened his gaze. "I have traveled the land on occasion."

Far more than a few infrequent trips. Few understood the dangerous cut of the mountains well enough to make such succinct plans without the aid of a map.

A gust swept through the forest thick with the scent of winter. Branches shook and clumps of snow tumbled to the ground. Another burst of wind howled through the trees.

Thomas glanced skyward, frowned. "A storm is moving in."

Angry clouds churned overhead, and she tugged her cape close. The last thing they needed was to become stranded in a blizzard. "We have ridden less than a day. Mayhap 'tis best if we turn back."

"Nay. After we left, the king and his forces departed. With the enemy nearby, 'tis too dangerous to retrace our steps. Come." He kicked his destrier into an easy canter.

After one last glance behind her, with a resigned sigh, Alesone followed.

Against the whip of wind, bare branches rattled overhead as she crested the next knoll.

Suddenly, an arrow whipped past.

Thomas glanced over his shoulder, cursed. "Ride hard!"

Panic swept her as she caught sight of several men charging in her direction. Alesone leaned low and urged her horse into a gallop.

Another arrow hissed by.

Her horse stumbled. "Thomas!"

The fierce knight glanced over. With a curse he hauled her before him as her mount started to fall. "Hang on!" He dug his heels into his steed. Muscles bunched as his destrier jumped a fallen tree, landed with a smooth glide and raced through the forest.

Shouts of their attackers filled the air.

She glanced back, gasped. "There are at least fifteen men!"

Thomas shifted in the saddle. "Blast it!"

Alesone turned, caught the streak of pain on his face before he turned back. "Are you hurt?"

"Hold tight!" Thomas whirled his steed, raced toward a thick stand of fir. Brush slapped their bodies as they pushed through the thick-bristled limbs. Moments later the dense fir gave way.

"Bedamned!" Thomas cursed.

"What is—" Paces ahead the ground fell away. "There's a cliff!"

"Aye." His arm tightened around her. "Hold on!"

Muscles bunched beneath her.

A scream tore from her mouth as his steed jumped.

Air, cold and laced with snow, assaulted her as his warhorse half-slid, half-stumbled down the steep incline. By sheer miracle they reached the bottom without his mount collapsing against the slick surface.

Hooves scraped against ice and rocks as the horse steadied himself. "Good lad." Thomas reined him toward the stand of trees, and then urged him into a gallop.

Miles flew by, the fearlessness of the knight's every decision leaving Alesone stunned. Regardless the danger, the impossibility of the landscape they faced, he never hesitated; choosing numerous paths she never would have considered.

At the top of the next knoll, he drew his mount to a halt, his breathing hard. "'Tis growing too dark to keep up this pace."

Relief swept her. For a crazy moment, she'd believed he would continue riding hard throughout the night. "With the waning light 'twill be difficult for them to track us."

"Aye, and with luck, the continuing snowfall will cover our tracks." He paused. "How do you fare?"

Exhausted and her body aching, she was ready to collapse. "I am fine."

He grunted. "Cold and tired, nay doubt."

She turned, caught the paleness of his face, the fatigue he tried to hide. "As are you."

"We must keep moving," he said.

"Once they canna find our tracks, they should turn back."

"During normal circumstance, aye, but as you are essential to your father's plans, his knights willna stop."

She swallowed hard. The truth. "How much longer will we travel before we rest?"

"There is a monastery a half day's ride from here. We should arrive shortly after nightfall. If anyone is about, the darkness will shield our arrival."

"A monastery? You said we were riding south a few hours before turning toward the sea."

"I have"—he muttered a soft curse, shifted—"decided otherwise."

Surprised by the strain in voice, she glanced back.

His face taut, Sir Thomas kicked his mount into a gallop, forcing her to turn around and hang on. "I thought we were taking it easy."

"We are."

Too tired to argue, Alesone sagged against his muscled chest and let the miles rush past.

Hours later, with the moon edging into the cloud-muted sky, ahead of them lay a large copse of rocks smeared with the fall of snow.

Thomas guided his horse to the center, then drew to a halt.

Another burst of icy wind tore at her cape, slapping loose strands of hair against her face. She shivered against the chill. "Why are you stopping? With the moon bright, 'tis too easy to see us here."

"'Tis. Nor will we remain." With stiff movements, he dismounted. "I will be but a moment, dinna move." Wisps of moonlight slipped through the breaks in the clouds, illuminating the falling snow with an eerie shimmer.

Unease wove through her as Thomas collected and stacked twigs and brush. A fire, was he insane? "We canna."

He shot her a cool look, and then withdrew his dagger and flint. After several strikes, smoke, then flames, crept through the tangle of wood. Moments later, sparks swirled into the sky.

After tossing several larger limbs on top, his movements stiff, the knight returned.

Confused, Alesone frowned. "I thought we were nae going to make camp?"

"'Tis a decoy." Face taut, Thomas swung up behind her and took the reins. "If anyone is nearby, they will see the flames. Your father's knights are battle seasoned. Believing we are resting in the dense firs they willna rush in, but encircle the encampment to prevent our escape before they attack."

"Which buys us time to put more distance between us," she said, impressed by his shrewdness. "You have set up similar decoys before?"

"Aye."

Though swirls of snow, she caught the flicker of light. "What if the wind blows out the fire?"

"Shielded by the rocks, and with the tinder at the base, the flames should continue to build. If the fire dies, our pursuers will find ashes."

The confidence in his voice eased her nerves a bit. "You have fought in many battles?"

"I am a knight," he said, his voice cool.

"That accounts for your proficiency with a blade, but nae your tactical expertise."

A frustrated exhale sounded behind her. "Do you always interrogate the people you meet?"

Though tired, she smiled. "Only the interesting ones."

Ice crunched beneath the horse's hooves as his destrier picked his way through the litter of rock and snow down the incline.

At her protector's silence, she glanced back.

In the cloud smeared moonlight his gaze held hers.

At the intensity, a shiver swept through her. From their less than cordial start, she'd doubted they'd ever come to a point where she'd look at him as other than a man to avoid. Yet something about Thomas drew her.

Drew her?

An understatement. In truth, from the way his eyes held hers, his direct manner, and how he moved with predatory stealth, left tingles of awareness sliding through her body. He was unlike any man she'd ever met.

Thrown off balance by the feelings he evoked, she shifted to a safer topic. "I want to apologize."

"You have done naught to apologize for."

"I have. Although you were praised by our king, I doubted you."

"Lass," he said, fatigue weighing heavy in his voice, "your belief in me is irrelevant. Once you are safely delivered, never will we see each other again."

She stiffened, hurt that he could dismiss her with such ease when thoughts of him lingered on her mind. Why? 'Twas nae as if she wanted him to stay. Still, a foolish part of her needed to know. "And when you ride off will you forget me?" she teased.

He grunted. "Anyone who drives an arrow a finger's width from my heart I remember."

She smiled at the reminder. "That is all?" Why was she pressing him? Regardless of how he made her feel, their time together would soon be over, and he'd ride away. In the end, he'd be naught but a vague memory. In truth, this warrior she would remember. A woman didna forget a man like him.

"I would think a woman of your beauty," Thomas said, interrupting her musings, "wouldna need to rummage for compliments."

"You think I am beautiful?" Warmth swept her cheeks as she stared at him. "Never mind."

He chuckled. "If your private banter with the Bruce is anything like what we are sharing, I understand why he finds you intriguing."

At the mention of their sovereign, memories of Grisel swept over her along with her reason for fleeing southward. The lightheartedness faded. "'Tis loyalty that binds us," she said, smothering the heartache. "How did you come to know the king?"

"A common friend."

Alesone frowned. "You have a penchant for vague replies."

"And you have a penchant for prying into people's lives."

She leaned back against his muscled chest. "'Tis nae prying, only curiosity."

"Are you this inquisitive with everyone you meet?"

"Nay," she said, intrigued by the fact that something about this man threw her off balance. She'd believed him a simple knight when they'd first met, but by the king's faith in him, and judging by his split-second decisions, cunning, and determination, he was much more. Neither was he cold or hard. *Intense* was a better choice, driven to serve those who'd earned his loyalty, and ferocious to those he protected. "'Tis that you are unlike anyone I have ever met before."

A rock clattered beneath his mount's hooves and the horse shifted. Thomas swayed in the saddle, righted himself, and then guided his mount between two oaks. "I am unsure if that is a compliment...or nae."

She chuckled. "Now who is seeking flattery?"

"I seek naught more than to serve my king. Never forget that." The coolness of his tone matched the rush of air that howled past.

Grief settled in her heart. Nay, she wouldna forget, a fact he would ensure. How had she thought him neither cold nor hard; he was both and more. The day when they parted couldna come soon enough.

He guided his steed down the shallow incline. "Here." He held out a piece of bread.

"My thanks." Alesone ate, noting the snow on the ground reflected enough light to travel.

"Once you finish, try to sleep. I will wake you upon our arrival."

She wanted to argue 'twas unfair that she rested while he remained awake, more so when but moments before she'd silently called him cold and hard. With fatigue weighing heavy on her mind and the comfort of his presence, along with the steady sway of the horse's easy gait, she drifted into blackness.

* * *

A horse's snort broke through her sleep. With a frown, Alesone opened her eyes and stared into the darkness, the slow, steady steps of the horse assuring her they continued to travel, except somewhere along the way Thomas had slowed their pace to almost a crawl.

Thankful for the warmth of his body against hers, with a yawn she glanced up. Shimmers of purple light warmed the eastern sky, and explained why her muscles ached. They'd traveled throughout the night.

Odd, he'd said that they would've arrived at their destination by now. "'Tis almost dawn."

Silence.

"Thomas?"

"A-aye," he stammered, "we will be halting soon."

At his rough voice, guilt swept her. After the long hours they'd ridden, he was tired.

He guided his mount into a thick swath of fir and drew to a halt. His entire body trembled. "We w-will rest here."

Confused, she turned. The first rays of light exposed the paleness of his face. "Sir Thomas?"

With the reins fisted in his hand, he dismounted then stumbled forward.

"Sir Thomas, wh—"

"Dismount!"

Panic twisting in her gut, Alesone slipped to the ground.

Face ashen, the knight wavered on his feet, stumbled, and then caught himself on a nearby tree.

Her gaze riveted on the blood smeared across his left shoulder. "You are injured!" Furious that he'd hid the fact, that she'd missed signs of his weakening condition, she stormed over. "Let me look at the wound."

The knight's pain-filled gaze cut to her. "It can…" He gasped. "It can wait until we arrive at our destination."

"Is that why you are bracing yourself against the tree and struggling for each breath?"

Silence.

Disgusted, Alesone jerked the reins from his hand, then secured the horse to a branch.

Agony streaked his face as Thomas stepped toward his mount.

She blocked him.

Teeth clenched, he glared at her. "W-What are you doing?"

Alesone pointed at the log behind him. "Sit down."

Green eyes narrowed.

"Now."

The pig-headed dolt. Add stubborn to his list of his irritating traits. Careful to avoid his wound, she caught his shoulders and all but shoved him onto the fallen log. "Why didna you tell me you were injured when we halted before?" she demanded as she carefully removed his cape.

"T-too dangerous."

She glared at him, noting the sweat on his brown. "Only a fool would ignore an injury of this severity."

"The arrow went through," he rasped. "There was naught to remove."

"And you have been bleeding ever since." If he wasna in so much pain, she'd shake him. With a jerk, she tore strips from her chemise. Once she'd cleaned the wound, she pressed a fresh wad of cloth against the gash and then secured the bandage.

His body began to sag.

She caught him.

Barely.

On a groan, his eyes closed.

Bedamned, he was going to pass out! Without shelter, if they remained here they'd freeze. A fact he had to know, a sacrifice he was willing to make to bring her to safety.

Unsure if she was more humbled or furious, Alesone glared at him. "How much farther to the monastery?"

"C-close."

Thank God. She moved behind him, slid her arms under his. "Push to your feet."

Mouth set, he started to rise. His legs trembled, and he collapsed.

Smothering her panic, she caught him. "You must help me get you on the horse."

Eyes blurred with pain, he shook his head. "L-leave me." He braced his hands against the fallen log. "Continue riding south. You will reach a monastery. Ask for...ask for Brother Nicholai MacDaniell."

"Who is he?"

"A friend." He struggled to keep his eyes open. "Tell him..." He started to collapse.

Muscles rebelling, she propped her body against his. If he fell to the ground, Alesone doubted she'd be able to haul him back up.

Heart pounding, she scanned the unfamiliar forest. If she left him here, how could she ever find her way back, or give his friend directions? With the amount of blood Thomas had lost, she couldna risk a delay.

Aye, she'd ride to the monastery, but by God he was coming with her.

Cold gulps of air burned her lungs as she hauled him to his horse's side. Bedamned, how was she to get him up?

He started to lean to the left, and she pushed him upright.

She glanced at the fallen log he'd sat on moments before, then moved him, along with his destrier, to the stand at the edge of the trunk. "Thomas, you must help me get you on the horse."

A groggy murmur stumbled from his mouth.

"Climb on the fallen tree."

His head gave a shaky nod.

She caught his hand and laid it over the saddle. Through sheer will, she aided him onto the log. "Mount, damn you!"

His body began to teeter.

She shoved.

Thomas slumped into the saddle.

Tears of relief filled her eyes. She swung up behind him and held him tight. With a prayer, Alesone kicked his steed toward the south. If she didna find the monastery soon, he would die.

Chapter Four

Holding Thomas before her as he lay slumped in the saddle, Alesone guided his mount down the steep incline. The sharp tang of pine filled her each breath as she scoured the curtain of snow, making out naught but several trees nearby. With her sense of direction lost in the swirl of flakes, had she traveled in the wrong direction?

Where was the blasted monastery?

The horse edged around a clump of fir, and Thomas's limp frame rocked against her.

On edge, she pressed her fingers against his neck.

A low, steady pulse thrummed.

'Twas weak, but he still lived. Cursing the miserable weather, she narrowed her eyes against the fall of white, struggling to make out any sign of culled stone.

As the destrier crested the rise, she caught the faint scent of smoke.

"Whoa." Through the whip of flakes, Alesone strained to catch a shimmer of light, the outline of a building, anything to guide her.

Naught.

A gust howled past.

Icy shards buffeted them, and she tucked her cape tighter around Thomas. With the amount of blood he'd lost, if they didna find shelter soon he would…

Nay! After Grisel, she couldna lose Thomas as well. However extraordinary their first meeting, the warrior's actions were given to protect his king.

Like magic, the clouds overhead thinned. Within the sun's rays, the snow tossed about with mayhem moments before spiraled earthward like fairy dust.

The tang of smoke again slipped past.

On a relieved exhale, Alesone urged the horse down the steep terrain. They broke through a stand of fir, and the smell grew stronger. She dug her heels into the animal's flanks, the thud of hooves upon snow a potent reminder of the knight's life slipping away.

At the end of the field, a line of oak and ash arched skyward as if to bar her path. Refusing to give up, she guided her mount into the shadows, and then wove through the tree-laden maze. Without warning, the thick swath of trees fell away.

Far below, framed within a snowy blanket of white, smoke swirled from the chimney of a stone hut. It wasna the monastery, but at least it was a place where they could seek shelter.

She stilled. Was whoever lived below loyal to Bruce or Comyn? Were they kind hearted souls who would help without question? Or men who chose to live alone and wouldna appreciate her presence? With Thomas's declining condition, little choice remained.

By whatever means necessary, whoever lived within would help them. Alesone headed down the slope.

* * *

The fire in the hearth popped with cheerful abandon as a stocky man close to her age, with thick red hair secured in a leather tie walked over. He halted at her side, a bowl of warm water in his hand. "How does he fare?"

"The same," Alesone replied, thankful the stranger, John MacLairish, had nae only welcomed them without hesitation, but had carried Thomas inside and insisted on helping to tend to him.

He set the bowl on the table. "'Tis a nasty wound."

"Aye." She soaked the cloth, surprised and thankful to discover the depth of his healing skills. After wringing out the excess water, she wiped away any lingering dirt, and then threaded the needle. "He has lost a lot of blood."

John grunted. "From the look of the damage where the arrow went through, he is fortunate he didna die."

She smothered the rush of fear, well aware of the severity of Thomas's condition. The next few days would determine if he lived. "He is a strong man." And as determined and mule-headed as any she'd ever met. And loyal as well, a warrior she could trust. Unsure how to deal with the feelings Thomas inspired, she refocused on her task.

"You didna mention his name," John said.

Unease shivered through her. She kept her hand on the needle, and out of view, wrapped her other hand around her dagger. "Thomas."

"Is he from this area?"

Heat touched her cheeks at the reminder of how little she knew about her champion. He'd kept away from any topic that allowed her familiarity. Given the minimal time they would remain together, a situation that wouldna change.

Shame filled her at the personal details of her life that King Robert had disclosed to this stranger, the shared information more humiliating because she knew naught about Thomas. "I dinna know."

Confusion flickered in the man's gaze, and then he shrugged. "It matters little. I thought for a moment he looked familiar, but I could easily be mistaken. Many years have passed since I saw the man I knew, nor would I expect him to be traveling here."

Thankful his question came from naught but curiosity, Alesone released the weapon and returned to her task. With skillful ease, she pressed together the ragged edges of the wound and began to sew.

"'Tis a fine hand you have with a needle."

At the appreciation in her host's voice, she glanced up. "I was taught by a remarkable woman."

"Here, let me help." He pressed Thomas's skin together, and she continued to stich the gash closed. "I am sure she is proud of you."

Her hand trembled, but she steadied herself. "She was." After several more stitches, Alesone secured a knot, and moved to the next injury. A short while later, she stretched to ease the ache of her muscles. "That is the last wound that needs tending." She damned the tremor, aware 'twas driven by exhaustion and worry.

Alesone made a poultice, then cleaned and replaced John's needle and his remaining herbs.

"You are fortunate to have found my home. The storm was a nasty one."

An understatement. "I smelled smoke from your fire. The snow had stopped by the time I reached the craig, and I was able to see your cabin."

"Thank God you did."

Indeed. Nor were they out of danger. Comyn's men still searched for them.

On an unsteady breath she sat and laid her hand on his neck. However weak, the soft flutter of his pulse offered hope. "I pray he will recover." Her hand shook as she set the basket aside.

"Steady, lass. God willing, your man will survive."

Her man? With his firm resolve, she doubted Thomas belonged to anyone but himself. Once he'd delivered her to Avalon Castle he would depart and never think of her again. With so little time together, a part of her, however foolish, would miss him.

"You are traveling through?" John asked, breaking into her musings. At her frown, he smiled. "If you lived nearby, over the years we would have met."

Feeling foolish, she smiled. "Of course. Excuse me, I am tired."

Somber eyes held hers. "Aye, you would be."

"We are headed south." A lie. The stakes were too high to trust a stranger with the truth.

"What are you called?"

"Elyne," she replied, refusing to risk him recognizing her name. Regardless if Robert Bruce had stormed their surrounds a fortnight prior and seized the land, those who lived in this swath of the Highlands may still remain loyal to Comyn. Nor would she chance that her father's men had traveled through, given John her name, and bid him to alert them if he saw her.

After smearing the mix of herbs atop the sewn gashes, she wrapped them with clean strips of cloth. "We are headed toward the monastery." Alesone glanced over. "Is it far?"

He shook his head. "From the next knoll, through the break in the trees, you can see the roof."

A spark popped in the fire, and the red glow swirled skyward within the smoke.

John settled in a nearby chair. "I admit that I disapprove of your husband allowing you to travel in such a storm."

Caught off guard by his comment, she turned. "He isna my husband." At the flicker of interest in his eyes, she silently groaned. The last thing she needed was a man's interest in her, especially a stranger. Nor could she take back her words. "Thomas is my escort."

"Your nae being married doesna excuse his exposing you to such dangerous weather," John said, a touch of anger in his voice. "But I admit I am pleased to learn that you arena wed. Living near the monastery and miles away from the closest village, rarely do I see women, even less often one of such intelligence and beauty."

Unused to compliments, Alesone, fumbled with how to reply, and in the end decided to change topics. "Once he is well enough, we will leave."

At the nerves in her voice, a frown worked across the imposing man's brow. "Are you in danger?"

Dread crawled through her at his question. Had he recognized her? She covertly slid her hand next to her dagger. "Excuse me?"

The man's eyes narrowed on Thomas. "Did he abduct you? If so, dinna fear telling me the truth. I will protect you."

After years of being shunned, that a complete stranger would step into the role of her protector left her humbled. Moved by his kindness, Alesone shook her head. "Nay, he was kind enough to offer me aid."

Doubt simmered in the man's gaze. "I saw only one horse."

However gallant, they'd met but a short while before. Though he'd helped her without hesitation, his noble actions far from secured her trust. "I swear to you, Thomas has been naught but a gentleman. My horse grew lame, and he offered me escort." The truth, or as close as she would share.

The red-haired man studied her a long moment, and then nodded. "The reason for your journey must be grave to travel in such dire conditions."

Fleeing the Bruce's camp and barely escaping Comyn's men raced through her mind. "'Tis complicated."

An understanding smile touched his mouth. "Most things in life are." Thomas shifted.

Thankful for the diversion, Alesone tucked in the blanket his movements had shoved aside. "He is coming to."

On a groan, Thomas lifted his lids. "Alesone?" he whispered.

"I am here."

Pain filled eyes met hers, then narrowed on the man at her side, the confusion shifting to a scowl. "W-who are you?"

"I am called John," he stated, his voice gruff. "'Tis my home you abide in. The lass brought you to my door earlier this day. Given the weather, you are fortunate she found me before you died."

* * *

Fortunate? Pain swamped Thomas as he took in the binding over his shoulder. Aye, luck was behind them indeed.

"I stitched up your wounds a short while ago," Alesone said with quiet warning. "You dinna need to be moving about."

Guilt slid through him. Bedamned, 'twas he who was charged with her protection. And he'd failed. Worse, he'd passed out, forced her to face the threat of those in pursuit while stranded with a wounded and unconscious man. "I thank you for bringing me to safety. I owe you much."

Compassion darkened her gaze. "You owe me naught, 'tis what I do."

Thomas had met many women in his life, but none as selfless or courageous as Alesone. That she would dismiss her bravery when most would have broken down or abandoned him, assured him of her depth of character, the same strength he'd witnessed in Templar Knights.

Moved, he studied her through the blur of pain. As a man of strong will, regardless of how she made him feel, he'd kept her at a distance. Never had he meant her to become important to him beyond his duty. By risking her life to save his, regardless of his wish or hers, a bond had formed.

He muttered a curse, as drawn to her as he was torn to keep her at a distance. Now what? With his fealty pledged to Robert Bruce, was there a choice?

A movement to his right had him glancing over. Thomas eyed the stranger, and noted the man assessed him as well. What had she told him? With his allowing them to remain within his home, clearly naught that'd place them in danger.

Red brows narrowed. "I am John MacLairish."

As he took in the stocky man, a sense of familiarity tugged at him. In his youth a lad with the same name had lived within Dair Castle, the son of the castle's smithy. Although John was a commoner, he and Thomas had often sparred, and the two boys had shared the dream of one day becoming knights. Years later they had again met, this time on a crusade. John MacLairish had indeed achieved his ambition, but it had ended during a battle that had left his leg disabled. He could walk and ride, but nae to the standards required of a Templar Knight.

Thomas narrowed his gaze. God's teeth, 'twas John! "'Tis—" Coughs wracked his body.

"Your throat will be dry," Alesone said as she held a cup to his mouth.

Cautious, he took several sips, then pushed the cup away. "I thank you." He met John's gaze. "I am Thomas MacKelloch."

A grin creased John's face, and he laughed. "God in heaven, I thought 'twas you, and then decided I was daft, a result of living on my own too long."

Alesone's eyes widened with disbelief. "You know each other?"

"Aye," John said, his voice rough with emotion. "A long time ago Thomas and I fought side by side until…" He paused. "I shouldna have doubted 'twas you."

"Many years have passed," Thomas said. "'Tis good to see you, my friend." He glanced at the twist in John's leg. "How do you fare?"

"Well enough." He arched a brow. "I would say a fair piece better than you."

Thomas grimaced. "The truth. I am escorting Mistress Alesone to—"

"I dinna think you should be talking so much given your health."

At the nerves in her voice, Thomas realized that she didna understand the inherent loyalty of the Templars, one that with their oath sworn would always hold true. Nor would he explain. "Sir John and I have been friends since our youth. I trust him with my life."

"And," his friend said, "that I live is due to Sir Thomas. After he carried me from the battlefield, 'twas he who ensured that when I returned to Scotland, I would have a place to live."

Uncomfortable with the laud, Thomas exhaled. "'Tis Brother Nicholai MacDaniell who deserves the thanks for your home."

"'Twas your letter requesting his aid that guided him," John said. "An entreaty your father sanctioned."

Though their travel to the monastery would leave them leagues from Thomas's home, the soul-deep yearning to see his family caught him off guard. Since he'd fled those many years before, he'd smothered his need of those dear to him beneath his guilt, and had foolishly believed himself immune to any reaction to his family, however near.

Against the rush of unwanted feelings, Thomas focused on the fact that they'd traveled farther south than he'd planned. 'Twould add several days or more until they reached Avalon Castle.

He glanced over, caught Alesone leaning forward to catch every word. Blast it. His past was exactly that. He didna wish to linger on events that he couldna change.

Sadness darkened his friend's gaze. "Your father still laments your leaving."

That he doubted. After his younger brother's death, if his father thought of him, 'twas with hate.

John sighed. "Your family will be—"

"They dinna know I am here. Nor will they."

"Thomas, your father still grieves."

Mouth tight, he held his friend's gaze. "I willna discuss the matter."

"We were once close friends," John said, his words weighted with sincerity. "Friends who could talk to each other."

Tempted to accept his offer, Thomas shook his head instead. "Years have passed."

"Mayhap, but the man I knew was like a brother to me, and wouldna have cared."

Thomas ignored his subtle emphasis on their Templar connection and closed his eyes. After what he'd done, how could his family truly accept him back into their home? For a while they might open their doors, welcome a son they'd believed lost. But with each passing day, memories of his unforgivable act would fester in their hearts and erode any pleasantry until all that remained in his family's mind was hate.

Another wave of heat seared him, and he groaned.

A hand pressed against his brow. "Oh God," Alesone said, her voice faint through a blur of warmth, "he is beginning to fever."

"I have herbs to treat him," his friend said, "but far from enough." Clothing shuffled. "I will ride to the monastery."

Against the blast of pain, Thomas pried open his eyes. "I…" He gasped for a breath.

Her eyes dark with worry, Alesone took his hand. "Dinna talk. You need to rest."

Mayhap, but beyond the worry, he saw curiosity. The lass had questions, ones he wouldna answer. Weak, he sagged back.

John tugged on his cloak and limped toward the door. "I will return shortly." A shot of snow swirled inside as he stepped out.

The door scraped shut. Silence filled the hut, but Thomas heard Alesone's sigh.

The room blurred, then again came into focus. He coughed. "A drink." She lifted the cup to his mouth.

He swallowed, the cool slide welcome, and then sagged back. "My thanks." In the flicker of firelight, lavender eyes dark with worry held his. Blast it, he didna deserve her concern. His task was to protect her, to keep her safe. He'd done neither.

She pressed a damp cloth against his brow. "John is a fine friend."

The numerous times he and John had roamed the woods as children came to mind, how they'd shared their dreams of one day becoming knights and battling side by side. In time the ambitions of youth faded beneath the reality of a war, one that had almost killed his friend. "Aye, he is."

Alesone pressed the cool rag across his brow. "Why did you leave your home?"

"'Twas time," he said, his voice tight.

"Why did John say that your father still grieves since you left?"

Bedamned! Images of his brother's death and his mother's heartbreak stormed him, the grief he'd delivered his family unrepairable. "We will be together but days. My past matters little."

Hurt streaked her gaze. "I see."

God's teeth, she didna. Another wash of heat rolled through him and the room blurred. Prickles of knife-edged pain covered his body and threatened to take him under. He clenched his teeth until the sensation abated. As quick, the next wave stormed him; exhausted, he sank into the welcoming blackness.

* * *

The soft bongs of a distant bell rang through the monastery as Alesone sat beside Thomas while he slept. In the last few hours he'd calmed, and a touch of color warmed his skin, at odds with the deathly pallor he'd had when they'd arrived three days prior.

Her eyelids began to sag, and she caught herself. With a yawn, she snuggled deeper into the blanket Brother Nicholai MacDaniell had laid across her, and looked around.

The glow from the fire in the hearth illuminated the lone crucifix hanging on the wall. The simplicity of the chamber touched by the scent of herbs relaxed her further.

Soft steps sounded from the corridor.

She glanced toward the entry.

The door scraped open. A tall man garbed in a long brown robe stepped inside. Though a monk, he bore a warrior's build. She sat up. "Brother Nicholai."

He nodded. "How does Thomas fare?"

The deep, easy cadence of his voice soothed her. "He is sleeping soundly at last."

Hazel eyes warmed with relief. "A good sign. If he continues improving over the next day, I feel confident he will recover." He shook his head. "With all that Thomas has endured, 'tis a miracle that he is still alive."

"If you hadna brought him to the monastery…" Instead of returning with herbs, John had led Nicholai and several monks inside. In a trice, they'd secured Thomas beneath covers in a cart led by a team of oxen and rushed him to the monastery. "I thank God you and the other Brothers arrived in time."

Kind eyes held hers, those that'd watched her with steadfast strength and belief since they'd met. "Thomas lives because of *His* will."

Tenderness warmed her. "Yes, he does."

Thomas shifted.

At the rustle of covers, Alesone looked down. "He is coming to."

"Run, Alesone!" Thomas rasped.

"The danger has passed," she soothed, keeping her voice soft as she'd done throughout his rambling delirium these past few days. She pressed a damp cloth across his brow. "You are safe." A frown worked its way across his brow as Thomas lifted his lids. He glanced over. "Nicholai?" The monk settled in the chair beside the bed. "You awaken, my friend. I thought you had meant to sleep well into the winter."

At the teasing in the holy man's voice, a hint of a smile tugged at Thomas's mouth. He shifted, winced at the effort, and then sagged back. "I tried."

The warmth in the monk's eyes eroded to concern. "'Tis good to see you again, Thomas. I admit my surprise at finding you here after—"

"'Twas unplanned." Face pale, Thomas cut his gaze to her. "You have met Mistress Alesone."

"Indeed. And grand company she is."

A blush swept her cheeks at Nicholai's praise, and through the haze of pain, irritation slid through Thomas. His friend always had a way with women, to put them at ease, to say the right things, traits in war that held little value.

She cleared her throat. "I explained how you were escorting me and en route, we were attacked."

"With Scotland at war," Nicholai said, his voice grim, "'tis unsafe to travel without guard, more so with a lass."

"I agree, but our travel was by King Robert's decree."

Surprise flickered on his friend's face. "He is still nearby? After he took Urquhart, Inverness, and Nairn, I'd heard he marched toward Elgin."

"I see you still keep your ear to the ground."

"One of the many tasks I take care of," Nicholai said.

Nay doubt that and much more. Though his friend didna inquire further, Thomas understood that once alone, he would have questions, more than on the topic of Scotland's king.

"Now that you are awake," the monk said, "mayhap I can convince Mistress Alesone to retire to the chamber provided her and rest. Since your arrival three days ago, she has refused to leave your side."

Tenderness filled him at her concern, compassion far from deserved. The blush on her face deepened, and his body stirred with awareness, one far out of bounds of what she should make him feel.

She cleared her throat. "As I sewed your wounds, I wanted to ensure they healed properly. I assure you," she said, her words rushing out. "'Tis nay more than any healer would do."

It was, especially when they now resided at the monastery where others knowledgeable in healing could have seen to him, a fact they both knew. "Mayhap," he said, his voice tender, "but I insist you rest."

She hesitated as if searching for an excuse to remain. "I will if you promise that you willna try to get out of bed on your own."

"I will take care." When she made to speak, he held up his hand. "Nay more."

Alesone stood and wove, exposing her exhaustion. Brother Nicholai stood, but she shook her head. "I can make it without help."

"Mayhap," the monk said, "but I insist on walking with you." He glanced at Thomas. "I will return." His friend escorted Alesone into the corridor.

The door closed behind them. Silence filled the chamber broken by the echoes of distant voices, along with the bongs of the bell announcing the conical hour.

Memories filled Thomas. Even with the many years that had gone by, his time living here remained clear as if nay time had passed. How many mornings had he awoken within the monastery and struggled to accept his lot of having devoted his life to God? At the time he'd risen to face each day, nay duty too mundane, his every act atonement for his sins. However, then as now, naught could repair the grievous wrong he'd wrought.

At the scrape of the door, Thomas glanced up.

"I thought perhaps you might have fallen back asleep," Nicholai said.

"I was remembering my time here."

"Your time living here, or the reason for it?"

Thomas swallowed hard. "You always were able to figure out what I was thinking."

"And you, my friend, were always too hard on yourself." Sage eyes studied him. "I had hoped that by now you would find forgiveness for yourself. It brings me great sorrow to see you still cling to your pain."

Grief raged through him and the outrage he'd smothered over the years broke free. "I killed my brother! There is nay forgiveness for that!"

Chapter Five

Anger reddened Nicholai's face as he glared at Thomas. "By all that is holy, your brother's death was an accident!"

"One that could have been avoided," Thomas growled, damning himself over again. If he could recall the day, turn back the hands of time until that moment of his foolish arrogance, he would. "Celebrating my becoming a squire, having a bit of fun and shamefully full of myself, I taunted Léod before our peers. To save face, he agreed to my dare. Had I left him alone and focused on my achievement, my younger brother would be alive."

"Your teasing wasna out of malice," the monk said, his voice softening. "'Twas naught more than boys do, those who strive to become knights, lads who one day grow into fine men, and warriors who protect those whom they love."

Far from swayed by his friend's logic, Thomas dragged his gaze to the cross hanging on the wall. His younger brother's death had left his family devastated. The soul-tearing sobs of his mother as she'd wept at the news of a son lost, and the grief in his father's eyes, haunted him still. Nor could he forget the shock and fury of his older brothers and sister when they'd learned of the tragedy.

Regardless if a time came where any within his family could forgive him, never could he forgive himself.

Nicholai grunted. "I see you are as stubborn as ever."

On a deep exhale, Thomas straightened in his bed. "If 'twas so simple."

"Indeed." With a weary sigh, Nicholai settled into a chair at his side, the wisps of grey sprinkled within his brown hair a potent reminder of the passage of time. "'Tis good to see you again. I have missed our talks."

"As have I." Thomas shifted to a more comfortable position, winced at the shot of pain.

A frown creased the monk's brow. "You must take care, you are far from healed."

Given the dire circumstances, a choice he couldna make. By now he and Alesone should have reached the western coast. With almost a sennight having passed since they'd departed the Bruce's camp, he wasna sure where Comyn's men were, or where they had positioned themselves to keep watch for their passage.

However much he wished to ride toward Avalon Castle, 'twas wisest to continue detouring south. After a day, mayhap two, and as long as he saw nay sign of danger, they would head northwest.

"Once I am able to ride," Thomas said, "Alesone and I will depart."

Nicholai refilled a goblet with water. "You have had a fever for several days." He handed Thomas the cup. "I caution you to allow your body to heal before you depart."

He took a drink, the cool slide soothing his parched throat. Thomas nodded toward the chessboard in the corner. "It wasna here earlier."

"Delivered while you slept. I thought you might enjoy a match or two. For old times."

"Old times?" he said, relaxing a degree, thankful his friend hadna pushed further. Exhausted, and with his body aching, the last thing he wanted to do was argue. "Methinks you are determined to beat me. As I recall, 'twas a feat you rarely achieved."

A smiled touched his mouth. "There is that."

"Little doubt you have honed your skills since I left."

"I may have played a game or two since our last challenge." The smile fell away. "Many years have gone by since you studied here."

They had, time he'd hoped would lessen the painful memories of his youth. He set the goblet aside. "After you advised me to consider becoming a Knight Templar, I was torn as to what decision I should make."

Nicholai nodded. "Had you arrived at the monastery with God in your heart and sincerity in wanting to serve Him, I would have encouraged you to remain. Except your reason was due to guilt, and your each day in service here driven by a need for penance."

Regret balled in Thomas's throat. He released a shaky breath. "You were right. I needed to leave."

"And now?"

"The Brotherhood gave me purpose, an outlet for my anger, and I found immense pride in helping others." But never peace—nor did he expect to find such, a fact he'd accepted long ago.

Satisfaction filled the monk's eyes. "The travel and experiences have given you a broader understanding of people. Taught you that regardless of where you go, at the core of every culture is the need to belong, to care for those who matter, and however much one would try to ignore the draw, a need for family."

He swallowed hard. Nay, one didna forget family.

The monk arched a brow. "Does your father know you are here?"

Thomas heard the hope in his voice, the belief that the heartbreak between him and his family could be mended. "Nay. Nor will I tell him."

Nicholai's mouth tightened. "By all that is holy, havena enough years passed?"

"Dinna you understand?" Frustration roughened his voice. "I have caused those I love to suffer enough." He fought the burn of grief. "Nor does it matter. To them, I am naught but a painful memory."

"Thoma—"

"Blast it, my presence would do naught but tear open old wounds!"

"'Tis time to repair the bond."

Hope ignited deep inside that such a chance existed. Just as quickly, it faded. Thomas shook his head, damned that even for a moment he'd allowed himself to weaken to the prospect. "'Tis impossible."

"I believe otherwise." Nicholai steepled his fingers, shot him a measuring glance. "Your father visited me a few weeks prior. Sadness still lingers in his eyes."

Torn between nae wanting to hear and thirsting for every detail, Thomas fisted his hands as the ache built inside for his father, for his family.

"However much you deny it," his friend continued, "you miss him, but are too bloody stubborn to admit what is evident in your expression."

Bedamned! "I have stated my reason for staying away." The monk's eyes narrowed. "You have, but in truth 'tis naught but an excuse."

"I—"

"You dinna want to remember, but you do," Nicholai pushed, anger sliding into his voice. "Or wish to discuss Léod's passing, but your brother's death haunts you, tears you apart, and destroys any chance you will ever find peace. Until you face your past, you will never heal. Nor will your family." Hard eyes held his. "Havena those you love suffered enough? As your friend, I beseech you to travel to Dair Castle."

Bitterness twisted in Thomas's gut at the idea of returning to his home, of facing the people he loved, those he had hurt. However much he dinna want to remember, he did, every day, with every breath. But his friend was wrong. With the despair he'd served his family, any chance of overcoming the strife between them was insurmountable.

On a hard swallow, Thomas clung to his one saving grace. "Regardless of my wishes, the luxury to remain and visit Dair Castle or visit my family isna a choice I can make. I am on a mission for King Robert. As I stated before, once I am well enough, I will continue my escort of Alesone."

"I see." Nicholai tapped his finger against the time-worn wood as he studied him. "There are other issues that pique my interest."

With the hint of exasperation lingering in the monk's voice, Thomas understood 'twas courtesy that'd guided him to another topic. For now, Nicholai wouldna press, but he was familiar with his friend's strategy in winning an argument, and knew they were far from through with the matter.

"Such as?" Thomas asked.

"With news of King Philip's order to arrest the Templars in France, as you are one of the Brotherhood, I am surprised to find you in Scotland."

"An unplanned event."

"In addition, you mentioned that you ride on orders from King Robert." Sage eyes held his. "I believe there is more to your appearance in Scotland than merely as an escort for an untitled lass."

Nor should he be surprised that his friend, a close acquaintance to the Bishop Wishart, was so well informed. "There is. After the Templars protected King Philip against the riots in Paris, for him to press false charges against the Order and call for their arrest 'twas despicable."

Nicholai gave a solemn nod. "I pray, as do the other monks, that Pope Clement will intervene on the Templars' behalf."

Thomas grunted with disgust. "Dinna hold out for such an intervention. 'Tis well known within the Brotherhood that the pontiff wasna chosen for his strength of character. King Philip ensured the man selected to brandish the church's power was one he could influence."

His friend made a sign of the cross. "'Tis a sad day when the most holy position within the church can be manipulated. Thank God you have escaped France. I pray more of your Brothers were as fortunate."

Thomas glanced over his shoulder to ensure the entry was closed, and then faced his friend. "What I tell you isna to be shared."

"I swear it."

"Weeks prior to the Knights Templar being charged with heresy," Thomas said, smothering the rush of anger the memories wrought, "the Grand Master received word of King Philip's intent. To protect the Order's secrets, Jacques de Molay followed a covert plan, one constructed with Robert Bruce in case of such a threat years before."

"By all that is holy, what has Scotland's king to do with the Order?"

"Incredibly, everything." Thomas gave a wry smile. "Robert Bruce is a Knight Templar."

The bewilderment on his friend's face gave way to stunned understanding. "King Robert's religious exclusion, and the Scottish clergy's refusal to acknowledge his excommunication, would allow the Bruce to offer all Knights Templar entry into his realm with impunity."

Thomas nodded. "Exactly. In secret the Grand Master dissolved the brotherhood and ordered select knights to load critical Templar secrets and treasures onboard our galleys. Before the arrests began, beneath the cover of darkness we fled St. Rochelle. Five ships sailed to Scotland, and the remainder headed to Portugal."

"A man of the Grand Master's caliber," his friend said, his voice somber, "would have planned for such a horrific event. Thank God you were forewarned, but 'tis tragic so many Templars were left behind."

Thomas fought for composure against the swell of misery. "I, as the others, despised leaving any of the Brotherhood behind. But to ensure none loyal to King Philip were alerted of our escape with the Templar treasure, Jacques de Molay explained the Order's daily routine must appear unchanged." He paused. "Have you learned of any details of the arrests?"

"Aye." Nicholai's hand trembled as he set aside his goblet. "Within days after the arrests began, numerous Templars were killed, many others tortured; horrific stories that chill me to the bone."

His friend's words conjured dreadful images of the Brotherhood who'd suffered, and he muttered a curse. "France's king may have confiscated the gold remaining in the Paris Temple," he rasped, "but never will he claim our true wealth or seize the holy relics we protect. Those are forever out of the bastard's grasp."

Grave eyes held his. "He will search for them."

"He will, but they are hidden, a location he will never learn. A fact by now I believe King Philip has realized…" God's teeth, the reason for King Philip's pact with Comyn! Why had he nae put the pieces together before? Regardless he knew now, a revelation that must be passed to King Robert.

"How do you know?" the monk asked.

His mind a rush of outrage and grief, Thomas met his friend's gaze. "Because in private, France's king has crafted a foul scheme with Comyn."

Nicholai's face paled. "Tell me."

"With the Templars' gold filling the French sovereign's coffers, and aware of Comyn's dire financial straits along with his lack of men to ward off King Robert's assaulting force, King Philip has offered the Scot both."

"The price?" the monk whispered.

"That Comyn's bastard daughter wed one of King Philip's nobles."

"A bastard daughter? That makes little sense. Why would King Philip let a by-blow marry one of his powerful lords?"

"Robert the Bruce believes the French king's offer to Comyn is but a ruse. Once the fighting is over, if Comyn is successful, King Philip will crush him and then claim Scotland for himself."

What little color remained in Nicholai's face fled. "'Twould be an atrocity!"

"Aye, and as established by his betrayal of the Templars, evil he willna hesitate to commit." He grimaced. "Before I departed Robert's camp, we both believed the goal of France's king was only to claim Scotland. Now I realize that somehow King Philip has learned the Templars have brought their treasure to Scotland. If he gains control of our country, he could plunder with disregard until he discovers where 'tis hidden."

"By all that is holy, this wedding must never occur!"

"It willna," Thomas stated. "King Robert has ensured that the lass is hidden away where none will find her."

"Thank God that he…" His friend's eyes widened in disbelief. "The lass—'tis Mistress Alesone. And 'tis you who is charged with her safety, which nae only explains your determination to reach your destination, but your urgency."

Thomas gave a curt nod. "God forbid if Comyn learns where she will be hiding."

"Indeed, 'twould be the beginning of Scotland's end." Nicholai paused. "Does she know of her father's intent?"

Memories of Alesone's pallor at news of her father's treachery rumbled through him. "She does, and wants nay part of him. Nor is she weakwilled. To her credit, she is an excellent archer." Pride filled Thomas as he shared how they'd first met.

The monk chuckled. "I believe you have met your match."

He shrugged, amused by his friend's mirth. With her wit, cunning, and strength of character, aye. "There is much to admire about her."

"Including her beauty." Nicholai raised a brow. "Dinna tell me you havena noticed."

Lavender eyes that would lure the stoutest man flickered in his mind. "I noticed, but her comely face and intelligence dinna change my plan. Though the Templars are dissolved, I shall abide by my vows given, which include forbidding marriage."

"Because you willna allow any chance for love in your life," his friend charged, "your penance for Léod's death."

Anger slapped him. "I—"

Nicholai shoved to his feet. "After all these years I believed you would have come to understand that your brother's death wasna your fault? But you havena. How long will you push away anyone whom stirs your interest?" His face darkened to a fierce scowl. "Dinna say that she doesna intrigue you. I saw how you watched her when you first awoke, your expression unguarded!"

"I—"

"Do you believe," Nicholai continued, rolling over Thomas's reply, "that Léod would have wanted you to sacrifice any chance at happiness?"

Years had passed since he'd heard his brother's name, but the mention still cut like a dagger to his heart. "We will never know what my brother wanted," he rasped.

"Will we nae?" Nicholai charged. "I knew him well. We played together as children. He was a lad full of happiness and caring. I doubt he would have wanted your life to be void of love or dredged in despair."

"Enough!" Thomas boomed, his head pounding, his distress so fierce 'twas storming his senses with brutal accuracy. "Despite what you wish, or the feelings the lass inspires, Alesone is but a duty."

His friend arched a brow. "Feelings she inspires?"

God's blade, where had that come from? "My thoughts concerning the lass matter little. I refuse to allow her to be more than a charge."

"Refuse?" He folded his arms over his chest. "Who are you trying to convince, me or yourself?"

He glared at his friend. "I have stated my intent."

"And what of her happiness? Would you deny her an opportunity for such?"

Thomas started to reply, then began to cough.

"Here." The monk handed him a goblet of water.

After a sip, he settled back. He set the cup aside, forced lightness into his voice, needing to smother his friend's beliefs. "You are mistaken, I have little to do with her happiness."

His gaze intent, he settled in the chair beside the bed. "You didna see how she remained by your side since your arrival, her growing concern with each passing day."

"She is a healer."

"Which explains her initial care, but nae why I couldna pry her from your chamber even after your fever broke. She refused to leave until after you had awoken."

And when he'd looked up and seen her there, a sense of rightness had filled him, a bond that crossed the lines of duty. Shaken by the need she stirred within him, he stowed the emotions deep inside. His life path was decided, one that didna include her.

"Cloistered within the monastery over the years, your mind convolutes loyalty to her craft with passion," Thomas said. "However much you wish to see otherwise, Alesone is my charge, nay more."

"Interestingly enough, when I questioned Mistress Alesone about you, she grew as defensive." His friend held up his hand as Thomas made to speak. "Talk of what exists between you and the lass can wait. Like her, you need to rest." He stood and started to turn.

"Have you achieved what you came here for?" Thomas asked, understanding his friend's intent too well.

He glanced back. "I did. You are very astute."

"You were a good teacher."

A smile flickered on the monk's face. "I will see you on the morrow." With quiet steps he departed the chamber.

On edge Thomas stared at the door, far from pleased by his friend's insight regarding Alesone. 'Twas easy to understand why the Bruce had allowed her into his trusted circle to become his healer, and the king's fierce resolve to ensure her protection. The lass inspired loyalty, trust—and if he were honest, more. A woman devastated by her own grief, however much she hurt, she pushed on.

A life alone.

A life without a bond.

A life buried beneath service to others.

Much like his own.

Nor did she linger on her troubles, but with her each breath she carved out the path she chose, forging the hurt of her youth into a fierce, unbreakable shield.

When they'd first met, he'd wanted to shake her for daring to threaten him. Now he found only respect. Alesone was unlike any woman he'd ever met. Dangerous to her enemies, a protector to those she loved. Nor had a woman's smile ever thrown him off balance.

Regret built inside at thoughts of leaving her, but 'twas for the best. However much she intrigued him, naught had changed. His service to the Templars, to God, had fulfilled him over the years and 'twould do so in the future.

Except emptiness lingered at thoughts of a life without her.

Thomas damned the truth. When he rode away from Avalon Castle he would fade from her memory, but she would forever be etched in his mind.

The soft chime of bells sifted through Alesone's sleep. Groggy, she lifted her lids. A gutted candle with a blackened wick sat atop a simple night stand like a harbinger of her empty life ahead. Uneasy she focused on the embers glowing in the hearth, flickers of hope that refused to yield.

She rubbed her eyes, the tang of fresh rushes and smoke scenting the air as she scanned the chamber. A cross hung upon the far wall.

The monastery.

Memories of the harrowing journey to the friary several days before erased the last wisps of sleep. Her legs unsteady, she sat.

She smoothed the rumpled sheet beneath her hand, paused as she remembered the fear that had filled her as they'd ridden to escape, each turn bringing them against another unknown. Throughout, Thomas had demonstrated horsemanship unlike she'd ever seen, and hadna hesitated in his every decision to keep her safe.

Even at the risk of his life.

More humbling, even wounded, he'd kept her ignorant of his injury along with the pain. A healer, she'd tended too many with similar wounds to nae understand the suffering he'd endured. But he had.

For her.

Humbled by his bravery, at how he'd risked his life to keep her safe, she slipped from the bed. Alesone padded to the hearth and laid several pieces of kindling atop the embers. Puffs of smoke swirled from beneath the dry wood. A flame flickered to life and grew.

Against the snap of the fire, memories ignited. However afraid she's been, she had found trust, belief in him to keep her safe. And he had.

Until he'd lost consciousness.

But he had awakened, and thank God, would survive.

Relief swept through her, unlocking unbidden thoughts of how he'd wrapped her within his powerful embrace and drawn her against his muscled chest. She shivered at the remembrance of how his breaths had brushed against the curve of her ear, teased her skin until she'd wanted to turn her lips to meet his.

Shaken by the yearning he inspired, she drew a steadying breath. Though she had met many warriors, none compared to Thomas. A knight. With the skills she'd witnessed, that she could believe, but naught about him was ordinary.

And his friends. John and Brother Nicholai were smart, steadfast, and trustworthy, men who wouldna call anyone a friend who wasna of the same ilk.

She picked up a piece of kindling from the fire. A flame danced on the blackened tip as if a beacon against the darkness, like the light Thomas had brought to her life.

On edge, Alesone shoved the dry tinder into the flames, watched as the wood was engulfed. With her linage mired with King Robert's enemy, how could Thomas view her as anything but a charge? 'Twas foolish to allow her thoughts to linger on him. He was a warrior, a man dedicated to his blade, both facts he'd made clear.

Pushing aside the tug of awareness, she brushed the dust from her hands, and jerked her gown off a nearby peg. Sunlight streamed into the room as she donned her garb. She'd see how Thomas was faring. The sooner he healed, the sooner they would be on their way.

As she stepped into the corridor, she smiled at the man exiting Thomas's chamber. "Brother Nicholai."

The monk pulled the door closed. "Good morning, Mistress Alesone. If you are wanting to see Thomas, he is a bit irritable. Likely due to the pain that he denies." A smile touched his mouth. "Considering everything— that his fever is gone and he is healing is a blessing."

"'Tis," she agreed.

"To allow time for his foul mood to wear off, I bid you to join me to break your fast."

"I really should go and—"

"Enjoy your meal with me." His smile grew. "'Twould be an honor, and a wee bit selfish. Rarely do we have visitors, much less a beautiful woman, to break the fast with."

Heat touched her cheeks at his compliment, and she nodded. She walked at his side as he started down the hall. "Thomas is blessed to have such a friend as you."

Mirth flickered in his eyes. "Depending on when you asked Thomas, he may or may not agree. At times we dinna see eye to eye."

"He is stubborn, you mean."

"Aye," he said with good nature, "the same as *other* people I know."

At the charge, Alesone laughed, the tension in her body easing. "I believe the trait is an admirable one."

"Indeed. And one that nay doubt intrigues Thomas as well."

She remained silent, embarrassed he would allude to Thomas or his feelings toward her. Neither would mulling over the fact change anything. The pad of leather upon stone echoed as they descended the turret.

"'Tis good to see him after all of these years."

"You knew him as a child?" Little harm would come in getting to know a bit more about Thomas, a man who regardless of his own feelings toward her, intrigued Alesone.

"When we were lads, Thomas and I would spar in the lists. Later on, I received the calling. When he arrived at the monastery intent on becoming a monk too, you can imagine my surprise."

Unsure if she was more stunned to learn Thomas had once intended to devote his life to God, or that he'd made such a complete change of direction and became a man of war, she frowned. "That explains his devout manner."

"What do you mean?"

"Several times since we met, I have seen Thomas praying, more than is common."

Understanding filled his gaze. "And have you noticed any other abnormal traits?"

At his teasing, heat stole up her cheeks. "Nay unusual," she rushed out, "but he is pious, more than most that havena become men of the cloth."

Torchlight illuminated his face as he nodded. "Dinna worry, I understood what you meant. I was but—"

Hurried steps echoed from below. "Brother Nicholai!"

Nerves shot through Alesone as a young monk, his expression panicked, rushed up the steps.

Worry lined Nicholai's brow. "Wait here." He met the younger man halfway down the turret.

Fragments of the man's terse whispers sifted up.

Nicholai nodded, quietly replied.

With a nod, the young monk hurried away.

Mouth grim, Nicholai returned.

Unease filled Alesone. "What is wrong?"

"'Twould seem there are visitors at the gate."

Fear slid through Alesone, and she prayed she was wrong. "Who?"

"Lord Comyn's men."

Chapter Six

Alesone turned away from Brother Nicholai and managed to bank the rush of terror, barely. Grisel had lost her life to her father's ruthless men, and by *His* Grace, Thomas's life was spared. All for what? To be found? For her father's nefarious plans with King Philip to succeed?

Nay!

The Brother cleared his throat. "Ales—"

She whirled, prayed she was wrong, but needed to confirm her worst fear. "Comyn's men are here for me, are they nae?"

The monk nodded. "They believe you are inside, but canna be sure. As long as you remain within the monastery, you are beneath our protection."

The amount of gold her father had offered for her capture could sway men to ignore the sanctity provided to those within these walls. However dangerous it was to leave, she couldna remain.

Where could she go? She was unfamiliar with the local terrain. With Thomas wounded and unable to travel and Comyn's men desperate to find her, traveling alone 'twould be foolhardy. "How did they find me?"

"Comyn's knight claimed they followed your tracks—"

"Impossible. Thomas and I evaded them during a storm. Any sign of our passing was covered by the falling snow." A shiver trickled through her. Was she wrong? As they'd forged through the Highlands, she and Thomas sharing a mount, had their combined weight left gouges in the snow, deep impressions even the storm hadna filled? The weather-mutilated trail would explain the delay until their arrival.

Still, it didna clarify how they'd…On an unsteady breath she stilled, prayed she was wrong. "Brother Nicholai, we didna ride to the monastery, but to Sir John's."

Grave eyes held hers. "Indeed. Comyn's men said they followed the cart's tracks from the crofter's hut to here."

"Nay doubt the knights questioned him." She breathed, "Neither would he have told them anything, whatever their methods of asking." Oh God, with her father's desperation to find her, his men's techniques to gain information could have quickly turned to torture. Her throat tightened. "We must ensure John is …"

"Alive," the monk replied, anger edging his voice. "We will soon learn. I have sent a man to ride to his home."

"My thanks," she whispered, and damned her father over and again.

"If you will excuse me, Comyn's men are awaiting my arrival."

She frowned. "Why you?"

"They requested to speak to a senior monk in regards to the matter. 'Twas my request to place you and Thomas under the monastery's protection, so I will entertain their questions."

She nodded. "Brother Nicholai," she said, despising what she must share, but as their champion, he must understand the enormity of the situation. "As long as Comyn's knights believe I may be here, they willna leave."

"Mayhap," he said, satisfaction shimmering in his eyes, "but they are unsure. A doubt I will exploit."

Though confident of the brother's abilities, after hearing of her father's twisted dealings over the years, doubts plagued her. "What if you canna convince them?"

"I have faith He will offer a way. Await me in Thomas's chamber. Once I am through speaking with Comyn's men, I will share what transpired." The monk made the sign of the cross and departed.

Alesone hurried up the turret. At the entry to Thomas's chamber, she paused, fought to steady herself. In his condition, the last thing he needed was for her to rush in as if they were under attack. Her father's men held suspicions that she was inside, naught more. She knocked.

"Enter," Thomas called.

She drew in a steadying breath, stepped inside, and then closed the door. Sweat clung to his face, which was battered with bruises. Was his fever returning? Heart pounding, she crossed the room and pressed her hand on his brow, then sighed with relief. "'Tis cool."

He grimaced. "I should be pleased by that."

"You should, 'Twas a miracle that you didna die."

"Is that what you think, my living is a miracle?"

Somber eyes held hers. Shaken at how important he was becoming to her, Alesone stumbled for a reply.

Confusion washed through her as she stared at the handsome warrior who'd risked his life to protect her. A man of his caliber, with green eyes a woman could drown in, he could have any lass he wished. His interest wouldna linger on a bastard whose own father didna want her, except as goods to barter.

Alesone shoved aside her foolish thoughts. However much she wished otherwise, her years ahead were best used to help others. With her family history, to invite a man into her life would, in the end, offer her naught but heartache.

"What I think is that you should rest," she said.

He grimaced. "I have tried, but I canna sleep."

Which explained the circles beneath his eyes. She retrieved a woven pouch from the basket, measured out a small amount of the herb. "You should have sent for me."

"You needed to sleep."

Though in pain, his concern was for her. Humbled and unsure how to reply, she double-checked the dosage. Except for Grisel and Burunild MacCheine, her mother's personal maid who had visited on occasion until Alesone was seven, few had worried how she fared. She mixed the herb with water. Nor could she forget the reality of the situation. His injury had delayed their parting. Once they reached Avalon Castle, he would be gone from her life forever.

"Alesone, something has upset you." He brow furrowed. "At times 'tis best if we share our troubles. Though we have spent less than a fortnight together, I have been known to be a good listener."

Her hand trembled as she handed him the cup, frustrated that even overtired, he missed little. She dinna need the bond between them to strengthen. 'Twould be hard enough now to watch him leave. "Drink everything."

With slow swallows, Thomas drained the contents. A soft clank sounded as he set the empty goblet on the bedside table. With a sigh he lay back. "I thank you. The chamomile will make me drowsy, but a touch of valerian might have been a better choice."

Impressed he knew his herbs, she stowed the unused portion inside the basket. She'd considered valerian, but had decided to wait. With her father's men downstairs and Nicholai's impending return with news, if for some reason the situation eroded, she needed Thomas alert.

"There is something I need to explain. Before I begin, know that Brother Nicholai is handling the issue."

With a grimace he sat up.

"What are you doing? You are too weak to be moving about."

His jaw tightened. "Tell me."

She said a silent prayer. "Comyn's men are below."

"What!" Thomas braced his arm against the bed and swung his feet over the side.

Alesone barred his way. "They are unsure if we are here."

Eyes dark with frustration held hers. "How did they find us?"

"They followed tracks left by the cart we used to bring you here."

Panic flared in his eyes. "John—"

"Nicholai sent a man to check on him." Her voice wavered at the last. "I pray he is…" She shook her head. "Once Nicholai knows more, he will let us know. Lie down, please. Moving about will tear your wound apart."

His eyes blazed, but he didna stand.

She considered it a small victory. Understanding his upset, her own nerves on edge, Alesone walked to the hearth and rubbed her hands before the flames.

"Alesone."

The quiet resolve of his voice had her turning.

"I will see you safely to Avalon Castle, that I swear."

"I know." When a man like him gave his word, he achieved his goal. A quiet yearning built inside. How would it feel if Thomas wanted her? Warmth slid through her.

Answering heat shimmered in his gaze.

Flustered, she looked away, but a soft burn lingered.

"Lass?"

Off guard, unsure what to say, she decided 'twas prudent to change the topic. She glanced over. "You are familiar with the healing arts?"

A shadow flickered in his eyes. "'Tis wise for a man who lives by the blade to learn cures that may one day save his life or that of his men."

Mayhap, but she sensed another reason lay behind his claim. She clung to the thought, needed the distraction to fill the void until Nicholai returned. "'Tis rare to meet a knight who has more than a minor interest in herbs."

Silence.

Far from discouraged, she walked over. "Did you learn the various uses during your stay within the monastery?"

A frown edged his brow.

"Nicholai told me you studied here."

"What else did he share?" Thomas asked, displeasure ripe in his voice.

"That you were smart, determined, and compassionate.'"

He grunted. "'Twould seem his memory fails him."

"How so?"

Thomas shrugged. "'Twas a time long ago."

Refusing to be put off so easily, Alesone sat in the nearby chair.

"You are close."

Green eyes met hers. "At one time."

"Naught has changed. The bond of friendship between you and Nicholai is strong."

His gaze flickered toward the hearth, softened. "Once, while we were in the woods collecting herbs, we found a robin with a broken wing. Nicholai insisted on bringing it to the monastery. He bound its wing and fed it each day. Once the bird healed, he set it free."

"He is a unique and compassionate man," she said, moved by the memory.

Thomas's gaze grew hard. "He is a man dedicated to fixing things that are broken, but at times, even he fails."

From the coolness of his words the topic had become personal. Why? What had occurred to make Thomas feel so undeserving? "I find it hard to believe Nicholai would spend time on anything, or anyone, that he found undeserving."

"He is a man," Thomas said, his voice empty. "He makes mistakes, as do we all." God's teeth, why was he rambling on? What was it about the lass that made him want to share? Was it because she was unlike any woman he'd met or that, because of her past, she was as broken as he was?

As if either reason bloody mattered? Comyn's men were below while he lay helpless to safeguard the woman he'd sworn to protect.

He glared at the door.

Blast it, where was Nicholai?

A dull pounding throbbed in his temple. Once they'd fled the Bruce's camp, he should have kept more alert, looked for signs of danger, taken a more strategic route. Now, because he hadna used every precaution, he'd placed Nicholai and those within the monastery into the middle of a dangerous political impasse.

The door scraped open. Nicholai scanned the hallway, then stepped inside. Face taut, he closed the entry, then glanced toward Alesone before meeting Thomas's gaze.

At the upset on his friend's face, Thomas understood. "Comyn's men refuse to leave."

On a sigh, Nicholai strode over. "I tried to convince them otherwise, but they are setting up an encampment at the edge of the woods."

Thomas cursed his weakened state. "Besides outwaiting them, what options do we have?"

"There are secret tunnels that you and Mistress Alesone could use to escape."

Alesone shook her head. "He isna strong enough. A fact he well knows, but willna admit."

"Blast it!" Thomas growled, "we dinna have much choice."

"There is another way," the monk said. "Your father—"

"Nay!" Thomas interrupted.

His friend's eyes narrowed. "'Tis prudent to reconsider."

Thomas straightened his shoulders. "My decision hasna changed."

Eyes narrowed, Alesone glanced from one to the other. "What decision?"

God's teeth!

A quick rap sounded at the door.

Temper simmering, Thomas glanced over.

"Enter," Nicholai called.

A young monk stepped inside, his face flushed. He nodded to Thomas then Alesone before turning to Nicholai. "The Duke of Westwyck has arrived and requests to speak with you."

A sharp, driving pain ripped through Thomas's shoulder as he shoved to his feet. "You sent for my father!"

Alesone fingers dug into his arm. "Sit down, please."

"My thanks," Nicholai said with soft words to the younger man. "Tell him I will be down momentarily."

"Aye." With a wary glance at Thomas, the monk rushed out, closed the door.

"Why did you tell him that I was here?" Thomas demanded, damning the pounding in his head.

"'Tis time you saw your father," Nicholai replied without apology. "If nae for you, for him."

Thomas silently swore. The last thing he wanted was for her to learn about the mire of his past. "Alesone, I wish to speak with Nicholai alone."

His friend shook his head. "She stays."

Fury edged through Thomas. Over the last few days the lass had endured more than any woman should. She didna need to be forced to remain or become tangled within his convoluted personal life. "I dinna want—"

"Alesone stays," Nicholai interrupted. "The king assigned you to be her guard. As long as you are together, 'tis imperative that she is familiar with the *situation*." His nostrils flared. "To toss the lass into the fray without understanding the issue is to leave her unarmed."

"There is naught to understand. Mistress Alesone will *never* meet my father or any others within my family." With his father's loyalty to Comyn, a risk he refused to take.

"The Duke of Westwyck is here. I willna ask him to leave without his first speaking with you. Blast it! Your father has suffered since you left, hurt that broke his heart. As I said before, the time has come to repair the bonds with your family," Nicholai continued. "As for any topics of concern, they can be easily be avoided."

"Blast it—" Thomas wrapped his hand around the wooden bedpost as he started to collapse.

Alesone caught his side. "Here, let me help you lie down."

For a moment he fought her, a shot of pain rewarding his effort. As his dizziness increased, he complied.

"However much you dinna like it," Nicholai said, "at the moment you have little choice."

Pained by the truth Thomas grimaced.

"I will be back shortly. Mistress Alesone, ensure that he doesna get up."

She nodded.

With a warning look, the monk departed.

Flames in the hearth crackled into the silence as Thomas met her troubled gaze. "I never meant to involve you in any of this."

"I know, but I believe your friend's decision is wise."

"You dinna know the situation." He cursed the ire in his voice, anger nae meant for her.

"I know you have family who wants you," she said, her words heartfelt, "something I would give anything to have."

Abandoned as a child, though raised by a woman who loved her, her own blood had shunned her. He understood her yearning to have a family, except she wasna aware of the reason that had torn his apart, a wound that couldna be repaired.

"You are blessed to have a friend who cares enough for you to intercede."

"Cursed is more like it. Nicholai knows how I feel about my family. He had no right to interfere." Thomas laid his hand over hers, needing to touch her. "Alesone, my frustration isna at you."

"I know," she replied, but he caught the soft waver. "I—"

The door scraped open, and Nicholai stepped inside, followed by Thomas's father.

Chapter Seven

Through the hot burn of tears, Thomas stared at his father. The thick mane of white evidence of the years past, the aged weathered lines carved in his face a testament to his strife, and the pale green eyes filled with anguish, suffering he'd caused.

A raw ache built in his chest. If he ever again faced his father, he'd envisioned the encounter a stoic if nae awkward event. A cool measuring look to the other, his father's scowl as he weighed the man Thomas had become, and a brief verbal exchange. Then, without incident, they would part.

He fisted his hands in the covers as he stared at the man who'd raised him, taught him how to wield a sword, and was stunned after all these years to find a need for his acceptance.

God's teeth! He was a Knight Templar, had led men into battle, and faced overwhelming odds in combat. Yet, with each moment, the defensive shield he'd carefully built around his heart crumbled.

Dark memories flooded him of the day they'd buried Léod, of the soul-tearing sobs of his mother and her inconsolable grief. Of how through sheer will he'd nae collapsed as they'd lowered his brother's body into the rain-drenched earth, and with each inch, numb, aching, how he'd cursed that it wasna him who'd died.

However much he wished to turn away, Thomas held. 'Twas his actions that'd caused his family's torment, and 'twas his guilt to bare. "Father." His voice wavered within the deafening silence.

The Duke of Westwick's lower lip began to quiver. "My s-son."

The pain in his father's voice drove another blast of misery through Thomas. Clinging to his composure by a thread, he remained silent.

With slow steps, the noble walked over as Nicholai moved to the side.

As he paused before the bed, Thomas noted how the man's jaw trembled, and that tears pooled in his eyes.

"I…" The duke shook his head. "Never did I think to see you again." His voice broke at the last.

Again Thomas cursed Nicholai's intervention. Didna his friend understand he'd done naught but ripped open old wounds, ones that would take many years, if ever, to heal? "I meant to keep away."

At his rough whisper, anger slashed the frailty in his father's expression. "I didna teach you to run from your troubles."

The ache in his chest drove deeper. "At the time 'twas best that I left. I would think, considering everything, you would welcome my decision to become a monk."

"I was wrong to allow you to escape to the monastery. I believed distance and prayer would help you heal. When I learned you had departed the monastery without a word to anyone in the family…" Aged eyes narrowed. "Your leaving broke your mother's heart."

A heart shattered by his brother's death, except his father refused to accept the truth. "'Twas never my intent to hurt Mother, she had already suffered enough." His voice trembled, and he silently cursed. "I pray she has moved past the torment I caused."

The little color in his father's face drained. "Y-your mother is dead."

Despair ripped through him, sucking his every thought until his mind blurred with grief. *Dead?* He looked away, his each inhale dredged with tears, the ache in his soul storming him with ruthless vengeance. When he thought he could speak, utter anything without again falling apart, he turned. "Ho-how?"

"Two years ago she grew ill. Healers tried to save her." A tremor shook his father's voice, but he continued. "In the end, there was naught that I, or anyone else could do but pray."

"I…" Thomas fought for composure against the swell of heartache. Throughout his youth, regardless the cause, he could always turn to his mother. Steadfast, calm when others were frantic, she was the cornerstone that'd held their family together.

That he would never see her again. God's teeth, how did one respond to such devastating news? Regret was a pathetic offering when one's soul lay ragged. Yet, he had naught more to offer. "I am sorry."

Sadness weighed on his father's face. "While I am sharing tragic news, your sister, Orabilia, came down with the sickness and died shortly after. And a year past, your brother Matheu died in battle."

Coldness clutched Thomas until he shook. Through the haze of shock, Alesone's soft sniffle cut through his sorrow.

The surprise in his father's eyes as he glanced toward her shifted to a scowl.

"Father," Thomas forced out, doubtful a way existed to salvage this situation. He shot Nicholai a cool look before turning to his father. "May I introduce Mistress Alesone. She saved my life."

The gruff expression faded. "Mistress Alesone, please accept my deepest gratitude."

"I…" She gave a shaky nod.

"Alesone," Thomas said, "may I introduce His Grace, Duke of Westwyck."

She curtsied. "Your Grace, 'tis an honor to meet you. My deepest regret for the loss of your wife and children."

"I thank you." The noble cleared his throat. "I regret your having heard our exchange."

As did Thomas, more so with Alesone still struggling to cope with the loss of Grisel. Never had he planned for her to know of his past, or to learn that like her, scars tormented his youth.

Bedamned, now wasna the time to linger on such troubling thoughts. With his father's fealty, he couldna risk him learning of Alesone's importance to Comyn. "I am escorting Mistress Alesone. En route, we were attacked, and through good fortune, we ended up here."

A grim line settled on the duke's mouth while he studied him. "Once healed and with Mistress Alesone delivered, did you intend to come home?"

He damned the question, nor would he avoid the topic. If naught else, he owed his father this truth. "Nay."

The cool expression on his father's grew fierce. "Where are you headed?"

Long seconds passed.

Shrewd eyes held his. "Blast it, Thomas, is the destination of such secrecy?"

Tingles prickled Thomas's skin. "'Tis naught anything I can discuss further."

The duke's mouth thinned. "As I rode into the outskirts of the monastery," he said, his words calculated, "I was halted by Comyn's men. They seek a man and"—his gaze shifted to Alesone "—a woman."

She gasped.

"I take it," his father said, his words ice, "'tis the two of you they are after?"

Thomas muttered a silent curse, glanced at Nicholai before facing his father. Blast it, he should have warned her of his father's loyalty. "Aye."

Face grim, the monk stepped beside them. "Your Grace, your son and Mistress Alesone are beneath the church's protection."

"Father," Thomas said, his head pounding and grief distorting his ability to select his words with care, "'tis best if you leave."

Veins throbbed in the elder's head. "By God, I am nae going anywhere until I find out the reason Comyn's men want you!"

* * *

Distraught by the conflict between father and son, and further troubled by how pale Thomas had become, Alesone stepped forward. Within the frustration and anger, neither had she missed the silent yearning in Thomas's eyes, the same reflected in his fathers. Though strife had torn their family apart, she refused to allow her situation to be the reason for continued conflict.

"Comyn's men are here because of me, Your Grace."

The Duke of Westwyck's hard gaze leveled on her, the intensity reminiscent of his son's. "Why?"

"'Tis *nae* your concern," Thomas snapped.

Aged eyes narrowed. "I asked Mistress Alesone."

Thomas shot her a warning glare.

With her father's claim of the blood tie and offering gold to whomever captured her, her vow to King Robert was void. "Lord Comyn is my father."

Shock paled the noble's face.

"Alesone," Thomas growled, "the duke's loyalty is to Lord Comyn."

She froze. The reason Thomas's hadna answered. What had she done! Refusing to show fear, she angled her jaw. "Neither will I return to my father."

Nicholai cleared his throat. "A choice sanctuary within the monastery provides her, Your Grace."

"Father," Thomas warned, "you willna interfere. Mistress Alesone is beneath my protection, a pledge I will die to keep if necessary."

The duke's eyes strafed his son. "Which I see that you have almost done."

"'Twould seem," Thomas said with soft violence, "there is little more to be discussed. 'Tis best if you go."

Regardless of the cause that'd torn Thomas's family apart, Alesone's heart broke at how after all of these years, and with silent yearning in his eyes, he pushed his father away. That the duke had rushed to see him when he'd learned his son was nearby spoke volumes.

Didna Thomas realize the gift he held, a bond however frayed, with time and nurturing, could be repaired? A relationship with her own father she would never experience.

"To have sent such a large contingent," the duke said, "you have upset Lord Comyn greatly."

Shame filled her at the truth. "He has offered a significant reward of gold as well."

"Alesone," Thomas hissed. "Dinna say more."

A decision she would heed if nae for the flicker of longing she witnessed every time the duke had looked upon his son, a need Thomas was working hard to ignore. Aye they were related by blood, both men of the same stubborn ilk.

"Your Grace, any right my father had to my welfare or loyalty has long since died." She angled her jaw. "Nor will I return to him."

Appreciation shimmered in the noble's eyes. "Neither would I expect you to."

At the pride in his father's voice, Thomas stilled. God's teeth, what was going on?

Tiredness settled on the duke's aged face, and the ire of moments before faded. "When Brother Nicholai sent a runner with news of your arrival..." He shook his head. "'Twas as if an answer to my prayers."

Skeptical, Thomas remained silent.

"When I learned you were wounded, I couldna ride here fast enough."

The sincerity in his father's admission left Thomas off balance. Need, deeply buried inside screamed in his mind to admit he'd yearned to see him, but guilt-ridden over the strife he'd caused, he shoved the confession aside.

When he didna reply, tense lines settled on his father's face. "I willna go without you. I lost you once, and by God I refuse to lose you again."

The words Thomas had longed to hear wilted beneath his shame. "With our fealties opposed to the other," he forced out, "it canna be otherwise. You must leave."

The duke shook his head. "Nay."

Blast it! "Father 'tis—"

"After the death of Margaret, the Maid of Norway," the duke cut in, "Robert Bruce was furious when The Guardians of Scotland refused to recognize his grandfather's claim as overlord to Scotland. King Edward twisted the law, ensured by whatever means necessary that his authority was recognized. Furious, I approached Bishop Wishart in private."

Thomas stared at his father in disbelief. "You confronted one of the Guardians of Scotland?"

"Aye, I informed Bishop Wishart that I was appalled by the treachery that he as the other Guardians of Scotland had allowed by King Edward I's hand. Further, I refused to swear fealty to John Balliol. But"—he gave Thomas a measuring look—"the bishop explained that when he'd learned how England's king had skewed any chance of Robert Bruce, the Competitor, claiming the crown, he arranged a secret meeting with the Guardians of Scotland. There, they made plans for Scotland's future, one that didna include King Edward I. Wishart beseeched me to appear loyal to Balliol, and in secret to conspire with him to ensure the Bruce gained his rightful crown."

Thomas stared at his father in disbelief. "You have been loyal to the Bruce throughout?"

The duke gave a curt nod.

"Never did you say anything," Thomas whispered.

Sadness touched the duke's face. "I had planned on informing you the evening after you had become a squire."

The day he'd killed his brother. After a desperate search for Léod in the river, Thomas had run to the castle. Frantic with the news, everyone had joined the search. With the last rays of the sun fading from the sky, they'd found his brother's body downstream, bloodied and shoved against the rocks.

"After"—his father's throat worked—"'twas nae the time for such news."

Guilt piled atop the already immense amount. The following day they'd spent burying his brother.

"Then you approached me about entering the monastery." The duke's eyes dark with anguish held his. "I cursed your self-condemnation, but you wouldna listen to anything I said. When you requested to become a monk, with the monastery but a half-day's ride from Dair Castle, once a month or so had passed, I had planned to visit and tell you the truth."

"Except when you arrived," Thomas said, the blackened memories rolling through him. "you discovered that I had left."

His father gave a weak nod. "I didna know where you had gone."

Thomas glanced at Brother Nicholai.

"I swore that I would never share your destination," his friend said.

Like the wind removed from his sails, Thomas sagged back, pondered his next move.

Shrewd eyes held his. "I would think," the duke said, "you would be pleased to know of my loyalty to Robert Bruce's grandfather, one that has transferred to our king."

He was, except his allegiance complicated everything. 'Twas simpler when his father supported the enemy, a solid reason why he must remain away. Now he had naught but the guilt of his brother's death.

"The news is a relief," Thomas admitted, "but it changes little."

The strain on his father's face softened. "It changes everything."

If 'twas only so easy.

The duke faced the monk. "I will be taking my son home."

"God's teeth," Thomas hissed. "What of Lord Comyn's men?"

"A simple enough task," his father said. "I will ride to Dair Castle and return with a contingent of men for an escort." He faced Alesone. "Mistress Alesone, as my son is charged with your safety, you will accompany us and, if you wish, care for him until he is healed."

* * *

Alesone held the noble's gaze, moved by his love for his son, saddened how Thomas's replies exposed that he remained mired in guilt. "I thank you, Your Grace, I am honored to be your guest."

Panic flickered into Thomas's eyes. "Your intervention is unnecessary. I am receiving proper care here."

"You will go," the duke said with quiet authority. He turned on his heel and strode out.

The monk followed.

Flames flickered in the hearth as the soft thud of the door echoed in the chamber.

On unsteady legs, she walked to the chair.

"You havena broken your fast this day," Thomas said, his voice ice, "a task you should see to."

Alesone arched her brow in defiance.

"I wish to be alone."

She sat. "Why do you push your father away?"

"You dinna understand what happened."

At the hurt in his voice, an ache built inside. "Then tell me."

Anger slashed his face.

"Do you think you are the only one that lives with guilt for the death of someone you loved?" she demanded, the ire she'd buried deep breaking free. "If I hadna brought Robert Bruce's man to our hut, never would Grisel's life been placed in jeopardy. How do you think I feel knowing that because of me, she was beaten, raped, and murdered?"

"You willna blame yourself! Your decision was one that anyone loyal to our king would have made."

"Knowing that and accepting the reality isna easy. A fact you well understand." She swallowed hard. "Tell me, how does one find forgiveness?"

"I dinna know," he rasped, his voice breaking at the last. "I-I am unsure if 'tis possible."

Chapter Eight

Alesone held Thomas's gaze, his struggle to find forgiveness for himself a battle she too fought. Would there ever come a time where she could find such, or, like Thomas, would she withdraw until she was but a shell of a person going through the motions of living?

Nor at the moment did her choices matter. Thomas had reached an important crossroads. "You have family who loves you, wants you to return." He glanced at the crucifix on the wall, and the strain on his face made her ache. If only she could help him.

"What if I go and after a fortnight, when my father looks upon me, all he sees is a tragic reminder of everything he has lost?"

She yearned to offer reassurances. Except none existed. However genuine the duke's request, until Thomas returned home he wouldna know. "What if while you are home, the bond between you and your father strengthens?"

He gave a cold laugh. "My mother, brother, and sister are dead. Little chance exists that naught but strife will ever remain between my father and I."

Tormented eyes shifted, and her chest tightened beneath the weight of his sorrow. "And will damning yourself for leaving change anything?"

"You know naught!"

"Then tell me."

His mouth tightened.

"A wise man once told me," Alesone said softly, understanding that he didna want to discuss the situation further, but needing to try. "That at times 'tis best if we share our troubles."

Anger flashed in his eyes. "What is wrong?" she asked, refusing to back down. "Is the advice only for you to give?"

"You dare much!"

"And you," she challenged, "dare nothing when you have everything to gain."

He closed his eyes.

An ember popped from the flames, faded into the thick silence like a subtle reminder that though we lose those we love, life continues.

Alesone's gaze lingered on his fisted hands. "Nae facing your troubles doesna make them go away, but allows them to fester inside, to destroy any chance at happiness."

Silence.

Irritated he would toss away a chance at family who wanted him, something she craved, Alesone shoved to her feet. "Cling to your anger like a bloody fool. I am going to break my fast." She stormed toward the entry.

"'Twas a celebration," Thomas rasped as her hand reached for the door.

She turned.

Intense green eyes held hers.

Humbled that he'd shared this painful piece of his past, she walked over and sat by his side. Guilt slid through her. She'd acted nay better than he and wouldna ask more. 'Twas his story to tell, and Alesone prayed she'd earned such trust.

Long moments passed.

Slowly, Thomas unfurled his fist. "Léod was the youngest in our family. A sister and four brothers. We were close. I had become a squire earlier in the day, which you discovered from my father's outburst." On a rough breath, he turned toward the flames, the reflection of orange and yellow bright in his eyes. "My younger brother looked up to me, but that day, caught up in my pride, my actions were reckless. I should have been taken to task for teasing Léod, for pushing him."

Her heart ached as his fingers tighten against the blanket until his knuckles grew white. "What happened?" she whispered.

He lifted his gaze to hers, the misery within almost dropping her to her knees. "I-I convinced him to spar, which isna out of the ordinary. Except on that day I dared him to accept my challenge on a fallen tree straddling a rain-swollen river. As we approached the edge, the thunderous roar of the raging water rose above the rain." He swallowed hard.

Alesone folded her hands in her lap, understood he needed to purge his memories, and prayed with the telling he could begin to heal.

"While we stood on the bank, I saw my brother's eyes darken with worry as he watched a small tree caught within the violent current rush past, the leafless branches ripping up clumps of dirt as it was dragged downstream," he continued, each word forced. "But with the challenge given before our peers, if he'd backed down, 'twould have brought him shame."

The snap of flames in the hearth filled the silence.

He rubbed the back of his neck, then dropped his hand to his side. "In position on the trunk, at first we traded swings. Once Léod realized I was but teasing him and had nay intention of a blistering match, my brother relaxed." He swallowed hard. "After blocking my next strike, he stepped back, rounded his blade in a maneuver he hadna yet mastered, nae doubt trying to impress me. Except"—he inhaled with a sharp hiss—"his foot missed the trunk and he lost his balance. Though I lunged to catch him, his fingers clung but a moment on the rain-slick bark before he tumbled into the dangerous current."

Oh God!

His face grew deathly white. "I can still hear his screams, his pleas for help as he was swept away. I s-swear on my life," he said, his voice breaking, "I tried to reach him."

"Thomas—"

"Terrified," he continued, his voice ripe with condemnation, "I ran along the bank as his arms flailed to reach shore, with me screaming that I would save him with every step." A tremor shook his body, then another. "I caught up to him several times, but when I waded in to grab him, the swift current hurled him out of reach."

Tears blurred her eyes at that sheer misery in his voice. "What did you do?"

His body began to shudder.

"Thomas?"

At the raw torment on his face, Alesone understood his anguish, distress that thrived within her at thoughts of how she'd cost Grisel her life.

"When I…" He shook his head. "When I realized I wasna going to reach my brother in time, I ran home. In the bailey, filled with well-wishers who'd traveled to celebrate the day, I screamed for help. As we searched, thunderstorms unleashed their fury. We scoured the rough water in the downpour for hours."

"You found him?" she asked, her heart breaking.

"My mother did," he strangled out. "When I arrived, she sat on the mossy bank clutching Léod's limp body. Her shattered wails will haunt me forever. The next day we buried Léod."

The last whispered with such desolation, Alesone strained to hear each word. She envisioned him collapsed against the fresh turn of earth, his tears staining the ground, and his sobs inconsolable. Or so filled with pain had he stood in stony silence through the service, his heart shattered. Once the last prayer was said, lost to his grief, how long had Thomas remained at his brother's grave? Had any of his family stayed beside him, or so blind to their own pain, had he remained alone?

"Why did you leave Dair Castle?" she asked.

"After the heartache I caused my family," he said as if a curse, "how could I stay? Each time they saw me, I would be naught but a reminder of what I had done, of the pain I had caused, and of the son they had lost."

She shoved to her feet. "'Tis unfair to think that."

Legs trembling, he stood, grasp the headboard to steady himself. "Is it? How can they nae hold me accountable when I took Léod's life!"

"So you requested to join the monastery."

"Aye. I believed giving my life to God would somehow make everything right."

She remembered his father's tormented claim of coming to the monastery and finding his son gone. "Except you dinna stay."

"I had intended to," Thomas said, the day he'd walked through the doors of the monastery etched in his mind. The grandeur of the hewn stone arches, the rich tapestries hanging on the wall, and the sense of a divine presence had offered him a glimmer of hope that somehow he would eventually find peace.

Understanding filled her gaze.

"As Brother Nicholai taught me the daily routine, and the tasks I was expected to perform," he continued, "over time he became more than a mentor, but a friend. After but a month, grief-stricken, I climbed the ladder to the bell tower and broke down." He stared at the hearth a long moment before turning to her. "Foolishly, I believed I had slipped away unseen."

"Nicholai found you?"

"Aye. When I opened my eyes, he sat on a stool but paces away. He said naught, allowed me to discuss my upset if I chose. After a long while, feeling as if I had naught to lose, I admitted the reason for my wanting to be a monk. Admitted?" He scoffed. "Nay. Nicholai prodded me until piece by piece he uncovered the truth. After he explained a man didna serve God as a penance, but out of love."

Humbled by the trust she inspired, Thomas studied her for a long moment. What was it about the lass that made him want to help her or share his sorrow when for years he'd said little of his past to but a few, men whom he trusted with his life?

Unsure, he focused on the possibly of his being there for her, like Nicholas had been for him so many years before.

"What happened?" she asked.

"Nicholai offered suggestions of occupations more *fitting* to a life where I could serve God as well as to help others."

"And still grieving for your brother, you left."

"Aye."

Curiosity flickered on her face. "What did you do?"

I became a Knight Templar. Regardless if the Grand Master had absolved the Order in secret, encouraged those who'd slipped away to blend into society and to marry, his life was dedicated to the Brotherhood, to preserve the treasures along with the secrets of the Templars for which many within the Order had died.

He closed his eyes against the painful thoughts of those falsely arrested on charges of heresy, and the many more innocent men whose fate lay in the hands of a traitorous king.

"Thomas?"

With his heart heavy, he opened his eyes, found her watching him with concern. "I fought in distant lands," he stated, shoving the anger beneath his shame.

She frowned. "You are a mercenary?"

He grunted. "Something like that."

"Your time studying in this monastery explains your devout manner."

"What do you mean?"

A blush slid up her cheeks. "Several times during our travel, I have watched you praying when you dinna know I was nearby."

What else had she observed? She was smart and quick of wit. Bedamned, he should have expected her to notice his actions. In the future he would have to be more alert. As if he wasna too blasted aware of her already. "Many knights have deep faith."

"They do, but…"

On a sigh, he nodded. "I see the question in your eyes. You may as well ask instead of badgering me in a roundabout way to find out."

Her expression softened. "'Tis about your father."

Blast it. After the days they'd spent together, he shouldna have expected her to shy away from topics that would upset him.

"Regardless of your wishes," she said, "your father will bring you home."

Drag him if necessary, and with Nicholai in on the scheme, he hadna further recourse. He shrugged. "Unable to get around on my own, 'twould seem I have little choice. Nor do I wish to place the monastery in the middle of a war. If you havena noticed, my father is a stubborn man."

"I heard stubbornness is an admired trait."

At the slight teasing in her voice, a smile touched his mouth, and he stilled.

Lavender eyes held his, firm with determination and incredible tenderness.

Never had he believed that he'd find happiness, but somehow, incredibly, she'd roused another emotion within him besides grief. Finding a desperate need to touch her, against his every reason why 'twas reckless, Thomas drew her hand within his. Stunned by an innate sense of rightness, he pulled away.

Tender confusion filled her gaze.

And why shouldna she be baffled? As he held her gaze, he felt the same. Never had a woman inspired a need to share his past with her, or to help her deal with her own troubles. She did both.

What was it about her that drew him? Her strength? Fortitude? Determination? Her innate gentleness? Or a dangerous combination? He'd thought her stubborn, but now he realized 'twas determination, one driven by the passion of her beliefs. Regardless if when they'd first met he hadna wanted a connection between them, the bond forged by pain and strengthened by understanding, grew with each passing day.

A part of him dreaded his return to Dair Castle and the upcoming confrontations with his father, but another looked forward to the time he and Alesone would spend together. An irrational yearning. However much she intrigued him, stirred feelings inside he hadna wanted, he could allow, nay more. In the end he would rejoin Robert the Bruce.

After her losing Grisel, 'twas best to keep things between them simple. And if he enjoyed her company, or found her pleasing to look on, 'twas expected.

*   *   *

"What are you doing sitting up?"

At the anger in Alesone's voice, Thomas turned, caught the bedpost to steady himself, the soft light of dawn filling his chamber. "'Tis a wound in my chest and arm, nae my legs."

She scowled. "You forget I sewed several stitches in your left thigh."

He grimaced. "Minor injuries."

Muttering something he had little doubt wasna a compliment, she stormed over. "You need to sit."

Tired, his body aching, he grimaced. "If you are here to badger me, you can…" From the turmoil in her eyes, her upset more to do with finding him on his feet. "What is wrong?" "Nicholai's men have returned with John."

"How bad is he?" Thomas said as he stepped toward the door, grimaced at the blast of pain.

Alesone blocked his path. "You must remain abed or you will tear open your stitches. Look at you all but swaying on your feet!"

Damning that he'd grown lightheaded, Thomas shot her a cool glare as he stumbled over and sat on the bed. "How bad is John hurt?"

"A few broken bones, bruises. I have already treated and sewed the cuts," she said. "He will survive."

"Thank God."

"J-John asked me to tell you that he didna tell Comyn's men where we were."

Thomas muttered a curse. "And almost died because of it."

"He made the choice. You would have made the same one for him."

"Aye," he ground out, understanding the code of a Templar, the offering of one's life for another without hesitation. "but it doesna make it easier."

"Nay." Dismay darkened her eyes. "I should have insisted that he travel with us to the monastery. Regardless of the storm, I should have expected Comyn's men to trail us. If anyone is to blame for his injuries—"

"'Twas nae your fault," Thomas broke in, furious she'd twist the situation in any manner and feel guilt. "That honor goes to your father."

"'Tis." Her voice wavered.

"You were tired and exhausted," he continued. "You made the best decisions you could at the time. 'Twas a miracle neither of us froze." He glanced toward the door. "Where is he?"

"At the end of the corridor." She hesitated. "First, you must try to sleep a couple more hours."

God's teeth. "Conditions?"

A becoming flush touched her cheeks. "You have already been up and about. It is clear from your trembling that your body is exhausted."

At his silence, she arched a questioning brow. Blasted stubborn lass. He gave a curt nod.

Alesone walked over.

"What are you doing?"

She settled onto the nearby chair. "Ensuring," she said with quiet warning, "that you follow through."

"I have given my word."

"You have."

Trying to conceal the pain his movements caused, Thomas scowled as he lay back, and then lowered his lids. After a long moment he peered out. She'd moved to the hearth and was adding several pieces of wood. Sparks spiraled within the flames, illuminating her soft curves with unsettling clarity. His body hardened, and he cursed.

Her brow furrowed, Alesone turned. "Are you in pain?"

"Nay. I am too restless to sleep."

"Restless," she asked with soft accusation, "or in discomfort?"

Nae wanting to linger on a topic that would only remind him of his growing need for her, Thomas glanced around the chamber, paused on the chessboard. "Do you know the game?"

Sadness flickered in her eyes as she walked over, picked up the queen with reverence. "Aye, 'twas Grisel's favorite."

"We dinna have to play," he said quietly.

She replaced the piece, then carried the game to the bed and placed the chessboard and carved wooden figures between them. "'Twill bring back fond memories. For fun we made up stakes the loser paid after each move."

"Stakes?" he asked, unsure what to make of such. "Such as?"

She gave a soft laugh. "Naught for anything of great importance. Who would prepare the next meal, an errand, or"—her eyes twinkled with mirth—"the telling of a secret."

Unsure if he liked the direction their impromptu game was heading, he hesitated. The last thing he wanted to do was share more about himself with her. Already they had too much in common.

"Dinna tell me that you question your skill against a simple woman?"

He grunted. After witnessing her proficiency with a bow, her sharp wit, and her bravery, there was naught simple about the lass.

"The secret you share *if* you lose a chess piece is nae the deep soul-searching kind," she teased, "but uncomplicated and a wee bit of fun." She arched a playful brow. "You do know how to have fun, do you nae?"

He grunted. "I have heard 'tis overrated."

A smile curved her mouth, and he found that he enjoyed having put it there. Nor with the grief she'd endured over the past few weeks would he steal her bit of happiness. John was here, had been tended to, and was expected to recover. For now there was little more that he could do.

Neither would he share that chess was one of the many games he loved, challenges he had won many times over. "Go on with your game then. Lasses first."

Mock surprise widened her eyes. "A gentleman." She moved her pawn. After a moment's deliberation, Thomas countered.

Several moves later, she slipped her carved wooden figure on the square to his right as she lifted his man. "Knight takes rook. You owe me a *secret.*"

Her playful whisper slid over him like a caress, and awareness slammed through him. Bloody hell, 'twas naught but a bit of foolishness! He smothered his body's demands, forced his mind to safer ground. A simple secret, how hard could that be?

"When I was a lad," Thomas said, welcoming the memory, one he hadna recalled in many years, "during the night I snuck down to the great room. My oldest brother, Donnchadh, had left a pair of his boots near the hearth to dry. While he slept, I filled the bottoms with cow dung," he said with a smile. "The next morning I awoke to him bellowing his outrage from a floor below."

Alesone laughed. "What did you do?"

His smile widened. "I decided 'twas prudent to sleep in a wee bit longer."

Her eyes sparkled with mirth. "Did he ever find out you were the culprit?"

"Nay. If he had, he would have sought revenge, and"—he shook his head—"siblings are a spiteful, brutal bunch."

"A wonderful memory," she said, and the warmth in her expression faded.

Thomas damned that he'd mentioned his family when she had none. Aye, she had a family, a father who was a pitiful cur and wanted her only as goods to barter.

Neither would he linger on the bastard. He'd made Alesone laugh, something she'd had little of as of late. A woman like her deserved more than the foul turn life had foisted upon her. If for the short while as they were together he bolstered her spirits, she deserved that and more.

And she was right. Regardless of the discord between him and his father, he did have family, one that loved him. "As the oldest, Donnchadh will receive the title of duke and inherit Dair Castle."

"Were you close?"

"We were. And before you ask, I miss him."

She studied Thomas a moment. "You are worried about seeing your brother?"

"Aye, and with good reason. With my having disappeared without a word after Léod's death, and absent when my mother, Orabilia, and Matheu died, Donnchadh will nae be pleased to see me."

"What if you are wrong?"

At the hope in her voice he shook his head. "I am nae."

"But what if you are?" she pressed.

Irritated, he shot her a cool look, then moved his bishop to the square at the edge. "Check."

"You canna always avoid talking about what you dinna wish," she said.

Blast it! "Your king is in jeopardy."

With a shrewd eye, Alesone surveyed the board. She slid her pawn before the king. "He is safe, unless you wish to take my man with your bishop."

"'Twould be foolish to sacrifice my bishop for a pawn."

She held his gaze, hers darkening in silent challenge. "That depends on what you are trying to win."

Chapter Nine

Pinpricks of tension rippled across Thomas's skin as he held Alesone's gaze. He damned himself for succumbing to the temptation of a verbal spar. 'Twas a perilous decision, more so with a woman who twisted his thoughts down a sensual path he had nay intent to follow.

Lavender eyes held his in soft challenge, and he fell into their depths, cursed the image of her moving into his embrace.

Stunned by the raw desire flooding his body, he shoved back his unwanted thoughts. Over the years never had a woman caught his interest, made him want.

Alesone did both, dangerously so.

This entire situation didna make sense. He was a man in control of his emotions, one who made his own rules of how to live, nae a green lad lured by a siren's call.

Guilt twisted in his gut. Nor was he fair to label her such. Her actions werena tossed out with the sensual expectations of an experienced hand, but those of a woman struggling to find solid ground. In truth, Thomas doubted she had any idea of her appeal to him.

Alesone hadna asked for her life to be cast in mayhem. As he, she'd been torn from a way of living that she loved. Now, they both were floundering against change, except he served King Robert, while she was left with naught but her doubts.

Given the circumstance, 'twas best to stow any interest she roused. God knew 'twas the logical solution. Except however much he tried, a part of him wondered if she, too, felt the stirrings of awareness.

Blast it, look at him rambling over a woman who had nay place in his life. Mayhap he wanted her, but by God if he chose such a foolish path, 'twould be a conscious decision, nae one spurned by desire.

Determined to put his reckless musings behind him, Thomas focused on her question of moments before. "And what is it you are trying to win?"

She sighed, and the defiant tilt of her chin lowered. "A life of my choosing."

Relief swamped him at her shift in topic, and he muddled back to safer shores. "With your being a healer, dinna you have that now?"

"What I have is a king's vow of protection, and a knight who almost lost his life trying to keep me safe. Both for which I am thankful. But a life of my choosing?" She released a slow breath. "With my father's offer of gold for my capture, and those who care naught but for the coin my seizure would bring them, never will I have the luxury of deciding how to live." She frowned. "As if during times of war anyone has such an option?"

Thomas cursed his draw to understand this complex woman. Whatever existed between them was moot. He should abandon this topic, return to their game, and focus on the lightness of moments before. And he would have, except he'd caught the soft yearning in her voice. "If you had a choice, what would you wish for?"

"I believe," she said, her fingers tightening on the pawn, "we are playing for secrets, nae wishes."

Driven by some inner demon, Thomas laid his hand atop hers, the smoothness of her skin in sharp contrast to his battle worn hands, ones that'd taken lives while hers had saved them.

Need rolling through him, he inhaled a slow, calming breath. Nay, 'twas naught safe about allowing his thoughts to linger on her, or to notice how her fingers lay intimately against his skin.

He should move away and end this madness. Instead, he skimmed his thumb along the silky hollow of her palm, and her hand trembled beneath his touch.

Her eyes flared, and his mouth went dry. Pulse racing he stilled, the innocent question of moments before having taken a direction he hadna intended. Except he needed to know. "But if you could have a life of your choosing?"

"'Tis dangerous to change the rules once the game has begun," she whispered. "Such a decision can open doors that you dinna intend to."

He glanced at the lush firmness of her mouth, and a burst of heat shot through him. Swallowing hard, he lifted his eyes to hers. "And staying within the guidelines is safe?"

On a soft inhale, her lips parted.

His mind a spiraling haze of urgency, Thomas released her, irritated at how she pulled her hand close to her body. How had he tumbled into such a convoluted mess? Blast it, his father should have left him at the monastery. Nor could he change the way of things now. However drawn to Alesone, 'twas foolhardy to allow a woman into a life as broken as his. She deserved a man who wouldna fail her.

While he...deserved no life at all.

With a forced smile he sat back. "So we will continue the game." Determined to keep his emotions under tight control, he withdrew his bishop to a safer location along with the whims of his pride.

She countered his move.

With a soft scrape, he placed his bishop on said square. Arching his brow, Thomas lifted her captured rook. "'Twould seem," he teased, "you owe me a secret."

"It seems I do." Humor shimmered in her eyes, and he drown within their hypnotic dance. "If I tell you, you canna laugh."

Her mesmerizing gaze lowered, and he chuckled, charmed by her unexpected shyness. Thomas made an exaggerated sign of a cross over his heart, the action more a reminder to him to keep his distance.

"You didna swear," she said.

He gave a mock frown and leaned closer. "I didna realize," he said, his burr deepening along with his desire for this fascinating woman. "that the secret was of such great consequence."

Her mouth trembled with laughter, the enjoyable sound pulling his gaze to her lips.

Full.

Lush.

God help him.

"Swear it," she said, "or I will be sleepless at night wondering if you will ever tell another soul."

"Now"—he held up her rook—"I am intrigued."

Devilment danced in her eyes as she reached for her rook.

Their fingers touched.

The burst of energy shot straight to his groin.

Her eyes widened, the flecks of silver within captivating. Her soft gasp drew his gaze back to her lips.

Unbidden, his thoughts tangled, clouding the reasons why he shouldna kiss her.

The king wobbled as he lifted his hand to cover hers, flesh against flesh. His breathing grew shallow. "You were going to tell me a secret."

"I..." Her lower lip trembled.

He clenched his teeth and through sheer determination, refocused on the game and their playfulness of moments before.

With forced lightness, Thomas folded his fingers over hers, the rook now firm between their palms. "You are nae going to renege on the deal, are you?"

"Why," Alesone whispered as she edged closer, "would I do that?"

Her intoxicating scent wrapped around him, and he fought the rush of desire.

"Thomas?"

Like a well-planned assault, the sultry whisper of his name slashed through his good intent. As the walls collapsed, all the reasons he'd vowed to keep her at a distance faded.

One taste was all he wanted.

Bloody hell, just one!

With lust scorching his every thought, Thomas hauled her against him. Chess pieces scattered as he crushed his mouth against hers.

On a throaty moan, velvet soft lips moved greedily beneath his, demanding, taking until his every breath was filled with her.

Fisting his hands in her hair, he pressed her against the bed, scraped his teeth across the soft flesh of her throat.

"Thomas," she moaned as she arched against him.

A primeval roar rose up. Hands shaking beneath his body's demands, he cupped her breast. "Ale—"

A scrape of the wooden door severed the sensual tangle blurring his mind.

* * *

With a gasp, Alesone jerked back. Pulse racing, she glanced toward the entry, struggled for coherent thought.

A tray of food balanced in his hands, Nicholai whistled as he backed into the chamber.

Shaken, she moved away from Thomas, neither did she miss the absolute shock on his face, or the fierce desire burning in his eyes. Thank God, the monk hadna seen them!

Trying to ignore the riot of emotions storming her mind, she snatched the carved figures knocked over during their kiss. Oh God, she wouldna think of that.

She shoved the pieces onto the board, avoided Thomas's hand as he did the same. How had she allowed their game to erode to such dangerous ground?

Allowed? As Thomas's lips had pressed against hers, for that too brief a moment, the realities that separated them had faded beneath the tangle of heat. She shivered at how his mouth had matched her own fierce demands. His each stroke, taste, had sent her higher. And when he'd laid his hand on her breast, pleasure had rippled to her core.

Heat stole through her at her wanton thoughts. Was she mad? With her father a powerful enemy, however much she yearned for Thomas, 'twas unwise to allow him, or any man, into her life.

Nudging the door closed, the Brother turned. Satisfaction filled his gaze as he walked over. "Ah, you are playing a game of chess."

"We just finished," she said, damning the tremor in her voice. "He won." With a grimace Thomas shoved to the edge of the bed.

Nicholas paused before the small table. "Aye, he has a penchant..." A frown creased his brow. "Your face is flushed, lass." His hesitated, glanced toward Thomas, and then back to her. "What is wrong?"

Heat burned her cheeks. "We had a slight disagreement."

"Slight?" Amusement crinkled the monk's eyes as he placed the tray on a nearby table. "Over the years Thomas and I have had"—he bent over, lifted the rook from the floor and handed it to her—"many disagreements."

"My thanks." She silently groaned as she set the piece onto its square.

"Have you come to a compromise," Nicholai asked.

"If only I were so lucky," Alesone muttered as she stared at the rook nestled next to the knight, doubtful anything could erase their kiss etched in her mind. Needing distance, she carried the chessboard to the table against the wall.

"I just finished talking with John," Nicholai said.

The worries of moments before faded as she turned. "How does he fare?"

The monk handed a steaming bowl to Thomas, nodded. "A bit of stew from the cook. She said 'twill make you feel better. As for John, as you warned when you tended to him, the few broken ribs are giving him discomfort, but he is thankful that he will make a full recovery."

Face grim, Thomas set the food aside, and sat at the edge of the bed. "I want to see him."

Alesone remained silent. However much she needed to remind Thomas of his promise to rest, with shimmers of pleasure storming her mind, at this moment, she was hardly ready for a confrontation.

At her silence, the monk's shrewd gaze shifted to Thomas, and he sighed his acquiescence. "Can you walk?"

With a curt nod, Thomas shoved to his feet.

Tension vibrating through her, Alesone held the door open as they moved past. An ache built inside as she glanced toward the bed, lingered on the rumpled sheets, where if only for a moment she'd tasted what should be forbidden.

* * *

Anger slammed through Thomas at the bruises on his friend's face, the stitches holding together severed flesh as John finished explaining the assault. Bedamned Comyn's men, the bastards would pay! Humbled by how his friend had revealed naught, even at the risk to his life, he stood. "You must rest. We have spoken overlong."

"I am poor company," John said.

Thomas grunted. "Nay more than I. 'Twould seem we are a fine pair."

A wry smile flickered across John's mouth. "Nor is this the first time we both have been beaten and left for dead."

Indeed. As Templars they'd fought side by side in the heat of the desert, their duty to God, to the Brotherhood, and to the faithful who wished to travel through the holy land.

From the other side of the bed, Alesone shifted.

Thomas didna glance her way. The few times their eyes had met, he'd caught the lingering desire within, a longing that still churned inside. What had he been thinking when he'd kissed her? Thinking? A hand's breath apart, and wanting her, coherent thought hadna entered his mind.

A knock sounded at the entry.

"Come in," Thomas said.

A young monk entered. "Sir Thomas, Brother Nicholai sent me to inform you that the Duke of Westwyck has arrived."

So the sojourn would begin. Resigned to his temporary fate, Thomas nodded. "I thank you. I will await my father in my chamber."

With a nod, the monk departed.

Hope shimmered in John's eyes. "You and the Duke of Westwyck have made amends?"

Thomas stilled. "I didna realize you were acquainted with my father?"

"We met at the monastery on one of my earlier visits to see Nicholai," his friend replied, his voice somber. "And before you ask, the duke didna tell me of the discord between you. That Nicholai explained."

"I see." Considering Thomas's entreaty to Nicholai, where he'd vouched for John, a Knight Templar wounded in battle and unable to continue his service to the Order, he should have anticipated that however innocently raised, the discord between Thomas and his father would have surfaced. "I willna forget what you have done."

John shrugged. "I did naught more than you would have for me. And, I pray that you repair the rift between you and your family."

Thomas's stiffened. 'Twould take more than a petition to God to repair the damage.

Sir John turned to Alesone. "I thank you for tending my wounds. You have a fine hand."

A smile touched her mouth, and Thomas's body tensed at the unexpected shot of jealousy.

"You are welcome. I thank you for your aid." Alesone moved to Thomas's side, and reached out for his arm.

With a scowl, he stepped back. He wasna a bloody invalid. Hadna he walked to his friend's room without aid? And if his legs were weak, 'twas expected. "You can remain if you wish while I speak with my father." After their smoldering kiss in his chamber, a move for the best.

The warmth in her eyes cooled. "'Tis time to allow John to rest."

Frustrated and wanting to storm out, his pride took another blow as he was forced to walk slow, dizziness threatening his each step.

A short while later, sweat beading his brow, he settled on his bed.

Alesone closed the door.

He glanced at the chess game then toward her. "I thank you for your help, nor do I mean to be short, and," he said, forcing the tension from his voice, "I am upset over my father's arrival."

"'Tis understandable."

He shook his head. "There is nay reason good enough to take one's irritation out on a person innocent of the situation."

Her expression softened. "I know you dinna wish to return to your home, but regardless of your past, of the tragedy, from your father's actions, he still loves you. I pray that you find the strength to allow the rift between you and your family to heal."

However much his father claimed that he wanted him to return, memories of Léod's death would always taint whatever would exist between them. "We will remain at Dair Castle until I am able to travel."

"Which should be at least a fortnight," Alesone said. "Long enough for you to make inroads with your family if you choose."

Doubting she'd ever fully comprehend the obstacles of such a goal, he remained silent.

A solid rap sounded at the door.

Thomas damned his weakness, more as he prepared to see his father, a man he'd always looked up to, and a man he'd failed. "Enter."

The Duke of Westwyck stepped inside. Flickers of caution tinged the smile on his face. "You are up."

"I am," Thomas replied, anxious for the day he and Alesone could depart.

His father nodded. "Mistress Alesone."

She curtsied. "Your Grace."

The lines of strain deepened on the noble's face as he looked over. "'Tis time to go home."

Thomas disregarded the tug of need. *Home.* As if such a place existed? Nor would he dwell on a topic that would cause his father naught but hurt. "What of Comyn's men? They willna allow Mistress Alesone or me to pass."

The duke's mouth tightened. "They willna stop us."

The cold determination of his voice sent a silent groan through Thomas. Bedamned his interference. "They dinna know that you are my father," he said, praying that by some miracle he could convince him to change his mind. "There is still time for you to—"

"My decision is made!"

God's teeth! Fighting the wave of dizziness, Thomas tugged on his cape.

In silence he and Alesone followed his father to the courtyard, as thankful as embarrassed by their slow pace.

The large contingent of mounted knights awaiting them in the courtyard left Thomas humbled. An ache built inside, that of a lad desperately wanting his family, pitted against the man who understood he didna deserve such a noble welcome. Gritting his teeth, he labored toward the cart, recognizing several men whom he'd played with in his youth. At the back of the wagon, he climbed inside.

Her expression tense, Alesone followed him up and settled on the wooden planks nearby.

Ignoring the throb of pain, he glanced over and read the unsettled nerves in her eyes. How could she nae be on edge? Comyn's men awaited them outside, and by the size of their escort, they faced a considerable force.

Again Thomas cursed his father's intervention, the fact that because of him, he'd placed his family and Alesone's life in jeopardy. Blast it, how could a simple task to escort the lass to Avalon end up in such a shamble?

The driver called out.

The cart jerked forward, the sting of the cold air sharp against his face.

Hooves echoed upon snow-crusted ground as they passed beneath the gatehouse, the scent of pine tumbled with the bite of the oncoming winter.

Sunlight smothered the shadows as they exited, the bright smear of the sun's rays sparkling upon the flakes of white like a fading wish.

Halfway across the open field, the thrum of hooves grew as a small group of Comyn's knights cantered to meet them.

His father raised his hand. "Hold!"

A knight at the front of the opposing force waved his men to stop, but continued forward. Paces before the duke, he halted his mount, then gave a respectful nod. "Your Grace, I must see all who exit the monastery."

"I have come to get my son," his father stated. "Move aside."

"Per orders of Lord Comyn, Your Grace, I am to—" The knight's eyes landed on Thomas, narrowed further as they shifted to Alesone. The knight cleared his throat. "Your Grace, in the cart are the man and woman we seek. I will—"

"Do naught," his father warned with insolent fury. "Move away or die."

Steel whispered against leather as the knights around them withdrew their swords.

"With you and your men greatly outnumbered," the duke continued, his words ice, "I believe your choice is simple."

The man's face paled. "I beg of you to reconsider, Your Grace. Lord Comyn—"

"Archers, ready your bows," the duke called.

The slide of nocked arrows hissed like serpents of death.

Fury flickering in the knight's eyes, he reined his mount back. "We will leave, Your Grace, but Lord Comyn will hear of your betrayal." He wheeled his mount. Hooves clattered upon the frozen ground as he cantered toward his men.

"God's teeth," Thomas spat. "You have made an enemy this day."

The duke grunted. "Nor will it be my last." He dug his heels into his steed.

The driver called out. The cart jerked forward, and the thrum of hooves clattered around them thick with foreboding.

Dread rolled through Thomas like blackened sludge. Comyn would come with a large force, of that Thomas had little doubt, except this time he sought more than he and Alesone, but his father, a prominent noble now branded a traitor.

Alesone glanced over. "Dinna be upset. Your father loves you very much."

"All he has done is made a very dangerous enemy."

She narrowed her eyes. "And what of his reclaiming his son?"

"'Tis sacrificing too much!"

"Sacrifice?" she scoffed. "Tell me, if you had a son whose life was in jeopardy, wouldna you do whatever necessary to protect him?"

Head pounding, he rubbed his brow. "'Tis nae that simple. By openly bringing us to Dair Castle, the duke provokes Comyn, who has the English king's ear, along with that of the king of France. A contingent will be sent. With the stakes so high, I wouldna be surprised if your father led the charge himself."

Any color washed from her face. "Oh God!" she whispered. "Regardless of how this began, the motive is because of me."

Bedamned Hades and back! "None of this is your fault. Neither will Comyn achieve his goal." To his last breath, never would Alesone be forced into a marriage to a cruel bastard who would break her strong will, and destroy this fierce, caring woman.

"I will deal with the future as it unravels," she said, her voice even, but he saw her tremble. "Until then, 'tis best to focus on you, and your family reunited."

"I—"

Against the rumble of the wheels she laid her hand over his. He stared at where her fingers pressed against his skin, and unwanted thoughts of their kiss poured through him with a searing heat.

"I know you are upset," Alesone said, "but can you nae see how fortunate you are?"

He squelched the slide of desire, focused on his being given a second chance. Thomas lifted his gaze to hers and admitted what perplexed him most. "I dinna know why my father has forgiven me."

The deep lines on her brow softened. "Because you are his son. For him 'tis enough."

"But—"

"'Tis a gift, one you are blessed to receive."

Emotion balled in his throat as Thomas stared at the stand of fir they rambled past, unsure how his father could offer compassion when he deserved none. "His decision makes little sense."

"Mayhap to you, but the duke is a man of wisdom. He understands what is important in life isna his holdings or gold but family." Her hand gently squeezed his. "I pray during your stay that you find the forgiveness for yourself that your father holds within his heart."

Doubtful such would ever exist, he glanced toward her.

"Naught is easy," she continued, her words somber. "There will be anger, theirs, yours, for old hurt and, if bitter words are passed once we arrive, new. But each day you push forward, you strengthen the precious bond between you and your family, one you are blessed to have."

The vision her words crafted tempted him to believe such a hope existed. "As if 'tis so simple to forget how my reckless behavior destroyed my family?" Thomas hissed.

Hurt darkened her eyes.

Ashamed of his outburst, more so as her advice wasna easily given, he shook his head. "I am sorry." Like him, Alesone carried the burden of another person's death. More than anyone else, she understood the silent war he battled, except unlike him, she had nay one left.

"We hurt," she said, her voice thick with torment, "but instead of focusing on the pain, we remember them with fond memories and with the laughter of times past. Neither do I delude myself in believing that the sadness of losing Grisel willna haunt me. 'Tis the risk of loving someone, a decision I dinna regret. Over time, however difficult to believe now, the sadness will ebb." She wiped the back of her hand against the tear trickling down her cheek. "Once I move beyond my grief, my guilt, I will be able to smile at the times we shared in life. Until you grow stronger and believe that you deserve your father's mercy, you can at least give him what he wants—his son."

Thomas stilled. She was right. After all he'd lost, for the time he remained at Dair Castle, he owed his father that. Thomas gave a curt nod. "For him I will try." Humbled by this woman who, beyond her own grief, tried to help his, he drew her hand into his. "Nor have I thanked you."

Tears glittered in her eyes. "I have done naught but offered advice."

He skimmed his thumb over the softness of her skin, her strength seeping into his battered soul. "You give yourself too little credit."

"And you," Alesone said quietly, "dinna give yourself enough."

Never in his life had he known a lass like her, stubborn, intelligent, and able to make him laugh. What would it be like to have a woman like her in his life? 'Twas easy to imagine waking up next to her each morning, her tendrils of blond hair fluttered against her cheek as she slept. And how those lavender eyes would open, and warm.

With stoic efficiency he smothered the appealing image. Regardless of what she made him feel, of how he wanted her, in the end he would ride off to battle.

Without her.

"What are you thinking of?"

Against the rumble of wagon wheels as the cart bumped over the snow-ridden land, hand trembling, he gently cupped her chin and drew her forward until her eyes flared with awareness. "That you canna become important to me, but," he whispered, "I fear 'tis too late."

Chapter Ten

Wagon wheels crunching upon frozen ground melded with the thud of hooves as Alesone stared at Thomas, stunned by his rough claim. From the unsteadiness of his voice, she believed that he didna caution her, but himself.

How in less than a fortnight could she have become important to him? As if with her own growing feelings for him made sense? What he made her need, made her want, defied logic.

The cart bumped over a rock breaking Thomas's hold. "I…" With a grimace he glanced at the knights riding nearby, then toward his father leading the contingent. "I shouldna have spoken."

Her entire life stilled as if on a fragile precipice. Had their kiss changed everything for him, too? Would she ever know? Apprehension shot through her, and she asked the question that could fill her with joy or leave her devastated. "Why nae?"

"We each have our own lives," he said with stoic firmness, "ones that dinna include the other."

Hurt that he could close her out with such ease, she drew father away. "And that decision is yours to make?"

"Alesone—"

"You are right, now isna the place to speak about this, but hear me well, this discussion isna done."

His cool gaze locked on hers.

Far from intimidated, she angled her jaw.

Irritation glittered in his eyes, and she dismissed his ire. She hadna looked for a man in her life, or wanted someone who inspired feelings best left buried deep. Except behind his fierce, uncompromising façade, each passing day she spent in this warrior's company unveiled a man bound by honor, loyalty, and a good heart. Traits that'd eroded her intent to keep him at a distance.

However much he was coming to matter in her life, if he believed he could toss out that she'd become important to him and then dismiss the topic as if she were day-old bread, he was wrong.

The cart lurched as it hit another rock.

As he caught her watching him, his expression pained, Thomas turned away, and her temper faded. "How far is Dair Castle?"

"A ways yet."

"Tell me about your home?"

He shrugged. "Many years have passed since I last visited."

"What does it look like?" she asked, hoping to draw his attention away from his discomfort. "Surely you remember that?"

Thomas gave her a measuring look. "'Tis built on the edge of a loch. When I was a child, I would climb upon a merlon, my fingers cold against the smooth stone as I stared past the castle walls and tried to imagine what lay beyond."

"Were you happy there?" she asked, envisioning him as young lad, full of hope, eager for excitement.

"Aye, but I wanted to travel." He shifted, tucked a handful of hay behind his back. "I yearned to begin the grand adventure that I had imagined. Except once I left, I didna anticipate how much I would miss the Highlands."

She scanned the rough peaks smeared with snow reflecting the sun like crystals tossed, their brilliance enticing one to believe fairies lurked beneath the flakes. "I can understand how you would miss it."

Thomas took in the harsh sweep of land, and like a door opened, more thoughts he'd banished over the years filled his mind. With each memory the barriers he'd carefully built to prevent him from thinking about his past eroded further.

Melancholy, he studied the woman who'd dared question him about his youth, one who intrigued him more than he wished. He should remain silent, sever any path to deepen their friendship. Already she made him care too much. Yet, however unwise, he found himself wanting to tell her about his childhood. Still sharing the memories would provide a much needed distraction.

As well, Alesone needed a friend who she could turn to in times of trouble. However unconventional their beginning, and though she hadna asked, he found his stepping into the role a natural move, more so with him charged as her protector.

In the future what she chose to do with her life was her affair, but for now she was beneath his guard. As well, until they reached their destination, for her safety, he would ensure any men about kept their distance.

He scanned the familiar track of land. "Once I am able to walk a distance, there are several places that I would like to show you."

As if a gift given, her expression softened. "I would like that very much."

Pleased, he settled against the backboard. "When I was a lad, at first light, with the smell of warm bread filling the castle, I would sneak into the kitchen and charm the cooks out of a fresh loaf." A smile tugged at his mouth. "If berries were in season, the lass crafting the loaves would give me a bowlful drizzled with honey."

"A charmer from your youth, why am I nae surprised?" she said. "With your having three brothers and a sister, neither do I believe you led a mundane life. If they were anything like you, your home must have been filled with antics."

"Aye," he said with a smile. "One time Matheu, Léod, and I caught Donnchadh trying to woo a kiss from a lass. The idea of pressing one's mouth against a woman's was a hideous thought to a wee lad, so we decided mead had muddled his mind. Our solution, Donnchadh needed but time to sober up and see the error of his ways."

"What did you do?"

"Once the lass departed, we jumped him. Amidst Donnchadh's demands to set him free, we tied him up, hauled him to the stables, and shoved him inside an empty barrel."

She gasped. "You left him?"

Tears of laughter blurred his eyes as he recalled his oldest brother's outrage. "We had planned on leaving him until morning, time enough for the drink to wear off, but spitting mad, he rocked against the barrel until it crashed to its side, and then he worked his way out."

Humor twinkled in her eyes. "Your father must have been furious when he discovered what you and your brothers had done."

"Except for my black eye, which I assured my father 'twas due to my having fallen while climbing the ben, he never learned of the event."

Her laughter warmed his heart. "Why do I have little doubt that you and your siblings' exploits over the years caused your parents much frustration?"

"Mayhap." Except the pranks they had played and the laughter that'd filled Dair Castle were long past.

Her face grew somber. "What is wrong?"

"'Tis…" An ache filled him, and he released a rough breath. "Never will I see those I love again."

"You canna, but for a while they were part of your life. You have memories of your time together," she whispered, her voice rough, "that nay one can take from you."

Emotion twisted inside. Damning his weakness when it came to her, Thomas stroked his fingers across her cheek. "My mother would have liked you." He envisioned her taking stock of Alesone with a shrewd eye and finding approval. "She would have appreciated your courage, your loyalty, and that you dinna allow anyone to push you around."

"Including when I first met you?"

He lowered his hand with a smile. "She would have been entertained by your driving an arrow into a tree but a breath away from me." The amusement in Alesone's eyes charmed him further.

"If your men hadna snuck up behind me," she said, "you would have been answering my questions."

"I would have," he admitted, "but more to learn how a woman of such beauty holds skills to rival the finest archer."

A blush swept her cheeks. "'Tis a clever way of asking how I became proficient at archery."

"And will you tell me?"

She shrugged. "'Tis a peculiar story."

"How so?" he asked, his curiosity piqued.

"When I was young, while out picking herbs, I came upon a well-armed knight who, while traveling through Comyn lands, had collapsed due to illness. A tall, burly man, though I tried, he was too heavy for me to drag, so I ran for Grisel's help."

"And the weapons?"

She arched a playful brow. "I should have known you would ask. Once he was settled inside the hut, I ended up making a second trip to retrieve them."

"With the effort required to bring the warrior to your home, 'tis understandable that you remembered him. Otherwise, there is little peculiar about the situation."

"A point with which I agree. Nor was making a second trip for a knight's sword or dagger out of the norm, until I saw his weaponry."

At the reverence in her voice, he stilled. "What do you mean?"

"Never had Grisel or I beheld such a finely crafted dagger. And his sword, though simple, was grand. On the hilt of both lay a cross."

Unease rippled through him. The emblem identifying a Knight Templar. "His name?" he asked with forced lightness.

"Sir Struan McRuer. He wouldna share his destination, but explained 'twas of great importance that he deliver the writ he carried."

"Did he say where he had acquired his weapons?"

The wagon bumped over another ditch, and she clutched the side. "I didna ask, but he mentioned he had been on campaign in Armenia, and that his weapons were the same as the knights whom he fought alongside."

Armenia, where the Templars had lost their last stronghold in Antioch. "Sir Struan sounds like an interesting man."

"Indeed," Alesone continued, ignorant of his inner turmoil. "And highly skilled with numerous weapons. In thanks for tending to him, for the few days he remained with us, while he recovered, he taught me how to improve my proficiency with a bow."

Which explained how she'd gained expertise rivaled by only a few, all knights within the Order. "You were fortunate to make an acquaintance of a man with such skill."

"I was. Though we never did see him again."

Only one reason made sense for a Templar to travel through the Highlands all those years ago, to meet with King Robert, a man few knew was of the Brotherhood.

From the knight's urgency, Thomas suspected his journey entailed a secret plan agreed upon by the Bruce and Jacques de Molay if the Templars ever had to evacuate. A strategy the Order had used to ensure that treasures held within the Paris Temple, along with the Templar fleet, vanished before King Philip began the arrests.

As they rounded the next turn, down the snow covered, rut mottled road, the stand of trees on either side fell away. His chest tightened as he surveyed the glen framing the loch, and how at the opposite end, Dair Castle arched skyward in brilliant defiance.

"'Tis beautiful," Alesone breathed.

"Aye." He took in the rugged sweep of land, wished back the years, ones that would never come. A movement to his side had him glancing over.

His father cantered toward them, reined his mount in paces away. "I sent a runner ahead to let Donnchadh know of our approach."

"I thank you." Though astonished by his father's forgiveness, little doubt remained that his eldest brother wouldna share the sentiment. After Léod's death, he and Donnchadh had argued, his brother's words laced with fury, and Thomas's rebuttal incited by guilt.

With his brother's blistering remarks scorching his mind and his guilt festering, he'd approached his father, explained that he wanted to become a monk. After a long discussion, and with his refusing to listen to any advice, though reluctant, his father had brought him to the monastery. And from that day, fueled by remorse, he'd vowed never to return home.

A promise he'd intended to keep.

"How do you fare?" his father asked.

Thomas shrugged. "Well enough."

Concerned eyes shifted to his side. "Mistress Alesone?"

"I am fine, Your Grace." She nodded toward the stronghold. "Dair Castle is magnificent."

Pride beamed on the duke's face. "'Twas handed down to me by my father, and through our family for hundreds of years. While here, you are free to go about as you wish. I will ensure that you are introduced to the healer. If you require herbs, she will have what you need."

"I thank you. You are generous."

"I am concerned for my son."

Thomas grimaced. He wasna on his death bed.

A castle guard's shout echoed in the distance.

Iron and wood grated, and the portcullis clanked upward.

Windcast snow swirled around them as they rode beneath the gatehouse. As the wagon rolled into the bailey, sunlight spilled through the clouds to shimmer across the daunting fortress.

Memories burned through Thomas as he took in the familiar surroundings. The smithy's, where he'd watched his first sword being forged, the lists where he'd learned to spar, and the chapel where he'd sought guidance from Him throughout his youth.

Years had taken their toll on the mighty stronghold. The curtain wall showed signs of recent repairs and several new buildings stood where naught had existed before but dirt.

A tall, sandy-haired man strode from the keep, confidence in every step, and anger burning in his eyes.

Donnchadh.

The driver halted the wagon at the center of the baily.

After an order from his father, the knights in accompaniment cantered toward the stables. The duke dismounted, and a lad ran over and led the mount away.

On a deep breath, Thomas pushed himself up.

Alesone stood.

Refusing to show weakness before his brother, Thomas ignored the pain and climbed from the wagon.

"I am thankful you made it back safe, Father." Donnchadh turned toward Thomas, his gaze filled with displeasure. "It has been a long time."

Mayhap, but from the coldness of his voice, his brother's anger thrived. Thomas gave him curt nod. "It has." He turned. "May I introduce Mistress Alesone."

His brother glanced over, and appreciation filled his gaze. "Mistress Alesone, welcome to Dair Castle."

A muscle worked in Thomas's jaw, and he placed a possessive hand on her arm. "Mistress Alesone, I would like to introduce you to my brother, Earl of Stratton."

"Lord Stratton," she said, "I am humbled by your father's generosity."

"I am her escort," Thomas added. "We will be here but days. Once I have recovered we will depart."

A muscle worked in Donnchadh's jaw. "It must be an inconvenience to be injured and forced to be hauled to Dair Castle like a cripple."

"Enough!" Their father stepped between them, shot his eldest son a cool look. "Regardless the circumstance, I am thankful Thomas is here. You *will* offer your brother welcome."

Donnchadh gave a curt nod. "Of course, Father, 'tis remiss of me to say otherwise." Eyes hard, he stepped back. "If you will excuse me, there is an issue of importance I must tend to." Turning on his heel, he strode toward the keep.

His father gave a frustrated sigh. "Excuse Donnchadh, Mistress Alesone."

She cleared her throat. "'Tis a difficult time for everyone, Your Grace."

"I take it a room has been prepared for Mistress Alesone?" Thomas asked. The sooner he was healed and they could leave, the better.

Sadness wedged in his father's brow. "Aye, the room to the left of yours has been readied for her. With you her protector, I thought 'twas best if she remained nearby."

"I thank you. I will show her the way."

"Thomas," his father said.

"Aye?"

"Regardless of what brought you here, 'tis good to have you home."

Guilt grew at the hope in his father's eyes, and he silently cursed. However much he wanted, neither could he stay.

"Do you need help?" the duke asked.

"Nay."

"I will leave you now, and order a tray sent up to your room."

Thomas nodded. "I thank you."

His father departed.

With his body aching from the long journey, Thomas glanced over. "Follow me." With slow steps, he started toward the keep.

Concerned eyes held his. "You are hurting."

"I am fine."

She scoffed. "You tried to hide your discomfort as you climbed from the wagon, but nay one was fooled. To salvage your pride, your father and brother said naught."

"I sincerely doubt my brother noticed my pain," he said, irritated by what likely was the truth, "or if he did, cared."

"Why?"

Thomas's muscles rebelled as he stepped forward, the effort leaving his legs trembling.

"Is the strife due to Léod's death?" she pressed.

He shot her a cool look. "Aye."

"How many years have passed since you left home?"

On a sigh, he pushed on. "Nae enough."

"I think your father feels otherwise."

Tired and wanting to reach his chamber, he grunted. "'Tis complicated."

"Anything worthwhile in life," she said, her voice gentle, "normally is."

Thomas jerked open the door.

As he led her to the turret, he scanned the great room, the arches a fine setting for the shields hanging upon the walls, the blades used by his ancestors beside each, and a coat of arms for the Clan MacDonald situated between. He slowed, his each step filled with reminders of his youth, igniting more memories. Never had he meant to return, except now that he had, God help him, he found himself wanting to remain.

Chapter Eleven

Wind buffeted the window as Thomas sat in the chair and stared at the hearth, the gentle waver of flames at odds with the storm howling outside. Grimacing against the pain, he leaned closer, held his hands against the warmth.

Another blast of wind screamed outside.

The air tinged with the scent of smoke, he tugged the blanket tighter around him, thankful this night he and Alesone were safe.

Out of danger was another matter.

A soft tap sounded on the door.

With a frown, he glanced over. What was she doing up so late? Nay doubt wanting to check on him. "Enter."

Hewn wood scraped, then his father stepped inside.

Unsure of the reason for his nocturnal visit, Thomas hesitated. He'd believed for the first day, mayhap two, his father would keep his distance. If for naught more than time to acclimate to his presence. "I didna expect to see you so late. 'Tis well past Compline."

"I had meant to arrive earlier, but there were several matters requiring my attention." Tired lines creased his brow as he settled in a chair close by. "I took a chance, as I believed you might be asleep."

"With the herbs Alesone gave me, so did I," he said, doubting his father's visit was to address such a mundane issue.

His father studied him for a long moment. "You have grown into a fine man."

Guilt tightened in his chest. "You know naught about me."

Aged eyes narrowed. "A fact," he said, his voice cool, "you ensured by remaining away."

Bedamned, he didna want to discuss this now. Or ever. "'Twas for the best."

"For whom?"

"As if you need to ask?" He shoved to his feet, clenching his teeth against the burst of pain. Blast it! "For you, for my family. My foolishness cost Léod his life."

Eyes dark with sorrow, his father unfurled his lean frame and stood. "I loved your brother, was devastated by his death, but when you left the monastery, I lost you as well."

And his family, the heartache of his decision so long ago, haunted Thomas still.

"You disappeared without a word, neither would Brother Nicholai reveal where you had gone." A wry smile touched his face. "I admit threatening him if he didna tell me, a sin I shall carry for the rest of my days. His assurance that you were in good hands gave me something to hold on to." He paused. "Will you at least tell me where you went?"

"Does it matter?"

"Aye," his father snapped. "I want to know what was so bloody important that you would disappear without a word." Anger flared in his eyes. "Did you think your leaving wouldna hurt me or your mother?"

"I needed time away, time to think, and a place where I could somehow find forgiveness."

"And the monastery didna give you that?"

Thomas shrugged. "If I had entered for the right reasons, mayhap." He stared at the sparks rising within the wisps of smoke. Nor would he mention his argument with Donnchadh before he'd left Dair Castle. The decision to leave had been his, but he would give his father a piece of the truth. "I believed by immersing myself in studies to become a monk, surrendering any chance of a family, 'twould be my penance for Léod's death."

The duke gave a shaky nod. "After your brother's death, our entire family grieved, but you were inconsolable. I thought your living in a holy setting would give you time to calm, to realize Léod's death 'twas naught but an accident."

"One caused by me!"

"Enough!" His father's brows slammed together. "I canna tell you the number of times throughout my life that I have made reckless decisions, ones that resulted in a people getting injured."

"But nay one ever died," Thomas said.

His gaze narrowed to dangerous slits. "And death is the bar of judging a poor decision?" he demanded, his voice rising. "So I should feel that if nay one died from whatever imprudent decision I had made, then 'tis excused?"

God's teeth. "That is nae what I am saying."

"'Tis," he said, his face red with anger. "Listen to yourself."

Thomas stared at the man he'd admired in his youth, one he'd wanted to emulate once grown, but after all that'd passed, he doubted he could ever begin to fill this great warrior's shoes.

Alesone's plea to accept his father's forgiveness echoed in his mind, but it wasna so simple. "I have listened to myself, tried to find a way to move on, and with my each attempt failed."

The duke's gaze softened. "You are nay longer alone, but with family."

Aye, a father who wanted him to remain, and a brother who wished that he'd never returned. A slow pounding thrummed in his temple. Thomas stumbled to his chair, wished he had more herbs to dull the pain.

He rubbed his forehead. What did he say now? Or was there anything left? "I am sorry I left the monastery without informing you. Never did I mean to hurt you." He blew out a rough breath. "I canna tell you how many times I wished the moment back, wished I had left Léod alone."

The duke settled in the chair at his side. "But you canna go back."

"Nay."

"Neither does ignoring the fact erase the tragedy. When you bury your misfortunes beneath the demands of duty, you dinna live, but exist." Hands scarred with age and time folded beneath the other. "Ask yourself what you want."

"If only 'twas that simple," Thomas breathed.

His father leaned back. "Why does it have to be difficult?"

He scowled. "Have you heard naught of what I said?"

"Aye, I have," he blustered, "your words spurned by grief, but none of your life ahead."

Bedamned! "I have..." Duty, as his father had said, nay thoughts for his own life. With his fealty given to Bruce and the upcoming confrontations as his king fought to unite Scotland, 'twas a fool's lot to make plans. A swing of an opponent's blade could sever any dreams made.

Weary, Thomas shook his head. "What do you want me to say? I doubt any reply I could give will rival those of your expectations. Nor do you have time to concern yourself with my aspirations. As Duke of Westwyck, you have responsibilities to fulfill, those with due time that will be passed down to Donnchadh, ones that dinna concern me."

He stiffened. "Try answering my question of what *you* want."

Panic swelled inside as Thomas he pushed his thoughts past duty, past a way of life that dictated his future.

His father arched a challenging brow.

"A home and a family," he blurted out, stunned the thoughts had been buried in his mind.

"*Both* within your reach."

"I am a knight. I own a horse and a few pieces of coin, nae enough to purchase a simple hut, much less attract a lass, nor will I accept a handout. Whatever I accomplish," he said, his voice tight, "'twill be achieved by my own hand."

Sadness touched his father's expression. "You are more than a knight, but the Earl of Kincaid."

"You are wrong, I gave up my title when—"

"'Tis still yours."

Blast it, why was he arguing? 'Twas a deed long since done. "I rescinded the title after I left the monastery, a writ you should have received."

"I did," his father stated, "and burned the bloody document as quick."

Burned it? Thomas stared at him in disbelief. "Why?"

"Because you are my son, and I had faith that one day you would return."

Emotion tightened in his throat. "I have done naught to earn such."

"My actions are nae your decision to make but mine. The right of a father, if you will." He rubbed his brow. "Wherever you went, regardless of the guilt that drove you away, I am confident that you achieved many things for which you are proud."

He paused. "Why do you say that?"

"You hold yourself with dignity, have a way about you that bespeaks confidence, and with your oath given to Robert Bruce, you are a man who isna afraid to fight for what you believe in." He grunted. "If you had led a disreputable life, I doubt our king would be charging you with the task of protecting Mistress Alesone." Shrewd eyes narrowed. "Where have you been all of these years? After everything, I deserve to know."

With all that his father had endured, suffered, Thomas agreed. In brief, he explained how Brother Nicholai had confronted him, suggested his becoming a Knight Templar, a life where, in addition to serving God, he could protect Christians traveling to the Holy Land.

Tears misted in his father's eyes. "I am so proud of you." He gasped. "Mary help us."

At his father's distress, Thomas stilled. "What is wrong?"

"A fortnight ago I received a missive concerning news of King Philip's charges against the Templars in Paris."

Memories of King Philip's scheme to arrest those of the Brotherhood flooded his mind. "The charges are false," he spat, "lies spewed to claim our gold."

Aged eyes held his. "As I suspected. I am thankful that you were among those chosen to leave. What of the Templars still in France?"

Thomas fisted his hands. "The Grand Master believes with Pope Clement's intervention mayhap they can find a way to save the remaining knights. A belief I dinna share. With King Philip's intent to claim the Templars' wealth, any attempt at negotiations are naught but a wasted effort."

His father paled. "You havena heard that France's king imprisoned Jacques de Molay?"

God in heaven, nay! He closed his eyes against the avalanche of heartache. A gentle hand lay on his shoulder.

"There is naught shameful in showing grief, more so when 'tis for men you cared for and battled beside."

Thomas met his gaze. "Nae, there isna."

His father withdrew his hand, the pride in his eyes leaving Thomas humbled. "I dinna know the right way to say…" Overwhelmed, moved by the depth of his father's forgiveness, he extended his hand. "'Tis important," he said, straightening his shoulders as his palm slid against the man's who shaped his world, "that you know how proud I am to be your son."

He clasped his hand. "You are a fine man." The duke gave a tight squeeze, and then let go. "I know you are in service to King Robert. Once you have finished escorting Mistress Alesone, I pray you will return, even if 'tis for a brief visit."

Warmth touched Thomas's heart, and for the first time in many years, a sliver of peace filled him. He nodded. "I would be liking that."

A gust battered the window, and his father grimaced at the blackness churning outside flecked with bitter tosses of white. "'Tis a brutal storm this night."

"'Tis." With a fragile bond forged between them, Thomas stood and walked over to place a log onto the flames. Sparks jumped, swirled within the churn of smoke that disappeared into the hearth. "John MacLairish was a Knight Templar as well. He is a close friend."

His father nodded. "I have always believed to be him a man of exceptional caliber."

Thomas settled onto his chair. "After he was injured in battle, I wrote a missive to Brother Nicholai beseeching him to help find John work where he could support himself. For all he sacrificed, he deserved a life he could be proud of. One serving the monks would be an honorable profession."

"Indeed."

"And," Thomas said, "'tis because of John that I am alive."

His father arched a brow. "Explain."

"After Alesone and I arrived at his hut, he rode to the monastery for help." Anger slid through Thomas. "Days later when Comyn's men trailed us to his home, John refused to give them any information of where we had gone, so they tortured him."

"By God I will have their heads!" his father roared.

"Nae if I find them first. Nor," Thomas said, his voice dry, "is the men's brutality the most imminent concern. Lord Comyn will be furious once he receives the blistering report of your threatening his knights when they tried to block us from leaving the monastery."

A satisfied smile curved his father's mouth. "Aye he will. Exposing my true allegiance for Robert the Bruce is a day I have long awaited. As for John, once he is able to be moved, for his loyalty, he will be brought here and stay until he is healed."

"I thank you. John is a good man."

"He is." His father rubbed his forehead, and then gave a tired sigh.

"'Tis late," Thomas said, finding himself weary as well.

Stifling a yawn, his father stood. "I think 'tis time I found my bed." Pride shown in his eyes. "'Tis good to have you back, my son."

Humbled, he nodded. "'Tis good to be home."

The duke departed and silence fell within the chamber.

With the strife between them eased, Thomas anticipated spending more time with his father, of learning about the man he'd become. More important, when the opportunity arose, he would return.

Flames flickered in the hearth. He shook his head in disbelief at the news of his nobility.

He still held the title.

Incredible.

At eleven summers he'd traveled to Conchar Castle with his father. A small but serviceable stronghold, he'd decided that when of age he would move there, marry, and raise a family. When he'd fled from his home so long ago and had revoked his title, a property he'd believed lost.

With the secret dissolution of the Knights Templar, the Grand Master had encouraged the escaping Brotherhood to marry and blend into society. After his strict way of life within the Order, never had he believed he would consider settling down in what the church defined as a normal life.

A thought his friend and fellow Templar Sir Stephan MacQuistan had shared several months prior. Thomas hesitated. Could he, too, find such happiness? Once his service to King Robert was complete, if he chose, he could reside in Conchar Castle. As for a woman to share his life, that was another matter.

Exhausted, Thomas closed his eyes, and embraced the weight of sleep. Wind slammed against the window as his mind began to blur, and he sank deeper into the numbing haze.

Without warning, the taste of Alesone's kiss rushed his mind, the softness of her mouth, and of how she'd pressed against him.

Body aching, Thomas sat, the fatigue of moments before shattered. He glared at the wall separating them. With but a few steps he could be with her.

God's teeth, what was he thinking? He was Alesone's protector. As if that explained their kiss in the monastery? Aye he was attracted to her, but a woman like her wouldna appreciate a simple dalliance, neither would he insult her with such an offer. Nor did the lass need complications when her life was riddled with treachery.

Except with thoughts of her haunting his mind, the slow burn pulsing within his body grew. With a muttered curse, he stood. A walk down the corridor to take in the paintings of his ancestors and savor the happier memories of his youth should provide a welcome diversion.

He grimaced at the stiffness in his legs as he crossed his chamber. Thomas exited, tugged the door shut.

The slap of wind outside echoed from down the passageway with a savage howl.

Torchlight wavered within the corridor illuminating several paintings he remembered. His gaze paused on the new portrait hanging across from his chamber, one of his father standing beside his mother on the wall walk, the Highlands a formidable backdrop.

His heart aching, he lifted his hand to the canvas and traced the face of the woman he'd never see again. "I am sorry," he whispered, the oils beneath his fingers rough like his words, "never did I mean to hurt you."

A soft cry sounded from the room to his right. Another sob, this time quieter broke the wind-whipped silence.

Alesone! Had an intruder slipped inside the castle? Furious, Thomas withdrew his dagger, rushed to her door, and shoved. Blade readied, he scoured the room.

Flames cheerfully swayed in the hearth, at odds against the hurl of wind against the panes.

He glanced at her bed. Uncovered, she lay curled in a tight ball in the center, her blanket twisted, hanging off the bed in a violent twist.

On a moan, she shifted, her hand clawing in the air.

A nightmare. With an exhale, he secured his weapon tried to ignore how shimmers of golden firelight caressed the curves of her body. Trying to smother the burst of need, he walked over and drew up the covers.

She gave another cry.

Thomas touched her shoulder. "Alesone, wake up, 'tis Thomas."

Lids thick with sleep lifted. Groggy eyes cleared, widened. On a gasp, she jerked the blanket around her as she sat. "What are you doing in my chamber?"

Bedamned! He glanced toward the door, half expecting his father to rush in. "Shhhh!" After a moment, thankful when nay one came to investigate, he turned. "I was in the corridor and heard you call out. You were having a nightmare."

White knuckled, she clenched the cover. "I…" Her eyes darkened with horror, and she looked away. "Go away."

And he would have, but she trembled. "What did you dream about?" he asked.

"C-can you just leave?"

The tremor in her voice had him sitting on the edge of her bed. "I want to know."

She turned. "Why?"

"Because I care about you." Bloody hell, how had he allowed that to slip out?

"'Tis unseemly for you to be in my chamber."

Unseemly was a poor choice to describe how he ached to touch her. "Aye, but to ensure you were safe, 'twas well worth the risk."

Her grip on the bed covering eased. "Given the circumstance of our first meeting, I dinna think I need a protector."

The reminder didna temper his desire. With her but paces away and looking like every man's fantasy he was a fool to remain. Except within her narrowing eyes the glint of tears lingered, and he suspected her bravado was naught but a mask to shield her upset. She needed a friend to listen to her worries. That he could give her.

"What were you doing up?" she asked.

"I couldna sleep and decided to go for a walk."

Suspicion darkened her gaze. "At this late hour?"

Thomas rubbed the back of his neck. "I havena been to Dair Castle since my youth, and I wanted to look around. There are so many memories here. Each curve, every room, brings more, some I had forgotten."

Her eyes softened. "'Tis hard."

"Indeed." Emotion tightened in his throat. "I keep thinking that I will hear my mother's voice, or see her."

Alesone edged closer. "I would feel the same if I returned to Grisel's hut." A comely blush dusted her cheeks, and she edged away. "I thank you for checking on me, but you can go now? I will be fine."

Naught but words, her distress easy to see. "Do you mind if I stay a while?"

Nervous eyes glanced toward the door.

"To talk," he said. Wisps of golden firelight shimmered across her skin in silent invitation, and he silently groaned.

She gave a shaky nod.

"What did you dream about?"

"I-I was being chased by my father's men and..." A tremor shook her shoulders, and then another.

The bastard! Reigning in his fury, Thomas drew her against him.

Alesone hesitated, and then laid her head against his chest.

Thomas wrapped his arms around her, and rested his chin atop her head. As long as he drew a breath, nay one would hurt her again. Several moments passed, but he remained silent, gave her time to calm.

"I dreamt my father and his men were chasing me," she finally whispered. "Then he was reaching out to grab me. I tried to fight him, but I couldna escape." She sat back, and he immediately missed her body's touch. Alesone sniffed. "'Tis ridiculous to be upset of thoughts found in one's sleep."

After having lived through his own night terrors he understood the traumatic visions nightmares could deliver. "At times in our life each of us struggle against memories, some awake, and some while we sleep. Though we could use the help of a friend, 'tis stubbornness that has us turning away from what we yearn for the most."

"Words of experience?" Her warm breath brushed across his neck.

Needing to touch her, he cupped her jaw, stroked his thumb along the curve of her chin, and his body tightened at the slide of silky skin beneath. "Aye."

Her gaze grew intense. Covers shifted as she moved closer, the mix of her scent her and lavender storming his senses.

If he leaned forward, their lips would brush, and he could taste her. Except he'd remained to offer her friendship.

"What are you thinking?"

Like a caress, her soft words stroked his need higher. "What I have nae right to."

She turned the slightest degree, but the movement aligned her mouth to his.

Heart pounding, he struggled for his next breath. "I must leave."

"A wise man said that there are times we all could use the help of a friend, but 'tis stubbornness that has us turning away from what we yearn for the most."

He swallowed hard, didna move, didna dare to, the grip on his desire tentative at best.

"And at this moment," Alesone whispered, "'tis you I yearn for."

Chapter Twelve

The ache to feel Thomas's lips upon hers smothered Alesone's intent to keep her distance. On a shudder, she pressed her mouth against his, and groaned beneath the explosion of sensation. As his taste flooded her, she shifted closer, stilled. He hadna moved.

Humiliation smothered the shot of desire, and she stumbled back. "I am sorry."

Thomas caught her arm. "Why did you kiss me?" he rasped, his gaze searing into hers.

"When we played chess you…" Heat stole up her cheeks, and she shook her head, wishing she could disappear. Throughout her life, outside Grisel and Burunild, she'd hadna allowed herself to become close to anyone.

How had this man had broken her carefully constructed barriers? More, made her yearn for his touch. "I believed you were attracted to me, that I…" She gave a shaky exhale. "Forgive me."

"Alesone." He stepped before her.

Tears clogged her throat. "I am sorry." She tried to jerk free, but he drew her closer. Their bodies aligned; she tried to ignore his muscled strength, his protective yet gentle hold. Until this aloof warrior had entered her life, never had she envisioned meeting a man that made her want. Except given the circumstance, however much she ached for him, 'twas wrong to embroil him in her debacle of a life as more than that of her protector.

"Alesone—"

"Let me go. Please." Before the yearnings rushing through her eroded her fragile hold and she asked him to stay and to lay with her throughout the night. Shocked by the yearnings he aroused, she awaited the flood of guilt, the remorse, but found only desire instead.

His hand skimmed up her neck to cradle her mouth. "And if I left," Thomas pressed his mouth over hers, along the curve of her jaw, and against her throat, and with each touch, she surrendered further. "I would be a fool."

"Thomas, I—"

"'Tis unseemly for me to remain."

Thrills shot through her at his quiet challenge, the unveiled need. "'Tis."

Something dangerous flickered in his eyes, and her heart slammed against her chest. With sultry slowness, he kissed each finger, and then drew her against him until their mouths were but a breath apart. "Your pulse is racing."

"I canna think." The truth, this close, wanting him, the words she needed to say to push him away vanished.

Green eyes darkened with heat. "Mayhap 'tis best."

"Is it?" she whispered.

"I am unsure." He again claimed her mouth, took the kiss deeper, and whatever she'd meant to say faded beneath the blur of heat.

They'd kissed before, but against this onslaught, what she'd experienced prior 'twas a simple exchange of desire. Now, his each touch, taste became vital to her very existence. His mouth feasted, and she gave, demanded in return.

With tenderness he freed the ties of her gown, and then his fingers skimmed across the sensitive curves. Her body trembling, she arched, giving him access, wanting more.

On a muttered curse, he caught her shoulders. "As much as I want you, we canna do this."

His rough words shattered the euphoria clouding her mind. Refusing to allow him to see her hurt, that if he'd chosen, wanting him with her every breath, she would have made love, Alesone turned away.

Gentle fingers turned her to face him. "Blast it, I am sorry. 'Twas wrong of me to touch you."

Angry that he would blame himself in any way, she pulled free. "I *wanted* the kiss!"

Dark eyes narrowed. "Dinna you understand? Intimacy between us is wrong."

"By whose standards?" Coldness filled her, and she stepped away. "You will have to forgive me if I dismiss decorum. Of late I tire of the standards of society, conventions I have followed my entire life, rules that have delivered me naught but contempt from those who wield them."

"You are upset," he said, "rightly so."

"And what of you?" she demanded. "In regards to us, what is it *you* want?"

He stilled.

A thrill swept her at the naked desire in his eyes, a mixture of yearning and dangerous heat. Aware she crossed every line, shredded convention with her next words, she didna give a damn. Here, now, was all that mattered. For the first time in her life she'd met a man who made her care, who considering their extraordinary introduction had befriended her, and a man who made her feel desire.

"If I wanted you to…" The bravado of moments before faded. What was she thinking? Nay, rational thought was the last thing on her mind. Moments before she'd awoken from a nightmare. Instead of thanking Thomas for his concern, she'd pushed him to where he didna wish to be.

Mortified, Alesone shook her head. "About what I…Ignore my words." Wide awake and with her safeguards restored, if possible, she needed to repair the situation. "You can leave," she said, forcing her voice to remain calm as if inside she wasna falling apart. "I am safe. Naught but a dream threatened me."

Tenderness softened his face as Thomas brushed his thumb against her cheek, and she savored the delicate tingle. "I willna depart allowing you to believe that I dinna want you, but 'tis nae so simple."

Fighting the ache in her chest, Alesone took in the finely crafted mantle carved above the hearth with intricate Celtic pattern, the stained-glass window, and the thick covering upon the bed embroidered with an elegant design. "As the son of a powerful duke, you have duties."

Anger flashed in his eyes. "Is that what you think I care about: power, status?"

"Nay," she replied, ashamed by her words, those cast from her own lack of self-worth. "You are a good man, one who any woman would be proud to have."

"Except you."

A fissure streaked through her heart. She inhaled a rough breath, then another as she fought for composure. "As the bastard daughter of King Robert's enemy, I am nae in a place where I could linger on thoughts of a normal life, much less allow myself to care for you."

Eyes holding hers with fierce intent, he moved forward. "But you do."

Another crack fractured her heart, and she cursed her weakness when it came to him.

"I think," he continued, as his thumb swept over her lower lip in a seductive slide, "'tis best that I leave."

A wise choice, a decision that would serve them both well. Except the thought of being alone left her empty, and she could feel the nightmares that'd stormed her dreams a short time before threatening to return. "I ask that you stay."

His body tensed.

"Only to talk," she rushed out. "If only for a while, please. I dinna want to be alone."

Thomas hesitated. Moments ago he'd cursed the desire searing through him until he'd wanted to take. Now he damned how shaken by her nightmare, at this moment she looked fragile. "I will stay for a while longer."

Her body sagged with relief.

Refusing to remain near the bed, Thomas gestured toward a carved bench paces before the hearth. As she sat, he stoked the fire, and then settled beside her.

Flames wavered over the wood, the simplicity of the moment calming.

With a hesitant glance, Alesone turned. "I thank you for remaining. I know you would have rather left."

He gave a dry smile. "'Twould have been prudent, especially if anyone were to learn of my nocturnal visit."

"You could say that you were sleepwalking."

"Or, I could explain that, feeling poorly, I came for an herbal potion."

Alesone arched a doubtful brow, but the concern on her face eased. On an unsteady breath, she glanced around. "'Tis a beautiful chamber."

"Aye, this room has always been one of my favorites," he said, allowing the memories to fill him. "It belonged to my mother."

Surprise flickered on her face. "Why was I given her chamber?"

"'Twas my father's doing. A choice which I admit pleased me."

A blush swept up her cheeks. "For me as well—to care for you that is," she blurted out.

He should accept her words, but after their kiss, and with his body still aching for her, he wanted her to admit that she wanted more. "And is that all?"

She stilled. "'Tisna fair to ask."

Unable to resist, Thomas skimmed his mouth over hers. "When I see something I want, I find it difficult to be fair."

Her eyes flared with nerves. "You canna want me."

He was pushing her, but for an unexplainable reason, her evasion drove him to hear her say the words. "Why would you think that I wouldna want you?" As a Templar, it was a question that weeks ago he would have sworn he would never ask. Then, he'd never expected to meet someone like her.

"I…" Her lower lip trembled, and she shook her head. "Tell me about your mother's chamber."

He hesitated, wanting to press her, but with her thoughts troubled from her earlier nightmare, now wasna the time. Neither was their discussion through.

Thomas scanned the room, and the tangle of need fading beneath the memories. "My father built this chamber for my mother when she wished to be alone to read, sew, or other quiet diversions."

A wistful smile curved her mouth. "That explains the beautiful details throughout. Never have I seen a mantle carved in such detail, or a stained window crafted with such an exquisite design. Both are breathtaking."

"My father," he said, struggling beneath the wash of sadness, "loved my mother very much."

"I am sorry. Your being here must be difficult."

"In truth," he forced out, "'tis hard to be anywhere within Dair Castle." There are so many memories."

Alesone gave his hand a gentle squeeze. "Will you tell me about your mother?"

Emotions flooded him as he thought of the woman he loved, one he would never see again. "She gave her heart to her family, and she was curious about everything." He shoved to his feet, walked over to a small case filled with books. He withdrew a thick tomb, the hand-tooled leather worn from often use. He stroked his thumb along the aged spine. "I had forgotten about his volume."

The quiet pad of steps sounded, then Alesone paused at his side.

Damning the burn of tears, he didna look at her.

"Tell me about this book," she said softly.

His fingers trembled as he flipped open the cover. Framed by the neatly penned prose, familiar drawings crowded the page, a bit of whimsy as several of the fey peeked out beneath blooms of heather.

She gasped with delight. "They are beautiful!"

"Aye. She enjoyed her time setting ink to paper. Claimed 'twas nae her, but the fey who guided her hand. Here." A smile curved his mouth as he flipped through the pages, paused. "See this?"

Alesone studied the wisps of powder shimmering upon the parchment. "It sparkles."

"Fairy dust she claimed, conjured from the mist of the fey when they'd sneak in at night to look over her stories and drawings. As a child I believed her." He shrugged. "'Tis foolish that I was so naive."

Her expression softened. "'Tis a special memory, one you are blessed to have."

Thomas nodded, wishing back the time with his mother. With a hard swallow, he traced his finger over the neatly written words and the sparkles scattered upon the page. "When I was young, she made up these stories for my siblings and me. When she read them, she'd nae recite a simple telling of a tale, but like a seasoned bard, she'd whisper when the story grew tense so we would be leaning closer, then she'd shout with the arrival of the villain. The lot of us would jump." With a chuckle, he shook his head. "You think we would have learned of her methods to lure us in until lost in the story, we awaited her each word and forgot her penchant for fun. At times I think we realized her intent, but if you could have seen the happiness in my mother's eyes." He smiled. "The stories were as important to us as to her." The joy of the moment faded. "Never would we take that away from her, and now…"

Throat tight, Thomas flipped through the pages, then closed the cover. "Can I see it?"

"Aye." He handed her the tome.

With reverence, Alesone leafed through the book, pausing to smile, and then continued. Tears misted her eyes as she returned the book to him. "What a precious gift. When you have children, you can retell her stories, and share a piece of your mother with each and every tale."

Moved by Alesone's heartfelt words, he nodded. Until this moment all he'd considered was the devastating loss "Aye, 'twill be her legacy of sorts. As much as I wish it," he said, sliding his thumb lovingly along the aged leather, "neither is this book nor the others mine. They belongs to my father. When the time comes to pass her drawings and her stories down, as the eldest, they will go to Donnchadh."

"I would think that your brother would honor your request for at least one volume of something so personal."

Thomas gave a cold laugh, replaced the volume. "I doubt Donnchadh cares what I wish. If 'twas his decision, I wouldna be here."

She hesitated. "What happened to cause the rift between the two of you?"

Hurt poured through him, the angry shouts, the accusations. He ran his fingers along the top of the leather binding, then let his hand fall away.

"Once we'd buried Léod, everyone left but me. Alone, I stared at the newly turned earth and wept until nay more tears would come, haunted by memories of my mother's sobs and my father's face shattered with grief. There was naught I could do to repair the travesty I had caused."

The old ache shuddered through him, and he faced the hearth, the flames charring the wood like the scars upon his soul. "As the sun began to set," he said, his words unsteady, "Donnchadh hauled me up. Eyes red with tears, he accused me of murdering our brother, told me I was unfit to breathe."

Alesone's eyes widened with horror. "'Tis a terrible thing to say."

Thomas grunted. "Anything he said was naught compared to what I had told myself in the hours that I had lain beside my brother's grave. Distraught, I told him that I would leave. Donnchadh cursed me, swore that regardless of where I went, never would I find a place that would bring me peace." The memories ripe, the words uttered all those years before scorched deep in his heart. "And he was right."

"'Twas an accident."

He met her gaze. "Mayhap, but in some things you are never able to find forgiveness for yourself."

Anger flashed in her eyes. "Like the guilt I bear for Grisel's death?"

Bedamned. "Alesone, I didna mean—"

"I know what you meant," she said, her voice raising a notch. "You think teasing your youngest brother makes you guiltier than my aiding a wounded man, but you are wrong. Innocent to the ramifications, each of us made choices, decisions that in the end led to the death of someone we loved."

Her voice broke at the last, and he damned himself. He reached out, but she stepped back.

"This isna about me," Alesone challenged, "but you. However broken inside, you have a family who loves you. Dinna you see, your father's forgiveness is the first step in making your family whole again. Though you and your brother are at odds, until you forgive yourself, quit damning your actions from so many years before, the rift between you and Donnchadh will never heal."

Humbled, Thomas stared at Alesone. Though she hurt, her only consideration was for him. And she was right. So caught up in his grief over the years, until this moment he'd never considered allowing himself even a shimmer of forgiveness.

Nor could he overlook the quiet worry in her voice. With her father's despicable interest in her, until Comyn was defeated, her life would be plagued by danger.

"Even though you damned your actions, you tried to find a way to absolve your sins," she said, breaking into his ruminations, "the reason you went to the monastery, to sacrifice any chance of a home or a family."

"A decision which infuriated my father." He fisted his hands as memories cascaded through him. "We had a terrible row over my leaving. In the end, as I refused to consider any other option, he agreed." He shrugged. "The rest you know."

Alesone nodded, smothering her heart-wrenching memories of Grisel, and focused on Thomas. "That you and your father have renewed a bond is significant, but I believe 'tis as important to mend the fracture between you and Donnchadh."

A muscle worked in his jaw. "For my brother and I, time has repaired naught, nor will the years ahead change that."

"Thomas—"

"Dinna you recall his welcome upon our arrival?" he demanded. "Tell me, has he come to see me since? Nay, nor will he. He despises me," he said, his voice growing hard, "and rightly so. Neither will I beg forgiveness from him when I deserve none."

"'Tis your brother!"

"By blood. There is naught more."

"Because you refuse to try."

The anger in his eyes wilted to resignation, and Thomas rubbed the back of his neck, and then dropped his hand. "I didna expect you to understand."

The man was pigheaded! "And I didna expect for you to walk away without trying to salvage the remnants of your family however tattered." Her eyes narrowed. "Dinna you understand how lucky you are? Nay, instead you cling to your grief, withdraw inside yourself when reminders of the old hurt arises." She fisted her hands. "Damn you, I would give anything to have someone who loved me, however remote, than to have a father who after years only acknowledges my presence because now he finds me useful for his devious scheme."

Stunned by her outburst, aware she'd overstepped her bounds beyond acceptable, Alesone shook her head. "I…" What? How did one apologize for her impropriety? "I am sorry." She turned and fled.

Pain tore through Thomas's body as he caught Alesone's arm.

"Let me go!"

"Wait." Anguish-filled eyes held his, and her words, however much he hadna wanted to hear them, made sense. "Stay, please. My anger isna at you, but me." He gentled his hold. "Your father is a fool to have shunned a woman who is amazing in her own right." Her expression grew tender, and he nodded. "Mayhap you are right, and I should try to repair the rift with Donnchadh."

"You will?"

The tension in her eyes shifted to hope, and to make her happy, the sacrifice of speaking to his brother a small price to pay. "Aye."

"Thank you."

Humbled by this perceptive woman, he brushed away loose strands of hair that'd fallen on her cheek. "'Tis I who should be thanking you. You make me see what I dinna want to, dare question me when I try to push you away." Thomas drew her to him, needing to feel her against him, her warmth, her spirit, and savored the rightness of her in his arms.

How in such a short time had she become so important to him? As if she had any place in his life? Like his thoughts of settling at Conchar Castle, they were little more than a dream. Until the day he walked away from the battlefield, even if he wanted to, he could promise her naught.

She leaned her head against his chest. "What are you thinking?"

He drew in her scent of woman and heat, ached from the rightness of her. "How I wish," he whispered, "that we could stay here forever."

In the firelight, she lifted her eyes to his, the desire within almost bringing him to his knees.

Unable to stop himself, he claimed her mouth, the earlier desperation lost to a slow need, something he couldna define, but touching her, feeling her tremble in his arms, 'twas as essential as his next breath.

Her breathing unsteady, she skimmed her hands up his chest, then her arms wrapped around his neck.

The rush of emotion built as he took, slow and gentle until she was kissing him back, her demands unleashing his own. Her taste pouring through him, he ran his hands over her skin, along the curves of her gown. Holding her gaze, he loosened the ties of her gown, skimmed his fingers along the soft swell of her breast, then lowered his mouth to taste, savor, until her body trembled.

"Thomas, I…"

"I want you," he whispered, stunned he'd spoken aloud. He should leave. To touch her now would do naught but make everything more difficult. Except against every reason, all he could think of was her, of this night, and of showing her all that she made him feel.

Doubt flickered in her gaze. "But you are hurt."

"I am fine. And I will be gentle. I swear it."

She glanced at the bed, turned and gave a shaky nod.

He ignored his body's roar to take her, and savored each movement as he released the last few ties. The gown puddled at her feet. Firelight caressed her skin within its golden glow, each curve crafted as if made to make a man beg.

She made to cover herself, but he caught her hand.

"Nay, you are beautiful." With reverence, he skimmed his fingers along her shoulders, and then cupped the silky weight of her breasts, and his entire body burned. "Perfect." He tasted each hardened tip, slow, savoring, until her breaths fell out in desperate gasps. His mind raw with need, he swept her in his arms and carried her to the bed.

"Thomas—"

"Dinna move. I want to see you. Touch you. Everywhere." With infinite slowness, he kissed her, caressed her until she grew restless beneath him, and her moans drove his control to the brink. Wanting to feel her fall apart, as he deepened the kiss, he skimmed his fingers lower, slid them into her moist heat.

She gasped.

"Just feel." With each stroked, her body arched up to meet his caress, her movements frantic. On a cry, Alesone called out, and Thomas covered her mouth and drank in her passion, absorbed her every shudder.

As she collapsed, he lay on his side and drew her against him, pressed a kiss on her mouth, her cheek, her chin, and then moved lower. "Now I—"

A knock sounded on the other side of the door. "Mistress Alesone?" his father called.

Chapter Thirteen

Embarrassed by her nakedness, more so with warmth still pulsing through her, Alesone grabbed the cover, wrapped it around her as she glanced toward the door.

His expression taut, Thomas pressed his finger over his lips.

Lips that had slid with aching slowness over her body, made her feel sensations she'd never imagined. Oh God, his mouth.

Another knock sounded at the door, this time louder.

"I must get dressed!" she whispered.

Thomas grimaced and moved away.

Cheeks burning, she gave Thomas a hurried kiss then tugged on her gown.

"Mistress Alesone?"

At the duke's urgent entreaty, she glanced over. "A moment, Your Grace."

Thomas caught her shoulders. "Let me speak with him."

"Are you mad! If he finds you here…" Shame filled her as she glanced toward the bed, her body still tingling from his touch.

"I came here because I heard you cry out. I came to check on you," Thomas said, keeping his voice low.

Unsure if 'twas due to the fact that they'd almost made love, or embarrassed by how she'd all but asked for their intimacy, she blurted, "If he finds you in my chamber he will—"

"Trust me."

However much she wanted to, what if he was wrong? What if instead of the duke accepting Thomas's explanation, his father became outraged and demanded…

What?

That he marry her?

Her heart plummeted. God in heaven!

However much she cared for Thomas, his being forced into a marriage wasna her wish. A foolish thought. As if a duke would demand his son wed the bastard daughter of his enemy?

With methodical efficiency, she collected herself. At this moment the only thing she had left was her pride, and with her having lain naked with Thomas that was in tatters. Still, when she left Dair Castle, however damaged, at least she would have that.

"Thomas, hide under the bed." She damned the tremor in her voice.

His mouth tightened. "I willna behave like a criminal in my home."

His home. Lost in his upset, he hadna realized what he'd said. Though his claim assured her that he'd begun to heal, it didna change the criticalness of this moment. "For me. Please."

"Trust me," he repeated, his voice tight.

"I want to, but 'tis too important." She cursed the hurt on his face, pain she'd caused, except the words had been said. Given the stakes, nor would she take them back.

Green eyes narrowed. "I willna hide like a coward, even for you."

Hurt by his charge, she shook her head. "Never did I intend for you to think that."

"Nay?" he said, his voice cool, "How was I to view it otherwise?"

"Thomas?" his father said from outside.

Eyes narrowed, he stepped back. "Come in, Father."

The duke entered. Confusion lined his brow as he halted within the entry and stared at Thomas. "Why are you here?"

"Your Grace," Alesone sputtered, "Thomas was—"

"I couldna sleep and decided to take a walk. When I stepped into the corridor, I heard Mistress Alesone cry out from inside her chamber," he said, his eyes holding hers with a flash of temper. "Worried for her safety, I rushed inside. Thankfully, she wasna in danger, but having a nightmare."

Warmth swept her cheeks at his simple explanation. Instead of trusting him to explain, she'd allowed her mind to create outrageous worries.

The duke's body relaxed. "After what you have endured, I am little surprised you had disturbing dreams." He closed the door and walked over. "'Twould seem a night for unrest. Nor could I sleep. With the sun beginning to rise, I came to check on my son."

Stunned, she glanced toward the window, noted the swath of color staining the eastern sky. Caught up in their talk that'd spun to passion, she'd lost track of time.

"When I discovered his chamber empty," the duke continued, "and as I couldna find him elsewhere, as he is in your care, I thought mayhap you would know."

Her care. God in heaven. Thomas was recovering from serious injuries. Instead of dismissing his assurance that he was fine and insisting that he returned to his bed, she'd allowed him liberties. Allowed? Nay, wanted, and had thrilled at his every touch.

"Your Grace, I am sorry to cause you any concern." Neither did she wish to give any sense of impropriety. What had she been thinking?

Alesone bit back a groan. With the way he'd touched her, kissed her, made her body come alive, there hadna been a lucid thought in her mind. She'd wanted him, and if they hadna been interrupted, would have given him her innocence.

Irritated at herself, and with Thomas deservedly upset by her lack of trust, 'twas best if he went to his chamber. "I explained to your son, Your Grace, that I was fine and he could return to his bed. Except he insisted on staying until he felt that I had calmed."

Pride filled the noble's gaze. "My son is a good man."

He was, one she didna deserve, a man she should have trusted moments before. Frustrated, she met Thomas's gaze. "I thank you again for ensuring that I was safe."

"'Tis the least I can do after you have cared for me." He gave a curt nod. "I will let you try to sleep."

The men exited, and the duke tugged the door closed behind them.

Alesone collapsed on her bed, her body still trembling from his touch, and however wrong the intimacy, yearned for more.

After his father had departed his chamber, Thomas's thoughts shifted to Alesone. Her taste still teased him, that innate sweetness that lured him to go to her and complete what they'd begun. With how she'd responded to his touch, along with the urgency of her kisses, assured him if he went to her now, they could make love.

Except when he'd asked, she hadna given him her trust. Frustrated, he began to pace to smother thoughts of her, but however much he tried, the image of her naked in his arms remained all too clear.

With a curse, Thomas lay on his bed, tugged the blanket up, and closed his eyes. If his father hadna interrupted them, he would have taken her innocence. He stilled. What if she'd become pregnant?

Blast it, so caught up in the moment, he hadna considered the ramifications of his actions. With her born a bastard, she'd endured a cold life, even shunned by those of her blood. Though fortunate that the healer had raised her with love, many an unwanted babe didna share the same fate. Nor would he allow such. If she grew round with child, he wouldna avoid his responsibility.

He shifted to his side, frowned. Though he was drawn to her, he wasna seeking marriage. 'Twas best if he kept his distance, returned to the role of her protector, nae more. More, regardless of how much he cared for her, of how her body felt beneath his, she deserved a man without emotional scars.

Thomas turned over, grimaced at the shot of pain, and forced his eyes closed. Except with thoughts of her tangling his mind, he doubted that he would find sleep.

* * *

Early morning sunlight streamed through the window, glistening on the ice clinging to the glass as Thomas pushed the tray of food aside. He swung his legs over the edge of his bed. After two days with naught but a few walks down the corridor, by God he wouldna spend another moment cloistered inside.

Grimacing at his stiffness, he dragged on his garb, then glanced toward the closed door. The woman who'd brought him his meals had explained that Alesone was feeling poorly, but he knew the truth.

Since the night they'd almost made love, she had avoided him. Mayhap he hadna planned on their intimacy, but neither would he apologize. She'd wanted him as well. He could still feel her hands caressing him, the softness of her mouth, and her hungry demands. His exhaustion had lowered his shields, otherwise he never would have touched her.

Thomas muttered a curse. As if thinking about her and what they'd done helped this convoluted situation? Nor could he allow her avoidance to continue. When he explained naught could ever exist between them, then they could step back and continue as before. After he delivered her to Avalon, then he would leave.

Except he'd miss her.

With his fealty sworn to King Robert, and Scotland embroiled in civil war, however much his thoughts strayed to the unbidden, a relationship wasna a wise option to consider.

Once Scotland was united, with his father having reinstated his title of Earl of Kincaid, then he could consider the idea of a woman in his life. As well, he would need a son to pass down Conchar Castle and title Earl of Kincaid.

The image of Alesone round with his child whispered through his mind. He shoved to his feet. The lass deserved more than a man who in his youth had torn his family apart, and whose life as a warrior had let him see little but blood and carnage.

However much he was drawn to her, she didna need a man emotionally damaged, but one who understood love.

Love.

Thomas grunted. Look at him mulling over such foolishness when 'twas duty he should focus on. The sooner he spoke with her and put this matter behind them the better.

Damming his soreness and wishing they were en route to Avalon Castle, he walked to the door. The writ he'd sent to Bruce would explain their delay. Nor would the king be pleased to learn that the Duke of Westwyck had exposed his true allegiance.

King Robert would understand that once Comyn received the news of the duke's betrayal he would attack Dair Castle. The noble wouldna allow his daughter to escape. Without King Philip's support, the Scot would fail in his attempt to defeat Bruce. Before her father and his troops reached Thomas's home, Alesone needed to be far away. With the rate he was improving each day, he should be able to ride within a fortnight.

After they reached Avalon and he explained the situation to Stephan MacQuistan, fellow Templar and now the Earl of Dunsmore, his friend would ensure she remained safe. Thomas held little doubt that with Stephan's wife, Katherine, being woman of strong will, Alesone would find more than a safe haven at the island fortress, but an alley, and if she chose to accept their offer, friendship.

Weary, he rubbed the back of his neck. 'Twas long past time for him to rejoin the Templars whom he'd traveled with to his sovereign's encampment, knights who knew him, men he trusted, a life he understood.

With his focus clear, Thomas exited his room and crossed to Alesone's. He knocked.

"Who is it?"

At her lyrical voice, unwanted images of her naked body stormed his mind. Bedamned, he wasna here to seduce her. "Thomas."

Silence.

God's teeth! He shoved the door open, stepped inside, and shoved the door shut, refusing to allow his gaze to linger upon her curves. "We need to talk."

Nervous eyes held his as she stood paces away. "You must leave. 'Tis indecent for you to be alone with me in my chamber."

"Since you decided 'tis prudent to avoid me, I took matters into my own hands." Thomas stepped closer.

On a gasp she stumbled back. "What are you doing?"

"Ensuring," he said as he caught her arm, "that you dinna run."

The paleness on her face transformed to an angry red. She tried to pull free.

He held.

"You have nay right to barge into my room, much less make demands."

"Why didna you visit yesterday?" he asked, far from intimidated. "*Or* this morning."

Lavender eyes narrowed. "As if you dinna know."

"I know," he said, keeping his voice void of the emotions brewing within, "that what happened between us was unplanned, and isna a reason for you to keep away from me."

"You saw me naked!"

Saw, touched, and tasted her. Bloody hell! "Aye, but 'tis done. Nor is anyone aware of what transpired."

"I know," she stated. "How am I supposed to act around you when you have seen me…"

"Naked?"

"'Tis unseemly."

"God's teeth, you are a healer and have seen many people disrobed."

Her eyes blazed. "What we were doing wasna medicinal."

Thomas doubted she'd approve of his notion that touching her raised his spirits. "From this moment," he said, proud of his calm when his body burned for her, "I willna touch you further."

Hurt darkened her gaze. "Are you saying that you didna want me?"

Bloody hell! "Nay."

At the rough desire in his voice, hope ignited. "Then you did?" Alesone asked, and then wished she'd remained silent. But his declaration that he wouldna touch her further when for the past two days memories of their intimacy had filled her every thought, had forced her reply. He stared at her in disbelief, and she felt more the fool.

Mayhap moments before she'd heard naught but frustration in his voice. Ashamed, she again tugged her hand to break free.

He held tight.

"Release me."

Thomas glanced at her wrist but didna let go. When his eyes lifted to hers, she caught the struggle within. A part of her thrilled at the discovery, another grew wary of the heat. However much he made her feel, they came from two different worlds. He, the son of a powerful noble, and she, the discarded bastard of his enemy.

His thumb skimmed along the sensitive skin of her wrist, throwing her further off balance. "I want you," he said, his voice rough. "More than is wise."

Dangerous awareness pulsed within, urged her to throw caution to the wind and say the words that would bring him closer, his mouth upon hers until lost in his taste she could only feel.

And then what?

Would intimacy with Thomas be a decision she would regret? The feelings he evoked went far deeper than lust.

With almost a fortnight having passed since they'd met, that should be impossible. Except thoughts of the day when he'd leave made her heart ache. However much she wanted him, if he came to her bed, 'twould change the situation, a transformation she couldna risk.

Moments before, regardless of his feelings toward her, he'd given her a vow to keep his distance.

A request she should honor. Too much stood between them to hope for anything more. She released an unsteady breath, glanced to where his fingers held her wrist. "You can let go of me."

His eyes lowered to her mouth, lingered, then lifted to hers.

Her body trembled beneath his gentle touch, more so at the desire darkening his gaze. Wanting him with her every breath, she cleared her throat. "I think 'tis best if you leave."

With a soft curse, his breathing ragged, he released her. "However much I want you, you canna be more than a duty. Whatever is between us ends here."

"I see," she said, aching at his rejection.

A frown furrowed his brow and he began to pace. At the hearth he paused. "You couldna, nor do I expect you to. There is much about me that you dinna understand."

"Thomas, an explanation is unnecessary. As you stated, I am a duty."

"I didna mean it like that!"

"Then how did you mean it?" she asked, feeling foolish prolonging their discussion when it would deliver naught but more hurt.

"If you became pregnant with my child," he said with exasperation, "I would have to marry you."

"Have to?" she whispered, her heart fragmenting into tiny bits, collapsing beneath the slide of blood that wept like tears.

"Blast it, I am explaining this poorly." He stormed over and caught her shoulders.

"Release me," she said, her words ice, needing to protect her fragile composure. With a slight shove she'd shatter. A fate she refused to allow him to witness.

"Alesone—"

She broke free, walked to the entry, and jerked the door open. "Leave!"

Chapter Fourteen

Thomas grunted at the shot of pain as he worked his way down the turret. After he'd mishandled his discussion with Alesone, agony he deserved. Mishandled? A kind word for telling the lass she was naught but a duty.

He winced as he set his foot on the next step. She had every right to be furious. He'd botched the situation like a battering ram shoved in mud. Nor with his words in a mire had he been smart enough to quit.

Aye, he was a bloody ass. Hardly the Templar known for his finesse in dealing with difficult situations, a warrior sought out by kings.

He shoved his foot onto the next level. He'd meant to seek her forgiveness, to make her understand how important she was becoming to him.

Except as her eyes filled with yeaning, trust and desire had held his, the tatters of his hard-won calm had collapsed.

Never had a woman made him lose control, or made him want her with such mindless disregard. To allow the bond between them to continue to strengthen would do naught but create further complications.

Shoving aside memories of her silky skin, of how her taste infused his every thought, Thomas grimaced as he took another step down. Though he'd made a debacle of the situation, however poorly achieved, he'd achieved his goal of placing distance between them.

He should be happy, pleased by the fact.

Emotion clogging his throat, he reached the great hall. He scanned the large chamber filled with lingering scents of venison, porridge, and herbs from the earlier meal.

Empty benches lay shoved against trencher tables where a short while before knights had broken their fast. In the hearth, a fire blazed bright, illuminating the tapestry upon the wall emblazoned with his family's heraldry. In the center, and spun from threads of deep red and white, a vine pattern framed a knight's helm atop an intricate weave, which had graced the great room since Dair Castle was built.

'Twas as if he could blink and nay time had passed. He would still be a child, and his entire family alive.

With an unsteady breath, he struggled against the wash of emotion. However difficult, he needed to face his past.

Thomas shifted his steps to offset the discomfort and made his way toward the entry. He nodded to several women working to clear the trencher tables, bent to pat of one of the deerhounds lurking close by in hopes of an errant scrap, then continued. At the door he glanced back, thankful nay one followed. For the task ahead, he wanted to be alone.

Flurries thick with the whip of snow lashed him as he stepped outside. Tugging the door shut, he stared at the graveyard near the far wall. An ache burning his soul, he tugged his cape tighter and started across the bailey.

With each step his chest squeezed tighter, but he pushed on, needed to face the consequences of his actions.

Frozen ground crunched beneath his boots as he paused before the somber display, the weathered gravestones like bleak sentinels against the stark, ice-hardened ground. A lump in his throat, his gaze settled on the first of four gravestones closest to the curtain wall.

Snow clung to the curve of his mother's precious name to create a softness, like she did in his life. On an unsteady breath he stepped over and brushed away the accumulation.

Heart wrenching sorrow slashed him. Tears blurring his eyes, he dropped to his knees. A shudder raked through Thomas, then another. "Mother," he rasped, his soul-torn words ripped away by the whip of wind.

His shoulders shaking beneath the force of his grief, he leaned forward and clasped the aged hewn stone. The piercing images of her wailing as she'd held Léod's body seared his mind. "I shouldna have fled like a coward. I-I never meant to hurt you. Yet 'twould seen in the end I caused you and the rest of the family naught but pain." And for the suffering he'd inflicted, never would he forgive himself.

Chest aching, after he finished an Our Father, he shifted to the next stone. Another sob wracked his body as he traced his finger over the *M* chiseled in cold stone. "Father told me of your bravery, Matheu. A fierce warrior. I regret nae saying good-bye." Now he would never have a chance.

An icy blast of wind howled past as if mocking his torment as he bowed his head and recited the Lord's Prayer.

Bitter cold pierced him as he shuffled to the third gravestone.

Memories of his sister's face dredged through his sorrow, her smile so sweet that many claimed 'twas a gift from the fairies. "Orabilia," Thomas rasped, "Father said you had grown to a beautiful lass. Nay doubt many a man vied for your hand. Any fortunate enough to win your affection would have been blessed. I am so sorry for nae being here to say goodbye." He whispered a Paternoster.

Thomas moved before the final grave. The edges weathered by time, streaks of a grey staining the cut stone. On a broken sob, he pressed his head against the weathered granite. "Léod, I am ashamed I ran. From you, Father, and everyone. 'Twas fate that brought me Dair Castle." He scoffed. "Fate? Nay. When father learned that I was at the monastery, he stormed over and hauled me back." He wiped his eyes. "Otherwise, I wouldna have returned."

"Nor should you have!" Donnchadh snarled.

Thomas shoved to his feet.

The shimmering fall of snow sifted past his older brother in stark contrast to the raw fury slashed across his face.

The anger blazing in his sibling's eyes he more than deserved.

"Father should never have brought you home," Donnchadh growled. "He has revealed his fealty is to the Bruce. And why? Because of you."

"I dinna deserve what he has risked." Anguish building within, Thomas stepped closer. "Nor did I wish to return."

His sibling's scowl deepened. "You are a coward. After Léod died, instead of facing his death you ran."

"As if you wanted me here, then or now?" he said, his voice rising. "I saw the hatred in your eyes, remember how we argued." Argued? A pitiful excuse for the painful words, the slam of fists that'd left them both bruised.

"Léod was dead because of your foolish challenge." With a curse, Donnchadh pushed Thomas back. "You couldna allow our brother to celebrate the day of your becoming a knight, had to force him to accept your dare given before our peers." He again shoved Thomas's chest.

Thomas stumbled back.

"Our brother looked up to you, admired you, and then…"

"He was gone," Thomas finished, damning each word, the horrific memories of that day knifing through his mind as if hours had passed instead of years.

The anger on his brother's face collapsed to grief, and he looked away. "Aye." Snow howled a mournful sound as it eddied past and then was swept away. "I found our mother sobbing and cradling Léod in her arms." Eyes reddened by tears cut to him. "I have hated you since that moment."

"N-nay more," Thomas strangled out, "than I despised myself."

His sibling's eyes narrowed. "How could you leave?"

He stared at Donnchadh in disbelief. "God's teeth, after our words, how could I nae!"

"Our brother had been dead but hours, and our mother had locked herself in her chamber with her sobs echoing down the corridor, and our father so distraught that he'd drunk until he was numb. Tell me," his brother demanded, "how was I supposed to feel? Had I have prodded Léod into sparring with me that day and he had fallen and drowned in the river, you would have been furious at me as well, wanted me gone."

The truth changed naught. "Except 'twas *me* who challenged Léod," he rasped, "*me* who caused his death." Thomas's shoulder's sagged. "Dinna worry, I will leave within a sennight." Sooner than he'd planned, but after their discussion, he'd stay nay more.

Donnchadh eyed him a long moment. "You will nae be healed enough to travel by then."

"Wanting me gone," he said, his voice dry, "I would think that you would care little about the state of my health." A fresh wave of misery swamped him. Refusing to break down before his brother, Thomas brushed past him as he headed toward the keep.

Donnchadh's fingers dug into his arm.

Furious, Thomas whirled. "Release me."

Hard eyes held his. "I was angry then," his brother ground out, "and aye, I still am. But I willna lose another brother over a tragedy that happened so many years ago."

Stunned by his declaration, hope ignited. Thomas smothered the emotion as quick. "What are you saying?"

"We are brothers, we have differences, but we are family," he stated. "We work things through and dinna give up. However much I didna want to, I have missed you."

Humbled by Donnchadh offering, Thomas fought for the words to reply, floundered to find the right ones when he didna deserve his compassion. "How can you forgive me when I canna forgive myself?"

His brows slammed together. "Is your destroying yourself with guilt what Léod would have wanted?"

"Our brother didna deserve to die!"

"Nay, he didna. Nor is death particular in whom it chooses." His body rigid, he stared at the chapel. "'Tis those it leaves behind who struggle to go on. But we have memories of our time together," he said, his voice softening. "To forget those we love is to bring them dishonor."

His chest tight, Thomas gazed upon the gravestones. "I will never forget them."

"Nor will I."

"I have an admission," Thomas said quietly. "When we were younger, I envied that as the firstborn, you would one day receive our father's title of duke. With the man you have become, I realize my concerns were those of an untried lad. I am proud of you, and know you will bring naught but honor to the title."

"I will try." Donnchadh glanced toward the keep. "I have a meeting with the steward. Know this: what we have discussed today willna take away my upset, but the words needed to be said. You already have our father's forgiveness. Now you have mine." With a curt nod, he strode away.

Humbled by his brother's compassion, Thomas stared at Donnchadh's broad-shouldered outline as he disappeared into a swirl of white. Another snow-thickened gust battered his face. He tugged his cloak tighter, the chill easing around his heart. He didna deserve his father's or brother's mercy, except both had offered a new beginning nonetheless.

Against the batter of flakes slipping beneath his cloak, after Thomas knelt before Léod's grave and said an Our Father, he headed for the chapel.

Wisps of frankincense and myrrh filled the air as he stepped inside. Candles flickered in wall sconces, lending a golden cast over the serene setting where he'd said many a prayer. Easing out a breath, he skimmed his hand along the polished top of the nearest bench as he gazed past the well-worn pews and paused at the cross hanging on the wall behind the alter.

He clenched the smoothed wood. How many times had he knelt within this house of God, his mind lost to thoughts of the future, of excitement of what he would find beyond the walls of Dair Castle? Yet however proud of his service as a Templar, he'd always yearned for his family.

Surrounded by the familiar, he walked forward, moved into the pew, knelt before the cross, pressed his hands in prayer, and thanked God for the blessings he'd received. With his brother and father's forgiveness, he'd been offered a chance for a new start.

Guilt swept him over how he'd treated Alesone this day. Blast it, she deserved better!

The scuff of wood had him turning.

Lines of concern weighed heavy on his father's face as he entered.

Ignoring the aches, Thomas stood. "What is wrong?"

His father motioned for him to sit as he walked down the aisle. After kneeling next to the pew and making the sign of the cross, he sat beside him. "I just spoke with Mistress Alesone."

Dread rippled through him. "She came to see you?"

"Nay, I found her sitting alone in the solar. When she saw me, she made to leave, but I bid her to stay. The lass wouldna explain why she was upset." Inquisitive eyes held his. "She is *very* loyal to those whom she cares for."

"I doubt you sought me out to discuss Alesone's loyalty," Thomas said, refusing to discuss the discord with him.

"While we spoke," the duke continued, "with my each mention of you, her expression grew further strained. It doesna take a man of great wit to deduct the reason for what, or rather *who*, is the cause of her strife."

He muttered a silent curse. "We had a disagreement." An understatement. He'd pushed away, hurt her, both unthinkable, which made him despise himself further. "Neither do I owe you an explanation."

A wry smile touched his mouth. "Long ago, I looked forward to the discussions we would have once you were a man, except I negated to factor in your stubbornness." The smile faded. "Aye, 'tis your right to keep whatever is between you and Alesone to yourselves. Neither will I pry. What you choose to tell me is your decision."

Thomas straightened in the pew.

His father watched him a long moment. "I think she is a fine lass."

He swallowed hard. "She is, and your enemy's daughter. How could you approve of her?"

"She is, but we dinna choose who we are born to. I would be a fool to judge a person by such."

"I didna know—" Thomas blew out a rough breath. "I wasna sure what to think if you discovered that I…"

"Cared for her?"

"Aye."

His father laid his callused hand on Thomas's shoulder, the weight bringing comfort. "I am honored that you would trust me with such a confidence. If you are asking my opinion, 'tis simple. Any man would be proud to have Mistress Alesone in his life."

"I agree," Thomas said, "but 'tis a choice I canna ponder. I must rejoin our king when he confronts Comyn, nor can I assure her I will return."

"I understand your concern, one each man who fights for Robert the Bruce shares. Sadly, many Scots will die before our country is united." He paused. "I remember how your mother would fret when I prepared for battle. Is the lass distraught because she is afraid for you?"

Thomas shrugged. "I didna allow the discussion to go that far."

Shrewd eyes studied him. "I thought Alesone was important to you?"

"She is."

"You are an earl, you can—"

"She doesna know." Frustrated, he leaned back.

"Why?"

The quiet warning had Thomas stiffening. "Because my title isna significant in what exists between her and I."

"But you care about her?"

"Aye," he said through clenched teeth.

"And you prove that by shielding secrets from the lass?"

"My nobility never came up."

"A fact," the duke stated, "I am confident that you ensured."

"Nor is how much I care for her relevant. Once I deliver her to Avalon Castle, I will never see her again."

His father grunted. "If you leave her without admitting what you feel for her, 'twill be a decision you will regret for the rest of your life."

Blast it! "You dinna know how I feel!" Thomas rubbed his forehead. "I apologize, you dinna deserve my anger."

"True. But what you *deserve* is to find a woman who loves you, one whom you love in return."

"She couldna love me. We have known each other but a short while."

"You care for her. Do you believe you could feel more?"

He shrugged. "It matters little," he said, his voice somber. "For the reasons I stated, naught can exist between us."

"Thomas, we are only given one life. None of us know if we will die on the morrow, within a fortnight, or years from now. Dinna throw away happiness you might never find again." He paused. "Your mother and I didna have the luxury of knowing if we would have tomorrow. Neither do you."

So caught up in thoughts of duty, the Templars, and his service to the king, he hadna considered such.

"If you feel strongly for the lass," the duke said, "I wouldna wait too long to tell her. Those living beneath Comyn's control may have avoided Alesone due to fearing her father's anger. Removed from his tyranny, and once she has escaped marrying King Philip's noble, a beautiful woman like her willna want for suitors."

He frowned. With him healing in his chamber and her in the great room while she broke her fast, nay doubt many men had studied her with more than a passing interest. "I thank you for your advice."

His father nodded. "Earlier you said your brother was looking for you."

Donnchadh's stern acceptance came to mind. "We spoke. You will be pleased to learn that we have made amends…of sorts."

"Good." The duke released a long sigh. "I will be sad to see you go."

"For now it canna be any other way, but I promise when the opportunity arises, I will return."

Happiness crinkled his aged eyes, and he stood. "Take care, my son."

The soft tap of steps echoed upon the floor. A creek, then sunlight streamed inside the holy chamber. Moments later his father closed the door behind him, severed the wash of light.

Alone, Thomas stared at the cross upon the wall, anguish twisting inside his heart. A part of him wanted to go to Alesone and admit his feelings for her, the other hesitated against the dangers ahead.

Naught was guaranteed, but after all she had endured, neither was it fair to admit how much she was coming to mean to him when he didna love her.

At thoughts of her in another man's arms, he shoved to his feet, started toward the door. Aye, he would talk with her, but until he knew the depth of what he felt for her, he would say naught. Still, as long as she remained under his guard, neither would anyone court her.

Chapter Fifteen

The scent of herbs melded with the tinge of smoke from the hearth as Alesone adjusted the lad's elbow. She glanced at the healer, struggled to focus on her task, nae linger on Thomas's hurtful claim that if she became pregnant with his child, he'd have to marry her. The oaf. Regardless of what he made her feel, he could rot in Hades if he believed she'd ever bind her life with his.

"Is this the angle you wanted?" Alesone asked, fighting for calm.

The elder woman nodded. "Keep your grip firm while I secure the binding." Aged eyes shifted to the boy. "Dinna move." With expertise she wrapped his arm, then looped a swatch of cloth secured to the bandage around his shoulder. "'Twill keep you from moving your arm about. Next time when your father warns you to nae run behind the horses you will listen."

Eyes filled with tears begging to come out met Alesone's, then darted toward the healer. The wee lad sniffed back a sob. "I willna."

The old woman stepped back. "Along with you, then. And dinna run."

"Aye." With another sheepish glance, the boy sped from the chamber.

As the door closed behind him, her anger at Thomas melting beneath the lad's fortitude, Alesone smiled at Forveleth. "'Twas courageous of the lad to shield his tears."

"He has had much practice. 'Tis the tenth time this year I have treated him for what his father has forbid him to do. Nor do I believe 'tis the last I will see of him." A twinkle shimmered in the elder's eyes. "He reminds me of Lord Thomas in his youth."

"Nay doubt he was quite handful," Alesone said.

"Indeed. Once he became stuck in the latrine shaft trying to frighten Donnchadh. It took three men to pull the fearless lad out." She chuckled. "I assure you, none were pleased with the task."

Curious to learn more about his past, Alesone sat in a nearby chair. "And Thomas?"

"His father ordered him straight to bathe, except even after two days and several extra scrubbings, you could still smell the foul stench whenever he walked by." A smile touched her mouth as she shook her head. "I had little sympathy, 'twas culled by his own doing. But did he learn? Nay. And a fortnight later, trouble and Thomas were back together."

Alesone imagined him in the thick of the mayhem, traits nay doubt his children would inherit. With the clarity Thomas had stated his future didna include her, a child she would never see. 'Twas for the best. However much she yearned for Thomas, she didna fit into his life. For a foolish moment she'd allowed herself to believe a chance existed, nay longer.

Emptiness filled her at thoughts of a future alone. Neither would she dishonor all Grisel had taught her. She was strong, knew how to protect herself, and was skilled as a healer.

"So Thomas was a handful," Alesone forced out, struggling to keep the melancholy from her voice.

"Nay more than his brothers or sister," the healer replied. "Often times, two or more of them were in trouble at the same time for banding together to pull a prank."

The emptiness of her childhood rattled in her chest. Though Grisel had raised her with love, and her mother's personal maid had visited on numerous occasions, she'd yearned for siblings.

"What of you? Do you have brothers or sisters?"

"Nay."

Tenderness touched her face. "Your parents were blessed to have a daughter such as you. Your mother—"

"Died after I was born."

Sadness welled within the healer's eyes. "I am so sorry. And your father?"

"He never wanted me." She shrugged. "'Twas a long time ago."

Aged eyes studied her for a long moment. "But you still hurt."

Surprised by Forveleth's insight, Alesone gave a shaky nod. "How could you know?"

"Watching you with the lad, along with the way you have helped me tend to others," she replied, "'tis easy to see that you have a tender heart."

Alesone stifled the surprising build of tears and laid her hand on the healer's arm. In their short time working together they'd become friends. Except for Grisel, she'd never shared her thoughts with another woman. Until now. "I thank you for your kind words. I…" Heat stole up her cheeks, and she sat back. "I was raised by Grisel. She was a healer and taught me about herbs, and how to care for people."

"And a fine job she did."

She released a rough breath, the ache of the loss too fresh. "Weeks ago she was killed."

"You are still grieving," she said softly.

A tear slid down Alesone's cheek, and she gave a shaky nod. "I think of her every day."

"Of course you do." The healer sifted a mix of herbs into a cup, filled it with steaming water. "Drink this. 'Tis valerian root tea."

Familiar with the elixir's soothing properties that aided many to sleep, Alesone took a sip, savored the warmth, the tingles easing her mind. "I thank you."

"Tell me about her," the elder said, "if you choose."

Though she hadna intended to say more, with the question asked and a friendship between them forged, Alesone found herself sharing stories of her years with Grisel. "And though nae her child," she whispered, her voice trembling with emotion, "She raised me as her own. I loved Grisel so much and will never forget her."

The healer took a sip of her own tea. "You were fortunate to have her in your life."

"I was."

"What will you do now?" the elder asked.

"I…" The coldness of her life ahead, one without Thomas or a place to call home stormed her mind, and she stumbled for a reply. "Once the chaos in my life settles, wherever I end up, I will continue my work as a healer."

"Wherever you end up?" She frowned. "Have you nay where to go?"

"Nay, but I shall be fine."

"Of that I have nay doubt." Forveleth paused, and her face warmed. "I dinna know what troubles you, but when 'tis over, you are welcome in my home. And with your having tended to Thomas, nay doubt the duke would welcome you in Dair Castle."

Humbled by the healer's offer, Alesone shook her head. "I couldna—"

With a hearty laugh, she patted her hand. "You can, and in the future, I expect to see you on my doorstep."

Emotions welled inside. "Y-you are too generous. I dinna know what to say."

Her smile widened. "Say aye."

"I shall consider your offer," Alesone replied.

"I am taking that as an aye," the elder said as she drew her into a fierce hug. She sat back. "I look forward to having you here." Forveleth winked. "Nor have I missed how Lord Thomas watches you with favor in his eyes."

"'Tis nae favor," Alesone said, needing the reminder to quell her unwanted yearnings, "To him I am naught but a duty."

Mirth danced in the elder's eyes. "Far from it. I have seen him watching you." She smiled. "Look at me rambling. Then, again, I admit that Lord Thomas was my favorite."

Confused, Alesone frowned. "'Tis the third time you called him Lord Thomas, why?"

"Because he is the Earl of Kincaid."

An earl? "I see." But she didna. How could he have concealed such an important fact from her? Then she understood. His nobility explained everything, damnably so.

You canna be more than a duty. Whatever is between us ends here.

Because of her blood tie to his enemy.

Tears burned in her eyes, but she forced them back, angry she'd allowed herself to nurture a foolish flicker of hope.

The chime of the church bell echoed from outside.

Alesone forced a smile to her lips. "I didna realize 'twas so late. I thank you again. If you will excuse me."

"I appreciate your help this afternoon." The healer patted Alesone's hand. "Go on now."

On shaky legs, Alesone stood. As she headed toward the entry, the door opened and Thomas entered.

Through sheer will, she forced her breathing to remain even, at odds against the pounding of her heart. "If you will excuse me, I was just leaving."

Frustrated eyes shifted to the healer and then to her. "I wish to speak with you."

Why? Hadna he said enough? At least she hadna given herself to him, then her shame would have been complete.

"I canna, I have an important errand to tend to."

He opened the door wider and motioned her forward. "I will accompany you."

She glanced back, noted the interest in the healer's face. Angling her chin, she strode into the corridor, then hurried off. The soft thud of the door closing, and his footfalls, echoed in her wake.

"Alesone."

At the frustration in his voice, she picked up her pace. She half ran down the turret, through the great hall, and into the windswept baily. Snow, flung within the whip of wind, prickled against her exposed skin. Ignoring the bite of cold, she rushed across the frozen ground.

"Alesone, wait."

"Go away!" She hurried into the stable, then darted toward the far exit.

Thomas caught her wrist as she ran past the fourth stall.

Alesone rounded on him. "Release me! I have a life ahead of me, one that doesna include *you*."

Regret shadowed his eyes. "I shouldna have said what I did this morning. I was upset."

Upset? A pale emotion compared to how pain had lanced her heart.

Hay crunched beneath his boots as he stepped closer. "We need to talk."

She grabbed a nearby rake, positioned it before her as if a sword. "Need to?" She narrowed her gaze. "Lord to serf."

A frown lined his brow. "What are you—"

"I know you are the Earl of Kincaid," she accused. "A fact nae important enough to share with someone who is naught but a duty."

He gave a rough exhale. "I need to explain."

"Why? Do you think I am impressed by your title or care?" she attacked, struggling against the hurt. "I was doing just fine before you barged into my life. I assure you, *Lord Thomas*, when I watch you depart Avalon Castle 'twill be the happiest day of my life."

"Blast it, Alesone! Listen to me!"

"I have listened, much to my regret. To think that I almost…" Heat stormed her cheeks. Damn him! She slapped the wooden handle against his arm when he reached for her again.

He yelped. "Ale—"

"Go away!" She gulped in much-needed air as she scrambled for control. "Until we depart Dair Castle, I expect you to keep your distance." She tossed the rake and aside stormed toward the exit.

God's teeth, he'd made a mess of the entire situation. He bolted after her and caught her hand.

Shards of afternoon sunlight illuminated the stable as she fought to break free. "Let me go!"

Aching inside, Thomas drew her against him, wrapped his arms around her when she tried to pull away.

"I despise you," she hissed, her claim shattering beneath a broken whisper.

"Anger I deserve," he said, wanting to ease her hurt, and damning the cold words he'd tossed at her hours before. "I was wrong to treat you so. And as for my title, I didna lie to you."

She arched a skeptical brow.

"As a child I was bestowed the title Earl of Kincaid. When I left the monastery, I sent a missive to my father renouncing my rank and returning the ownership of Conchar Castle."

Dubious eyes held his. "Without the protection of the monastery or that of your father, why would you abandon your either?"

"Because…" Few knew of his joining the Brotherhood, nor was it a topic he wished to discuss, except she deserved the truth. "What I am about to tell you, you must swear nae to tell anyone."

Silence.

"Alesone, I will have your vow."

"I swear it, but know this," she stated with ice, "I will listen to you, but I doubt whatever you tell me will sway my mind."

A compromise of sorts. How had he forgotten the warrior he'd first met weeks before? Humbled by this fierce woman who moved him as nay other, Thomas released her hand.

She stepped back and crossed her arms over her chest.

He glanced around. Neither would he talk where anyone could walk in and hear them. "Follow me." At her hesitation he nodded. "What I tell you must be said in private."

Alesone gave a curt nod, then followed him to the tack room. The rich scent of leather permeated the air as she stepped inside.

He closed the door.

With an appreciative eye she looked around, noted the gear for the horses hanging on pegs in an orderly manner along the wall. Her gaze wary, she faced him.

"What I have told you about my past is the truth, but…there is more."

Alesone remained silent.

She wouldna make this easy for him, nor had he expected her to. "As I explained, after Léod's death I entered the monastery. Brother Nicholai, whom you met, was my tutor."

"The reason you and he are close."

He nodded. "He is a very intelligent and observant person. Within but a fortnight, he had discovered my reason for wanting to join the monastery."

"As penance for your brother's death?"

"Aye," he replied.

Her stance relaxed a degree more. "And why you left?"

"'Tis, but I departed following his sage guidance." He paused, weighing how much detail he should give her. "I became a Knight Templar."

Surprise widened her eyes.

"And," he continued beneath her assessing gaze, "Brother Nicholai was right. Fighting for God's cause did fulfill me. I canna say that I found peace. Through the demands of my service, of those we aided, I did find a sense of purpose," he said, his voice rough. "I loved being part of the Brotherhood, and miss it still."

She frowned. "But you left?"

"Left?" Memories of how he, and many of his Brother's fled beneath the cover of darkness ripped open his soul. "Never would I leave what I loved."

"But—" Despair filled her eyes. "Oh God, the whispers of King Philip ordering the arrests of the Knights Templar but weeks ago are true."

Nor was he surprised by the rapid spread of news of the Templars' demise. Nay doubt the shock of the French king's declaration had fed many a tongue, and with those envious of the Templars' wealth and power, jealous righteousness as well. "Aye, except unknown to King Philip, before the charges of heresy were publicly disclosed on Friday, the thirteenth of October, the Grand Master had been forewarned of the monarch's nefarious intent."

Her hand tightened on a weathered post. "Thank God."

"Against such dire circumstance, our being alerted 'twas indeed a blessing. Under the Grand Master's orders, prior to the day of the arrests, many Templars boarded our galleys and escaped. "With regret"—his throat tightened against the horrific truth—"many within the Brotherhood remained ignorant of the king's treachery until their arrest."

Horror darkened her gaze. "Why didna the Grand Master warn all of the Templars? A fighting force of such caliber, you could have confronted the king, challenged his lies?"

"With the Brotherhood scattered in several countries, we didna have the luxury of time to contact everyone, much less organize a formal denial," Thomas explained. "Even if we exposed the truth, with the growing dissent of those jealous of the favor given to the Templars over the years, we wouldna have found enough support to confront France's sovereign."

Tears shimmered in her eyes.

"Our first priority," he pushed on, his voice rough, "was to ensure that the secrets the Knights Templar guard were kept safe. However difficult the decision to depart without alerting all within the Brotherhood, each knight chosen to leave understood the dire reasoning behind the Grand Master's decision."

Face pale, she frowned. "What is so valuable that weighs higher than the sacrifice of their lives?"

"I canna tell you," he said, haunted by the horror that due to the false charges, many men he'd fought alongside were now imprisoned, tortured, or dead. "Know this, we achieved our mission."

"And the cargo?"

Pride filled him at memories of their seizure of Avalon Castle, and how they'd hidden the goods they'd sailed away with in the secret catacombs beneath. "Where it will never be found."

On a shaky breath she stared at him. The defiance of moments before erased beneath her eyes haunted with grief. "I am so sorry. The Brotherhood are revered, known for their fierceness in battle, their honesty, and loyalty."

He gave a shaky nod. "I-I thank you."

"And," she continued, a waver in her voice, "your being a Templar explains much. Your confidence, skill with weapons, knowledge of tactics, detailed use of herbs, and more." She exhaled. "I should have guessed. You are unlike any man I have ever come across. When we first met and I placed that arrow but a hand's breath before your face, I expected you to jump back or yell. The most common reaction. Instead your face tightened with anger."

That moment lay etched in his mind. "I was upset at myself for being lost in my thoughts instead of keeping alert. If I had been paying attention, never would you have had a chance for a shot."

The edge of her mouth crooked a degree. "I did mention you were confident, and may I add, a wee bit arrogant."

At the subtle teasing, Thomas's body relaxed. "'Tis nae arrogance, but confidence in my abilities."

"I can see that, now. Still, I canna understand..." A wash of red swept up her cheeks.

"What?" he asked, confused by her embarrassment.

"'Tis only that I believed Templars were forbidden to..." Her blush deepened.

Understanding dawned, and his body tightened. "Be intimate?"

"Aye."

"They are, or rather were." Memories of that turbulent time swept him. "Before the Templars fled France, the Grand Master secretly dissolved the Order, encouraged us to marry, and blend in with the locals." He paused. "Now you know why I made you swear to tell no one before I explained."

"I do, but it doesna explain why you kissed me or…"

How they'd almost made love. Heat stormed his veins. She'd felt magnificent beneath him, her seductive taste still potent in his mind. Thomas glanced toward the closed door, the earlier needed privacy shifting onto dangerous, intimate ground.

His father's advice for Thomas to tell Alesone how he felt about her echoed in his mind. If he admitted that he cared, things between them would change. He silently swore. As if their intimacy to this point hadna done that? In the end he decided for a mixture of the two.

"When I sailed from France," Thomas said, choosing his words with caution, "never did I believe that I would find a woman who would intrigue me, or make me care. Then I met you. Between my loyalty to the Templars, my fealty to King Robert, and the complications of my family, I was torn if 'twas fair to allow you into my life." He exhaled. "Yet with you, 'twould seem that I had nay choice."

Hope flickered on her face, and he damned that he couldna give her the words she wanted to hear. "I lead men into combat without hesitation, remain calm in the midst of battle. That I am unsure how to proceed with how deeply I care for you leaves me baffled." Tenderness filled Alesone as Thomas struggled to explain, the strain in his voice betraying the difficulty of his admission. As a Templar, a fierce warrior who defied the odds in many a battle, to flounder with his growing feelings for her, or how she fit into his life, left him frustrated.

At himself.

Never her.

The need for him she'd smothered beneath her upset seeped through, erasing the anger she'd clung to, leaving only warmth. With her mind clear, she stared at the man who from the start had challenged her, dared push her as no man before, and broken down her every barrier.

Heart pounding she stilled, the realization of the moment leaving her stunned, and explained why when he'd pushed her away earlier, it'd hurt, horribly so.

God in heaven, she loved him!

The euphoria of the moment faded beneath reality. Though he admitted that he cared for her, 'twas a far cry from wanting her in his life.

After being treated as an outcast by her father and the men in the surrounding village during her youth, she'd vowed to never allow a man such power over her. Except against her every barrier, he'd claimed her heart.

A fact he didna know.

"Now what?" she asked.

Desire darkened his gaze, and he skimmed his thumb along the curve of her cheek and then across her lower lip. "Though I have nay right to ask, I would be wanting to kiss you."

Tingles ignited over her skin. Her body tensed, aching to hear his words of love.

For now naught but a wish.

His admission of moments before exposed the difficulty of his transition from a knight serving God to a warrior free to a life beyond the strict rule of a Templar.

Would he ever come to love her? Was she foolish to nurture such a dream? Dare she give him the intimacy she desperately wanted?

And if she walked away, never would she know what they could have had. However terrifying to yield to her desire, Alesone found 'twas more frightening to walk away and never know.

Chapter Sixteen

"Aye, 'twould be your kiss that I am wanting," Alesone said as she leaned her body against Thomas's muscled length, aware if he choose he could haul her against him and take what he wanted, but this close, she didna feel fear, but desire. "And more."

His mouth hovered over hers, his breath skimming across her lips, soft, teasing as if a dare. On a groan, he kissed the edge of her mouth, along the curve of her jaw, and then returned to skim his lips over hers.

"I thought," she rasped as heat burned inside, "you were going to kiss me."

"I," he whispered as his tongue worked miracles against her skin, "am working my way toward that."

"I..." she moaned as his mouth pressed intimately over hers. With mind-teasing slowness he deepened the kiss until her thoughts blurred and her every breath tasted of him. Unsure at which moment they'd moved, she found her back against the door and their bodies flush. Heat pouring through her, she skimmed her hands along his back, over his arms, desperate to feel every inch the man who against her every caution had stolen her heart.

On a rough breath, he lifted his head. Green eyes churning with hunger burned into hers. "I want you."

Alesone pressed her body brazenly against his hardness. "I want you as well."

On a rough hiss, he released the ties of her garb. Whisper soft, her gown tumbled to the bed of straw. Air crisp with the morning caressed her nakedness, and her body tingled beneath his sensual appraisal.

His heated gaze holding hers, he stroked his thumb across her nipple, then cupped her breast.

"Thomas," she gasped as his hands slid lower, touching, teasing her until beneath the onslaught, her knees threated to buckled. Without warning he took the kiss deeper.

His body shuddered and he lifted his head, his breathing coming in sharp rasps. "You are beautiful."

The lines of strain on his face assured her he was holding back, his focus on her. And if he thought to steady himself when she was but a blur of need, he was wrong. Alesone stroked his hardness.

On a sharp hiss, he caught her hand.

"I—"

"Dinna move." Eyes raw with desire held hers as his mouth worked with his hands as he touched her, tasted her skin until her body ached for him.

"Thom—"

His tongue swept across her most private place, and his name dissolved in to a whispered moan. He stroked her again, explored until sensation swelled inside until it felt as if she would explode. "Thomas," Alesone gasped, "I canna—"

He plunged deep.

A wave swept over her, then another. She cried out.

He stood and cradled her against him as her release rolled through her with destructive force, but it wasna enough. She wanted him, needed him more than she'd ever needed anything in her life. If their intimacy damned her, she didna care. "Thomas," she whispered, "make love with me."

Her taste burning in his mind, Thomas fought to steady himself, the softness of her body threatening to smother his every rational thought.

Bedamned, he had intended on leaving her untouched. In but weeks he would stand alongside their king to lay siege against her father. 'Twas reckless to entertain such thoughts, except with her naked against him and the desperation of her throaty plea, his last defense shattered.

Aye, they would make love, but with her wrapped in firelight, and her eyes illuminated within the soft glow as their bodies merged.

"I want you," he forced out, "but I willna take you in a stable. The first time, *our* first time, I want you embraced in candlelight and without risk of our being disturbed."

At the reminder of where they were, her face paled. "I forgot where we were."

"High praise indeed. A state I hope to achieve this night. For what I wish to do to you, we will need each hour of the night." A blush reddened her cheeks, one he liked putting there. On an unsteady breath, he started to draw away, but she caught his hand.

"Thomas, your wanting me is enough."

At the rough hope in her voice he yearned to admit that he more than wanted her, but needed her with his every breath. "You deserve a man who cares for you without question," he forced out, "one you can depend on."

Her eyes softened. "I can depend on you."

"As a warrior, a protector, aye," he said, refusing to linger on her belief in him. 'Twas a time for truth, nae emotions that in the end would leave her devastated. "I have many demons yet to overcome, including the reason I had intended to keep my distance from you."

"I know." Somber eyes held his as she covered his mouth with her own, slow with need, soft with understanding, and against his every intent, he hauled her against him, running his fingers over her flesh, his body aching as he skimmed across her slick folds quivering from her release.

Through sheer will he scooped the wisp of emerald silk from the hay and slid the gown over her shoulders, his fingers lingering on her every curve.

After securing her last tie, she lifted her eyes to his, the shyness there leaving him surprised.

He wrapped the errant blond lock that'd tumbled free around his finger, tugged her close. "How can you," he said pressing a soft kiss upon her mouth, "be shy after what we have done."

Red slashed her cheeks. "'Tis unseemly to speak so bluntly."

Enjoying that he'd thrown her off balance, he smiled. "I will do more than speak of it this evening, that I promise."

Her blush deepened. "I would be liking that."

His groin tightened, and he pressed his length intimately against her softness. "Once everyone has retired, I will come to your chamber."

"'Tis indecent," she said, excitement filling her voice.

"Aye," he said with a wink. With one last hard kiss, and after he'd assured her that she didna look properly ravished, they departed, his mind anxious for the night.

* * *

The day passed as if dragged by a stone, and with the ring of each bell announcing the next hour, Thomas willed the time to hurry. He worked his injured arm to loosen the taut muscles, grimaced at the shot of pain. Soon he and Alesone would depart Dair Castle.

In the solar he shifted in the chair before the hearth, returned his attention to his father, too aware of his brother, who sat at his side. Though Donnchadh had offered forgiveness, much still stood between them.

"Thomas, what of King Robert's intent?" his father asked.

"He is leading his forces through the Garioch and deep into loyal Comyn territory," Thomas replied.

The duke nodded.

"And Comyn?" Thomas asked.

"With the stakes so high, I believe he will detour around the king's men and attack Dair Castle to capture his daughter in order to finalize the agreement with King Philip."

His father grimaced. "With Bruce's forces closing in on Inverurie, I didna think he would take the risk."

"My thoughts as well," his brother said.

A solid rap sounded at the door.

"Enter," the duke called.

Wood scraped, then Sir John MacLairish limped inside, fading bruises still marring his face.

Thomas surged to his feet. "What is wrong?"

"On my way over here," John said, "I came across the Bruce's man critically wounded."

"What!" the duke boomed as he and Donnchadh stood.

John bowed and then held out a missive secured with the king's seal. "Your Grace, I carried the king's man to Dair Castle, and he bade me deliver this to you."

Eyes hard, the duke broke the imprinted wax round, unrolled the parchment, and skimmed the penned lines.

On edge, Thomas met his brother's worried gaze, then turned to his father.

The duke slammed his fist against the table. "A sword's wrath! Robert Bruce's health is declining with the auld sickness. He has delayed attacking Comyn and has rerouted his forces to Slioch until he is well enough to fight."

Donnchadh muttered a curse. "Nay doubt Comyn will be informed of both the king's shift in plans along with his ill health."

"Aye." Thomas agreed. "News that will have Comyn increasing the number of men that he brings to attack Dair Castle."

"Extra guards will be placed on the wall walk, and everyone within the castle is to prepare for an assault." The duke's eyes narrowed. "Any questionable activity will be immediately reported to me."

Donnchadh stepped forward. "I will pass along your command."

The duke nodded.

Though pleased with how his family was coming together, Thomas damned that 'twas because of his arrival, one that placed those within Dair Castle in jeopardy. However much he didna wish to raise the point, it needed to be said. "With your fealty sworn to King Robert, neither will Comyn be coming for his daughter alone."

His father scoffed. "I wouldna think much of Comyn if he didna confront me. Except any loyalty that I had to him is long since dead. 'Tis a grievous day when a Scotsman is in bed with the English, and betrays their country struggling to unite."

"Aye," Donnchadh agreed. "Beneath his bluster of aiding Scotland, King Edward wanted naught but to claim Scotland for his own."

"Regardless of his reasons," the duke said, "when Comyn arrives, we will be ready."

However prepared for the upcoming battle, Comyn's force was significant. If only they had the backing of the Knights Templar. Thomas stilled. But they did! "Father, several of my men travel with the Bruce. We must send word, explain the circumstance to our king. Given the gravity of the situation, I am confident he will honor my request to have my men, along with a contingent of his knight's, ride to Dair Castle."

The duke nodded, turned toward Thomas's friend. "How long did the rider say he had traveled after he was wounded?"

"A day, Your Grace," John replied. "He believes he is at least two days ahead of the contingent, mayhap more."

The noble muttered a curse. "Which leaves us little time."

"But enough." Terror shot through him at the thought of losing Alesone, but he refused to give up hope. "We can hold them off until the Bruce's forces arrives." They had nay other choice.

"I will write a missive to King Robert," his father said.

"Your Grace," Sir John said, "'twould be an honor to carry your message to the Bruce." At the duke's scowl, the knight stepped forward. "I swear that I willna fail."

Since the injury had forced John to leave the Brotherhood, Thomas understood that if only for a moment, his friend needed to rejoin the elite warriors as he had years before. "Father, I trust John with my life."

"Wait outside, Sir John," the duke said. "I will summon you soon."

"Aye, Your Grace." The knight departed.

"Donnchadh," the duke said, "once you have alerted the men, bring the lead knights with you to the war chamber."

"Aye, Father." Donnchadh departed.

"Once I have explained the events to Alesone, I will join you." Thomas stepped toward the door.

"Thomas."

He glanced back.

"We will keep Lady Alesone safe."

Pride filled him. For the first time since he'd left home he felt a part of the family. "Aye, Father, that we will."

Strategies utilized by the Templars ran through Thomas's mind as he strode down the corridor. He weighed the pros and cons of each, narrowing down their best option. As he neared the end of the hall, the melodic tones of Alesone's singing echoed from within her chamber.

Damn her father to bloody Hades! His time fighting in the Holy Land had taught Thomas the evil that men do, boundless malevolence for the sake of power and greed. Except in this he swore Comyn would fail.

A curse rolled from his lips. As long as he lived never would anyone harm her again. By God she deserved better, she deserved happiness, a life he wanted to give her.

Thomas halted before her chamber, her soft voice at odds with the emotions raging through him. How he longed to wake up beside her each day, and at night to slide into her slick heat. May Comyn burn in Hades for forcing a delay with his destiny.

His destiny?

Thomas's breath left him in a rush. He stilled, listened to her angel-sweet voice as the enormity of the realization stormed him.

God's teeth, he loved her!

On a hard swallow, he pressed his brow against the cool wood. He remembered months before, assuring his friend, Stephan MacQuistan, that unlike him, never would he give a woman his heart. Stephan would find great humor if he could see Thomas now, except with the news he needed to impart to Alesone, 'twas naught amusing about the situation.

All these years he'd believed he'd never find a woman he would love, and now that he'd found her, he would…

Say naught.

At least for now.

Little was guaranteed in war. If he told her that he loved her, and she admitted the same, and then he died during battle, 'twould leave a lass of her depth devastated. If naught else he'd learned that in her feelings for others that she cared for, she gave all. 'Twould be the same with her heart.

At the moment, an admission of his love 'twas naught but selfishness on his part. But the time would come. For now, the plans of this morning crumbled beneath grim responsibility.

Thomas opened the door and stepped inside.

Wrapped within the golden light she looked like one of the fey who'd slipped away from the Otherworld. Firelight shimmered across her moisture-dampened skin as she brushed her hair, each stroke sending ripples through her blond tresses.

With a silent curse, he damned the upcoming discussion and closed the door.

At the soft thud she turned. Lavender eyes softened.

"Your hair is damp?" he said, fumbling at how to begin, news that would destroy the warmth in her eyes.

"As I believed you wouldna be here until much later," she said, a hint of nerves sliding through her voice, "I enjoyed the luxury of a bath."

A drop of water fell from her hair and rolled down her golden skin. Mesmerized, he watched its errant slide until the droplet disappeared beneath her tunic, and he too easily imagined the feel of her damp skin beneath his hands.

Thomas cleared his throat. "We must talk."

At his somber tone, the smile in her eyes faded, and she lowered the brush. "What is wrong?"

However much he cursed the telling, she needed the truth. "Your father is en route to Dair Castle."

Chapter Seventeen

Alesone's hand trembled as she set aside her brush, stood and faced Thomas. "The guards at Dair Castle spotted my father and his men?"

"Nay." He strode over. "A runner carrying a missive from the Bruce to Dair Castle was spotted by your father's knights, and they gave chase. Though severely injured, King Robert's man was able to escape. John MacLairish found him, brought him here to recover."

"Will he live?"

"Aye."

"Thank God," she whispered. "What did the writ say that was of such importance?"

"That our king has grown ill with the auld sickness and delayed his attack and is making camp near Slioch."

"An affliction he has struggled with over the years." Her stomach tightened. "And with the king ill and nae able to lead his forces, you believe my father will ride straight here en force."

"Aye," he replied.

The ramifications of Comyn's arrival made her want to retch. Thomas's home and the family he loved would be under attack, and more lives would be lost because of her. Damning the situation and refusing to allow more people to die, she angled her jaw. "I will leave."

Thomas frowned. "What?"

"My father will attack Dair Castle," she said, her mind a blur of worry, "and you are still unable to travel. But, I could take a horse and—"

"Nay!"

Heartsick, she laid her hand atop his. "Do you nae understand? 'Tis the only way to deflect my father's assault. Once he discovers I am gone, he will leave."

Face grim, he drew her close. "The time for your escaping has passed. Nor does Comyn ride only for you. With my father having formally announced his fealty for the Bruce, your father's intent is twofold."

Tears blurred her eyes, and she stared at the stained-glass windows unsure what to say, ashamed to be tied to such a horrid man.

Strong hands caught her shoulders.

She stiffened. "I despise him."

"With good cause, but dinna blame yourself. Any acts of malice are because of your father's greed."

"Regardless, it changes naught."

"It doesna," he said, his voice grim. "We will hold Dair Castle. Comyn will achieve naught but frustration."

Alesone turned, needing to see the confidence in his eyes, the strength that was so much a part of him. "How can you be sure?" she asked, wanting to believe him, wishing a time would come when Comyn's influence over her life would end.

"My father sent a writ to the Bruce requesting a contingent," Thomas said, "and my entreaty for my men, who are Knights Templar and traveling with the king."

"But you said Robert the Bruce is making camp at Slioch?"

"He is, but considering the circumstance, I am confident he will send reinforcements. Though his forces are a two day march away, my men and many of his knights are traveling on horseback. A chance exists that they could arrive before Comyn."

Hope ignited in her soul. "And if they dinna?"

"Then we will hold off your father's forces until they do."

He made it sound so simple, when 'twas anything but. "How?"

"I believe once Comyn's initial assault fails, believing the king ignorant of his plan, he will order his men to form a blockade." Satisfaction glinted in his eyes. "While they await our surrender, 'twill give my men and the Bruce's troops time to reach us."

Alesone prayed he was right. "What can I do to help?"

"Food stores, water, and whatever else is needed to run the castle must be stockpiled."

"'Twill be my honor to help prepare." She paused, humbled by this man. "I thank you."

His thumb skimmed the curve of her cheek. "Dinna be thanking me so quickly," he said, his voice tender. "My motives for your safety are driven by more than duty."

Heat ignited inside. "Are they?"

"Aye." Thomas drew her against him, pressed his mouth against hers in a slow easy glide that left her breathless. "I find that when I am with you, I can concentrate on naught but the way you feel."

Her body ached to finish what they'd begun earlier, except he hadna arrived to seduce her, but to warn her of her father's impending attack. A confrontation that could cost many people lives, including the man she loved.

He raised his head, and his eyes darkened with concern. "Alesone—"

"Make love with me," she rasped, terrified for his life, desperate for each moment she could share with him.

In the firelight he pressed his brow against hers. "I want you with my every breath, but my father awaits me with his men in the war chamber. I needed to warn you of the situation."

"I want to help with the planning."

He nodded. "With your skill as an archer along with knowledge of your father, your presence will be welcome."

Many men would have dismissed a woman's presence within a council preparing for war, but Thomas was unlike any man she'd ever met. If she wasna sure that she loved him before, his decision to include her as an equal would have severed any doubt. "I thank you."

"We should leave, but first." He caught her mouth in a fierce kiss, all tenderness and seduction of earlier lost.

On a moan she savored his fierceness, demanded more.

Without warning, Thomas whisked her into his arms and carried her to the bed.

"What are you doing?" she gasped. "I thought we were going to—" Hands as tender as restless skimmed along her body, and she arched against his touch while his mouth worshiped the curve of her neck, and then dipped lower. She fought for control as his fingers edged lower, touching, stroking until she fell apart. He caught her cry of release with his kiss, until floating downward, her mind a haze of bliss, she lay back.

Thomas drew her against him as tremors rippled through her body.

"I thought," she gasped as she fought to calm the rush of emotion. "we had to leave?"

A satisfied smile settled on his mouth. "We do, but I wanted to ensure you thought about me, about what I am going to do to every inch of you before the night is through."

* * *

The duke guided the discussion at the war meeting of the best way to protect the castle.

Alesone was surprised and appreciative when the duke asked her several questions, and proud of how Thomas, his brother, and Father worked in unison to solidify plans.

However rough the start, 'twould seem Thomas had truly returned home. For that she was thankful. Nor would she linger on thoughts of wanting him. Their time together would soon end.

An ache built in her heart as the discussion of war echoed around her. Never had she believed she'd find a man that she could love, a man who respected her and wanted her as well.

Except he was a noble, and a man whose existence for many years was cultivated around war.

And she was the bastard daughter of his enemy.

Regardless of her desire for his love, mayhap after all of the horror's he'd witnessed as an elite fighter, for his own protection he'd buried his emotions too deep to ever be able to acknowledge love.

From her experience in treating soldiers, she understood the hardship wrought by years of combat. Some men withdrew so deep inside they were naught but an empty shell, nae living, but surviving, waking up to try to make it through another day haunted by their memories.

That Thomas still found hope made him extraordinary. If he never told her that he loved her, 'twas a small price to pay for knowing a man of his caliber. Though many would damn her for going to his bed without the sacrament of marriage, she found little shame in her decision.

Thomas wanted her, and she loved him.

In but a day, two at most, her father's men would attack Dair Castle. A battle in which many would die. Each day held nay guarantees, so she would take this moment and regardless what happened, regret naught.

The duke stood, and the warriors filling the room grew silent. Pride glistened in his eyes. "When Lord Comyn arrives, he will rue the day he dared attack Dair Castle!"

Cheers roared. The scrapes of chairs echoed as men stood and began departing.

Alesone watched as Thomas remained to speak with his father and brother, thankful for his strengthened bond with those he loved. 'Twould bring her peace knowing that for the rest of his life he would have family to turn to.

He glanced over. Warmth flickered in his eyes.

Anticipation slid through her as he walked over. Well she knew the warrior and the lover as well. He was a man any woman would want.

Thomas halted a pace away. "Donnchadh and I are meeting with the knights in the courtyard to review tactics and make detailed preparations for the castle's defense."

She nodded. "I will go help Forveleth prepare herbs."

"This day hasna gone as I had planned," Thomas said softly with heat in his eyes, "but nor is it over."

At his sultry promise, her breath left her in a rush, and as he walked away, her mind spun with heated thoughts of the hours ahead.

* * *

The afternoon crawled past. Alesone wiped her brow, noted the sun sinking in the west.

"Hold the bundle tight while I secure the tie," Forveleth said.

Embarrassed to have been daydreaming, Alesone tightened her grip. "We should have plenty of herbs for whatever treatment is required."

"Indeed." The healer set aside the sack. "Come, we have one more injured man to care for this night."

Alesone scooped up the basket and followed. "I thought we had treated everyone?"

"'Tis the king's man Sir John carried in. I tended to him when he first arrived. With his injuries, he will be in great pain. I want to give him some chamomile to help him sleep."

The scent of roasting venison filled the air as they headed down the crossed the great room.

The healer headed outside.

"Where is he?" Alesone asked, surprised as they started across the bailey.

"He wished to remain in the guard's quarters."

"'Tis odd that he made such a request. Most warriors look forward to staying in the keep."

Forveleth shrugged. "The knight seems a humble sort."

A horse whinnied in the stables, another snorted. Alesone tugged her cape tighter against a chill. "I am ready for the warmth of spring."

She grimaced. "Aye, my old bones grow weary of the cold."

"If you wish, I can care for him," Alesone offered. "We have been preparing herbs and treating people all day, and I see the fatigue in your eyes."

Nay, lass. I couldna let you—"

"You have been so kind to me." Alesone halted. "'Twould be an honor to help."

The healer paused.

"Please," she urged at Forveleth's hesitation. "'Tis nay a sin to sit before the hearth when the tasks are being done. And 'twould be my pleasure."

A tired smile touched the healer's mouth. "I thank you." She pointed toward a sturdy structure that rose to connect with the wall walk. "The injured knight is inside. His wounds need to be cleaned and repacked with herbs. Oh, and his name is Sir Iames."

A trickle of unease swept Alesone. She knew a man with that name who was a scoundrel of the lowest sort, a dangerous warrior who over the years she had avoided. She dismissed the disquiet. The name was a common one.

"I will be saying an Our Father at the chapel in thanks." The elder winked. "I wouldna want to commit a sin of laziness." She headed toward the church.

A gust of wind had Alesone glancing up. Clouds rolling in smothered the meager warmth. Neither would she tarry. With the sun beginning to set, soon Thomas would arrive at her chamber.

Shivers of warmth danced across her skin as she thought of the hours ahead. Though he'd touched her, left her body trembling with release, this night would be the first time they would join in the most intimate of ways.

A part of her wanted to tell him that she loved him, but another part was unsure.

She laughed. Look at her mulling like a dim-witted lass, but for this moment she enjoyed her bit of foolishness. For this night and until they reached Avalon Castle, he would be hers.

"Watch yourself, lass," a man exiting the guardhouse warned.

Startled, she stepped around the post paces before her. Heat swept her cheeks. Served her right for losing herself in a daydream. "I thank you."

The man nodded. "Did you need something?"

"I am here to tend to Sir Iames."

"He is on the cot near the back wall." The warrior stepped aside, and she entered.

The lingering scent of men and leather and smoke filled the large room as her eyes slowly adjusted to the dim interior. Illuminated by two torches in wall sconces along with the flicker of flames in the hearth, numerous beds lay against the far wall in a staggered fashion.

Alesone lifted her basket and made her way toward the injured man covered with a heavy blanket. As she approached, she noticed he was shivering. God in heaven, after his brave deed, please dinna let him have come down with a fever.

At his side, she set down the basket. "I am Alesone, and I will be tending to you."

"A…" The knight coughed. "An older woman was here earlier," he grumbled.

She began sorting through the herbs for the chamomile. "'Twas Forveleth; she is the healer at Dair Castle." She lifted the blanket and began unwinding a bandage. "I will be cleaning your wounds and—"

The man turned. In the shimmer of firelight he came into clear view.

Her chest constricted. Sir Iames!

Through the wash of pain, satisfaction settled on the fierce knight's face.

Alesone gasped. "They said you were…"

He gave a cold laugh. "Robert the Bruce's man?"

Dread filled her as her mind clattered with horrified understanding. "Where is Comyn?"

"By now," he said with vile satisfaction, "he has surrounded Dair Castle."

"You killed King Robert's man," she charged.

"Nae until he told us where you were." A smirk crawled along his mouth. "I was impressed by his loyalty, but there are inventive ways to make a man talk, some more pleasurable than others."

Bile rose in her throat. She had to warn Thomas! Heart pounding, she stepped back.

With lightning speed, the man caught her wrist.

The flare of panic darkened to fury. Despising this man, all he represented, with a flick of her wrist, her *sgian dubh* fell into her palm. "This is for the man you tortured." She slashed the blade across his hand clasped on her arm.

Shock widened the man's eyes as he cried out.

"And this," she rasped, "is for torturing and killing a man for my father's cause." She drove the dagger deep into his heart. As he slumped against the sheets, his blood dripping to the floor, Alesone sheathed her dagger and bolted toward the keep. God in heaven, she had to warn the duke!

Chapter Eighteen

Heart slamming against her chest, Alesone shoved open the hewn door, bolted into the war chamber. "'Tis a trap!" she yelled. "'Tis Sir Iames MacCheine. He isna the Bruce's man, but Comyn's."

Chairs scraped as Thomas, his father, and brother shoved to their feet. The other knights in the large chamber turned to face her.

The duke's eyes narrowed. "Explain."

"When I entered to care for the knight," Alesone replied, damning Sir Iames with her every breath, "I recognized him."

Thomas unsheathed his dagger. "God's teeth, I will slay the bastard!"

"He is already dead." She angled her jaw. "When he realized that I knew who he was, he grabbed me. I drove my dagger into his heart."

Satisfaction settled on the duke's face. "Tell us all you know."

"The king's man was tortured to gain information, and then killed," she explained, temper riding her voice. "Sir Iames was sent with the Bruce's missive to buy Comyn and his men time while they surround Dair Castle."

Thomas's face drained of color as he sheathed his blade. "God's teeth, Sir John MacLairish left earlier this day with a missive to update the king."

Line's furrowed Donnchadh's brow. "Do you think he slipped past Comyn's men?"

"I pray so," Thomas replied.

Expression grim, the Duke of Westwyck eyed the men. "We must immediately—"

The ringing of the tower bell fractured his words.

Shouts of an attack blared within the castle.

"To your posts!" The duke ran for the door, Donnchadh at his side, and his warriors hurrying in their wake.

With the press of men rushing past, his expression fierce, Thomas caught Alesone's hand. "Gather your bow and arrows. Meet me on the southern side of the wall walk."

Calls for reinforcements echoed in the castle, and fear tore through her. "Thomas, I love you," Alesone blurted out, the urgency of the moment making the heartfelt words tumble upon the other. "I needed to tell you in case—"

"Your father willna take you!" He caught her mouth in a hard kiss. "We must join the others, but know this, our discussion on what exists between us is far from through."

Alesone opened her mouth to speak, but Thomas joined the rush of men running toward their stations, the mix of warriors quickly smothering him from her view.

On shaky legs, she hurried toward the turret.

Knight's yells melded with curses and the scrape of steel as she entered the corridor. What did Thomas mean by their discussion about what exists between them was far from through? He cared for her, could he feel more? The joy of what he would say faded beneath the somber reality of the upcoming engagement.

Alesone scowled as she broke off from the mass of muscled bodies, then hurried to her chamber to retrieve her weapons. If her father believed that he could destroy the happiness she'd found, he was wrong.

With her quiver secured, she sprinted toward down the corridor. The stench of smoke assaulted her as she stepped onto the wall walk. She looked to the left, pleased at the numerous bubbling cauldrons of oil awaiting dispersal atop their enemy, then toward the baily where women and children carried replenishments for the imminent battle.

A horn sounded from the distance.

Nerves strung tight, Alesone glanced past the battlements.

Sunlight shimmered over the massive formation of mounted knights cantering across the frost bleached ground. At the forefront, a familiar standard rippled in the breeze.

Fury drove through her as she glared at the man riding at the head of the contingent. Disgusted with the man whose blood ran through her veins, she strode toward Thomas.

His eyes softened as she halted beside him, and he squeezed her hand.

Love for her stalwart protector swelled within. Nay, more than a protector, he was a Knight Templar, a warrior feared by many, a man who didna make promises he couldna keep.

'Twas surprising that she had not made the connection. The many times she'd caught him deep in prayer, or the focused, structured way about him, his expertise on many topics, the extent of his travel, and his knowledge of herbs, all indicators of his inclusion in the Brotherhood. Then again, she hadna known of the secret dissolution of the Templars, or of their sailing to Scotland.

Horns blared in the distance.

Thomas glared at the attacking force.

"Arrows readied," the duke yelled.

Cursing her father with her each breath, Alesone, knocked her arrow, aimed at the nearest enemy.

"Halt!" Lord Comyn yelled above the clamor.

The wall of approaching knights behind him halted.

Her father nudged his steed before the gatehouse. "Westwyck!"

"State your purpose," the duke called down.

"I dinna wish to attack," Comyn said. "I only want my daughter."

Anger and guilt tangled inside her. The bow wobbled in Alesone's hands.

Understanding eyes held hers, and the duke nodded. "Dinna worry, you are safe here."

She gave a shaky nod. "I thank you, Your Grace."

The noble glared at Comyn. "The lass doesna wish to go with you. Nor will I make her."

Anger reddened her father's face. "If you send her down, I will overlook your treachery of pledging fealty to the Bruce."

"Lying bastard," Thomas hissed, "if he had Alesone, he would still attack.

His father grunted. "Aye. Once he loses this battle, he will walk away with naught but disgrace. A fact that pleases me immensely."

"Westwyck, send her down," Comyn roared. "My patience is at an end."

"So you can barter her like sheep?" the duke demanded.

"What I decide has naught to do with you. She is of my blood." A scowl darkened his face. "'Tis my right to speak with the lass."

"I will give him an answer," Alesone seethed. Her hand shook as she sighted her arrow on Comyn. She no longer had a father, but Thomas and his family, whom she would defend with her dying breath!

The duke pushed her bow down. "Nae like this." He faced Comyn. "The lass doesna wish to speak to you. Go on with you, and none will be harmed."

"You dare threaten me!"

"If you attack, you will pay the consequence," the duke warned. "Pray God has mercy on your treacherous soul, because I willna."

Red mottled the noble's face. "You will regret your decision!" Comyn whirled his mount, shouted commands as he galloped toward his men.

Tears burned Alesone's eyes, and her respect for the duke grew tenfold.

A roar from below recaptured her attention.

Comyn's soldiers charged.

"Release the arrows!" the duke roared.

Archers along the walls let loose their arrows; screams of the enemy filled the air. Horses reared while others, wild-eyed, were caught by footed soldiers.

"Ladders on the north wall!" Thomas yelled above the fray.

"Bring the hot oil!" Donnchadh ordered.

Women hauled over steaming buckets of hot oil strewn with bits of heated steel. They balanced their vessels atop the crenels.

Wood scraped as the advancing horde began to climb the rungs.

Donnchadh nodded. "Pour!"

Buckets were tipped.

Screams echoed from below.

The stench of burned flesh filled the air as a fresh rush of attackers ascended the ladders.

More pails of steaming-hot oil spewed over the side.

Agonized yells rang out.

The woman backed up, then rushed away with their emptied pots.

Another wave of Comyn's men clambered up the ladders, this time several of the assailants reached the top.

Thomas swung. His blade slammed against the advancing attacker.

"Step back," Alesone yelled.

Thomas complied.

The arrow hissed from her bow and embedded in the invader's chest. With a cry, he tumbled back.

"Help me push off their ladders," Thomas called to several knights nearby.

Alesone joined them.

With a mighty groan they shoved. Scores of men clinging to the structures plunged to the body laden earth.

Amidst the flurry of arrows and the stench of blood, several men on the ground hauled one of the ladders up. Wooden slats slammed against the wall.

In a trice, Thomas and others pushed the ladder away.

The sky lay savaged with raw yellows and bloody reds like a brutal portrait to the devastation below as Alesone reached for another arrow.

"Halt!" Comyn yelled.

She hesitated, glanced at Thomas. "Do you think he has given up?"

Thomas damned having to extinguish the hope in Alesone's voice. "Nay. Comyn is desperate. Without King Philip's aid or England's support, he knows his hopes of winning against the Bruce is slim."

His aged face streaked with splatters of blood, the duke strode over, grimaced toward where Comyn and his men were withdrawing. "He is trying to convince us that he will wait until dawn to attack." He grunted. "Once night falls, I suspect his men will try again."

"A belief I share," Thomas said.

Sweat and blood streaking his mail, Donnchadh joined them. He sheathed his sword. "All is secure—for now."

His father nodded. "Indeed, 'tis far from over. Pass to the men to remain in their positions throughout the night, and to take turns catching sleep."

"Aye, Father." Donnchadh strode down the wall walk.

He faced Thomas. "And you—"

"Aye, Father," he said with pride, "I shall inform the men on the far side."

Alesone wiped the sweat from her brow as she watched Thomas pause and speak with several knights before moving on.

"They are good men," the duke said, "sons any father would be proud to have."

She smiled. "They are, Your Grace. You are fortunate."

"I am." Beneath the glow of torchlight, he rubbed the back of his neck, then dropped his hand to his side. "There are many nobles who rule with a fair hand, and sadly, a few who become caught up in the need for power."

Like her father. From her birth he'd shunned her, until he'd found her of value to his cause. "A person's decisions create consequences. I find little forgiveness in people who ignore the blood spilled for their gains."

"Well said." The duke paused. "'Tis late. If you wish to go below and rest, do so."

"I will remain," she said, ignoring the fatigue weighing on her mind. "'Tis my father plotting another attack. However much I wish otherwise, he has made the confrontation personal."

Approval shimmered in the noble's gaze. "Comyn is a fool to overlook what an exemplary woman you are."

Humbled by his praise, she shook her head. "My life is one far outside that of inviting commendation, more so with my skills as an archer."

Aged eyes crinkled with warmth. "Aye, your skills with the bow compare to few archers I have seen, and your spirit and courage, those," he said with pride, "are traits to admire."

Humbled by his praise, she nodded. "I thank you."

"I agree," Thomas said as he halted by her side as she finished. "'Tis how we met."

Heat stroked her cheeks.

Against the fading light, the duke arched a brow. "You didna mention how you were introduced."

"'Tis a long story." Thomas paused. "The knights have been informed of our plans."

"I thank you." On a heavy sigh, the duke strode toward Donnchadh who was halfway down the wall walk, then they headed toward the far tower.

Murmurs of men talking, errant scrapes of steel as knights cleaned their weapons, and the whisper of wind filled the air as within the golden shimmers of torchlight as Thomas studied her. "How do you fare?"

"Tired," she replied, "but nay more than anyone else."

A fatigued smile touched his mouth. "With your expertise with a bow, several times I thanked God that you were on our side."

"I am proud to be fighting alongside your father's warriors. They are skilled men."

"They are." His eyes darkened with warmth.

She drew a steading breath. Was he thinking about her earlier declaration of love? Was this the *later* he'd mentioned? Nerves tangled her mind as she scanned the flicker of distant fires beyond the wall walk. What if he didna share her feelings? Once they'd reached Avalon Castle and he departed, would he forget her? Her heart ached at the thought.

Mayhap she was creating strife where none existed. Until he explained, she wouldna know. Neither would she press him. Well she understood the struggle to bear one's soul.

Tension churning inside, she glanced toward the heavens darkening to a milky purple. "I can see a star."

"The sky is clear," Thomas said. "'Twill be cold."

"My father's men have started several campfires. Mayhap they willna attack this night." And she prayed 'twas true.

Thomas grunted. "The fires are but a decoy. Before this night is over, Comyn will strike again."

"'Twas what I feared." Shivering, she tucked her hands beneath her cloak. On edge, she glanced over, frustrated that shadows had claimed his face. "About earlier...when I said I loved you."

He remained silent.

The building of nerves overrode her intent to say naught until he was ready. "With the battle upon us, and unsure of the outcome…" She blew out a rough breath, and an icy cloud misted between them faded. "I wanted you to know."

Moved, needing to touch her, Thomas cupped her face, his words of love trembling on his lips. On a rough breath he stilled them. "Never have I met a lass like you.

Within the cast of torchlight, hurt flickered on her face, and he damned that he couldna give her the answer she wished. He stroked his thumb across her cheek. "You are an amazing woman, never doubt that."

"I shouldna have told you," she whispered. "'Twas foolish."

She tried to turn away, but he held her. "When a person speaks her heart, 'tis never foolish."

Memoires of their plans for intimacy this night left him aching. Thomas refused to utter promises he couldna keep, nor would he leave her with naught. "I spoke with my father earlier. If Bruce agrees, once Comyn is defeated, you are welcome to live in Dair Castle. Your skills as a healer and archer are welcome."

"And you?"

"I will fight alongside our king until Scotland is united."

"I see."

He damned the tremor in her voice, and his intent to say naught of what she made him feel dissolved. His father was right, naught was guaranteed. Thomas took her hand, love for Alesone filling his heart

"They are scaling the wall on the south end!" a knight shouted.

"Ladders are hitting the east side as well," another warrior on their left yelled.

With a curse that he'd allowed his thoughts to wander from duty, Thomas glanced over the side. "There are ladders on north side!"

"Prepare for a full scale attack," the duke roared.

Scrapes of steel melded with the cries of death as Thomas drove his blade into an ascending knight, the falling man quickly replaced by another. Hours passed as he battled until slowly silence filled the night. Nae convinced the enemy had left, he scoured the night, the lingering stars nae lending enough light to detect where their enemy had withdrawn to.

As dawn's faint glow shimmered in the distance, his brother, exhaustion lining his face, walked over. "They have extinguished all of their fires."

"To move to new positions, nay doubt." Thomas wiped the sweat from his brow.

The clack of authoritative steps sounded. His father paused beside them. "Have you seen or heard any movement?"

"Nay," Donnchadh replied.

Thomas scanned the roll of land blackened by shadows. "Nor I."

"The bastard's havena given up," their father growled. "They are out there. The question is where and what will be their next move."

A gust of wind raced through the castle, casting flakes of snow from the merlon into the air. Spirals of white shimmered against the backdrop of fading stars, and then the flakes drifted toward the blood-stained earth below.

"I know one thing," Thomas grunted, "wherever they are hidden, they are freezing their arses off."

His brother laughed. "They are at that."

Unease filled Thomas as he spotted Alesone down the wall walk with her bow lowered, staring into the darkened void of night. He damned the second assault that had interrupted them, nor would he make the mistake of discussing something so important when they could be interrupted. Once the battle was over and the castle secure, then he would tell her that he loved her.

He grimaced. What of John MacLairish? He prayed his friend had reached the Bruce. Still, they must take every precaution that the king was warned. "Father."

"Aye," the duke replied.

"I think 'twould be wise to send another runner to King Robert," Thomas said, damning his words.

"Had I of known the enemy was so close…" His father gave a weary sigh. "Another man will be sent."

Donnchadh glanced over. "Whoever goes, we must choose wisely," he said. "Given the situation, I believe we have but one chance for a runner to make it past the enemy."

Thomas nodded. "As I am familiar with where Bruce was camped and given my experience, I am the best choice to make the journey."

"With your injury, I only allowed you to fight as each man is necessary," his father said, temper sliding into his voice.

"My injuries are all but healed," Thomas pressed. "I could steal a horse and slip away before anyone notices."

"Your wound will slow you," his brother snapped. "I should be the one who—"

"Enough," their father interrupted. "In a day, mayhap two, if the battle continues, then I will decide who rides to our king."

Thomas muttered a silent curse. Many things could change in a day. A force could lay siege, or they could wake up to find Comyn and his men gone. As much as he wished, with the stakes so high, he didna expect the latter.

He glanced toward Alesone. She now sat with her back against the stone. "I will check on the lass."

The soft tap of steps grew closer. Alesone shifted, but she didna open her eyes.

"Are you well?" Thomas asked.

At the concern in his voice, she peered out. "As anyone else." He settled beside her, and any chance of her drifting off faded. As if she could sleep without thinking of him? As of late, Thomas filled her every thought. She opened her eyes. "Are their campfires still out?"

"Aye."

Hope slid through her. "Do you think they have left?"

"They are staying. It is what they are planning that causes concern."

She frowned. "What do you mean?"

"With their failed attempt to scale the walls, mayhap they willna lay siege and have decided upon another method."

Frustration rolled through her. "Do you have any thoughts of what they could be plotting?"

He shrugged. "There are several possibilities. Until sunrise, 'tis too dangerous to send anyone outside the walls to check."

Alesone worried her fingers on the curve of her bow. "I dinna like it."

"Nor I, but 'tis the way of war."

"As a Knight Templar, how do you endure it?" she asked, emotion sliding into her voice. "The waiting, the fighting, watching those you care for die, only to pick up your sword and continue?"

"There is little place in war for emotion," he said, his voice cool.

"But you do feel," she said, trying to understand. "How do you keep the hurt of the loss of your friends, the sight of the slaughter from marring your soul? And dinna tell me that you are unaffected by battle. You are a deep and caring person. However much you wish, you canna smother it all."

The flicker of torchlight wavering across his face, accenting the tautness of his mouth. "For some, incredibly, they are unmoved by the blood, screams, and gruesome sights of war. Then there are those who after the first battle fall apart at the witnessed atrocities."

He paused, the strain on his face a testament to the suffering he'd endured.

"Many men, as I, stow the terrible memories deep inside," Thomas said, his expression grim. "Aye, it does affect me, and at times the horror threatens to overwhelm me where I want to walk away from the bloodshed. Then I remember why I fight, understand that if I, as the other Templars, didna champion the Christians in the Holy Land, they would be slaughtered."

Tears burned her eyes as she stared at him, the appalling events he'd witnessed leaving her aching inside. This day's fighting was naught compared to what Thomas had endured. "I had never considered such, but you are right. With each believing their faith supreme, or with the desire for power, the fighting will never end."

"Which is why 'tis important to live, to experience, and to thank God each day for the blessings in our lives." He gently drew her into his arms. "As I do with you."

Her throat tightened.

"I never meant you to become important to me, you were to be naught more than a duty." A wry smile touched his mouth. "In that I failed."

Emotion stormed her. He hadna said he loved her, but given the mayhem of this day, she embraced his confession. The morrow would bring its own questions, and mayhap he would admit more. For now 'twas enough.

"Lie your head on my shoulder and try to sleep," Thomas said. "We both need to catch a bit of rest."

Alesone glanced around, surprised to note many of the knights along the wall were asleep while others stood watch. "We do." Thankful for this man in her life, she complied and though naught was guaranteed, savored the rightness of this moment.

* * *

The low thud of steel on wood had Thomas opening his eyes. Blood-red hues streaked the morning sky littered with clouds, broken by errant rays of light. At the slap of steps, he glanced over.

Donnchadh was rushing toward him.

Ignoring the aches, he shifted. Alesone lay against him still asleep. With regret, he carefully extracted himself from her warmth, stood, and walked over to meet his brother. At the deep scowl on his face, unease filtered through Thomas. "What is wrong?"

His breaths coming fast, his brother pointed toward the east. "Look!"

Thomas turned. Stilled. A short distance from the castle, the enemy lashed together sturdy hewn logs, with a basket secured at the end of a long beam that they'd use for the counterweight once filled with stones. "God in heaven. A traction trebuchet!" Tension churned inside as Thomas took in Alesone's pale face as she sat beside him. Cursing the situation, he glanced toward his father standing before the knights filling the chamber.

Expression grave, the duke scanned the warriors. "With the speed Comyn's knights are building the siege engine, 'twill be finished on the morrow. If given the opportunity, beneath heavy cover of their archers they will move the trebuchet to a lethal distance, which we canna allow." Wizened eyes narrowed. "We must destroy their war machine this night."

Grim faced men nodded.

Thomas stood. "Beneath the cover of darkness, I will slip outside and destroy the siege engine."

Donnchadh shoved to his feet. "I will accompany you."

The duke frowned, but remained silent.

As much as his father worried over the last two of his sons risking their lives, he would have been ashamed if they hadna offered. Thomas nodded to his brother. "Once 'tis dark, meet me in the great room."

"I could arrange a small contingent of men to accompany you," his father said.

Thomas shook his head. "'Tis best to keep our number small. Once we signal that we are ready, if you start a diversion, 'twill distract them while we set the trebuchet ablaze."

His father nodded. "'Twill be done."

Once the last of the plans were finalized, the warriors departed for their positions along the wall walk.

Thomas entered the corridor, and Alesone fell into step at his side. "I thank you for letting me lean on you last night to sleep."

The lyrical flow of her voice wove around him like a blanket of hope, the memory of her lying against him bringing its own comfort. "You needed rest."

"Thomas…"

At the concern in her voice, he glanced over.

Her lower lip trembled, and worry darkened her gaze. "I will pray for your safety."

For the first time in his life the danger of the battle ahead weighed heavy on his mind, of the risks, of what he had to lose.

He took her hand and skimmed his thumb across her palm, wishing they were alone, the castle was safe, and that uninterrupted hours lay ahead of them where he could take her into his arms and show her how much she meant to him, tell the words filling his heart. "I shall come back to you."

"What if—"

"With the throng of flaming arrows raining upon Comyn's men," he interrupted, wanting to ease her worry, "the enemy will be too busy defending themselves to notice my brother and me setting their siege engine ablaze."

Eyes churning with emotion held his. "They will be."

But he heard the nerves edging her voice, ones that lingered inside. 'Twasna a simple battle they fought. The outcome of Comyn's attack could shape more than their future together, but Scotland's history.

Like an omen, torchlight cast angry shadows as they hurried up the turret. Thomas glared at the mix of darkness and light, hurried past.

As Alesone stepped onto the wall walk, a snow laden gust tugged at her blond hair. "How can you slip back inside the castle without being seen?"

"Hidden tunnels are scattered about known only to family."

"What of their stockpile of beams near the forest?"

"Once the siege engine is burning, we shall torch any supplies they could use to rebuild." He grimaced at the distant stack of timber. "We only have this one opportunity. Once your father realizes we can sneak out of the castle, he will double the guards around any weaponry or supplies."

She released a shaky breath.

Waves of the oncoming night scarred the last wisps of the sun's rays on the horizon as Thomas paused beside the corner tower. "We canna fail. If they destroy the curtain wall, naught can prevent them from storming the castle."

"Mayhap," she said, her voice unsteady, "Sir John MacLairish has reached our sovereign."

"However much I pray he has, unless my men and the Bruce's forces arrive, we canna count on such." He rubbed the tense muscles in the back of his neck. "My hope is that destroying their siege engine and stockpile will dissuade your father from believing that he can take you and that he will leave."

"Given the stakes," she said, her words unsteady, "do you believe he will ever go without me?"

On a curse, he hauled her against him. "Nay."

* * *

Heart pounding, Alesone again scanned the night, waited for the sign from Thomas to begin the diversion. With clouds smothering any starlight, blackness drenched the land.

A flash from a flaming arrow flew high into the air.

The sign!

"Fire," the duke boomed.

Pulse racing, Alesone, along with the other archers lined along the wall walk, lit their arrows. Lethal gold cut through the sky, punctuated by shouts of enemy knights caught beneath the fiery barrage. Time dragged as she released arrow after flame-tipped arrow.

Her arm ached, her muscles bunched in knots as she pulled back her bowstring. An arrow hissed past a breath from head. Narrowing her gaze, Alesone aimed toward the blur of movement, released.

A scream sounded.

She jerked another arrow from the quiver, took aim on the next victim.

"The trebuchet is on fire!" the duke roared.

Alesone released her arrow, turned. Outlined within the lick of flames, the nearly built siege engine burned bright. Cheers thundered around her, but she scanned the pile of timber stacked near the forest's edge.

A distant blur of moment wavered within the wash of flames.

Thomas!

The echo of wood against stone slammed to her right.

"Ladders on the wall!" a knight warned.

Snow lashing her face, Alesone whispered a prayer that Thomas and Donnchadh reached the safety of the tunnel, and then focused on the men scaling the wall.

Leaning forward, with deft accuracy, time and again she loosed her arrows, the roars of anger melding with pain-filled screams of her enemy.

The stench of blood and rancid oil from the earlier pots dumped over the side burned her lungs as she nocked another ash arrow, aimed, then released. Weaving on her feet, she glanced toward the east. A wash of purple smeared the sky. Her fingers tightened on the bow. God in heaven 'twas almost dawn, where were they?

"A ladder to your right," a nearby knight called.

Alesone ignored the ache in her shoulders, aimed, and took out the lead man.

Two women hurried over, lifted a steaming bucket of oil.

She stepped back.

"Heave!" the woman on the right called. They upended the container.

Screams rang out.

The women carried the empty container away.

Several knights rushed forward, caught the tip of the ladder, shoved.

"They are withdrawing," the duke called. "Cease fire!"

Fingers numb, Alesone lowered her bow and flexed her hand. "Thank God."

"Aye," Thomas agreed, his voice rough with fatigue.

Alesone whirled. On a cry, she launched herself into his arms. "You are safe!"

He wrapped his arms tight around her. "Did you ever doubt me?"

Her eyes blurred, and her body trembled with relief. "Nay."

"Here now." Thomas lifted her chin, and a tear she fought to control slid down her cheek.

"I-I was so afraid for you."

Tenderness softened his gaze. "I swore that I would come back to you."

She sniffed, wanting to laugh, to cry, the emotions storming her making her feel strong and weak at the same time. On an unsteady breath, she stepped back. "And look at your face all covered in soot."

"Donnchadh looks the same," he said with pride. "We slathered a mixture of lard and ash onto our skin to blend in with the night."

She wrinkled her nose. "Please tell me that isna you that I smell?"

Thomas chuckled. "Penance for success."

Her heart warmed. "And here I was thinking of kissing you. Now 'twill wait until you have scrubbed up."

Laughter in his eyes, he brushed a swath of hair from her face. "Are you saying that you dinna want a kiss?"

At his teasing, the remainder of the tension weighing heavy upon her faded. "Nay, I—"

"You and your brother have bought us much-needed time," the duke stated with pride as he strode toward them.

In the wash of the first rays of golden light, Thomas studied the charred outlines of the trebuchet, the weave of black smoke littered with sparks curling into the lightening sky. "Aye."

On edge, Alesone glanced into the murky light where Comyn's men battled the blazes, a potent reminder of the dangers Thomas and his brother had faced.

"Once all of the fires are put out," Thomas said, his voice grim, "they will be deciding their next plan of attack."

"They will." The duke paused. "Donnchadh left to scrub off at least the top layer of grime." Humor touched the noble's face. "I canna say that I envied either of you smearing on such filth."

"However foul," Thomas said, "it allowed us to accomplish the task."

His father nodded. "That it did."

Alesone prayed that repelling the attack had gained them enough time to allow King Bruce's men to arrive. Or had the enemy killed Sir John MacLairish before he could deliver his missive? Dread crept through her. If so, this entire night been for naught.

Chapter Nineteen

Through the soft fall of snow, Thomas cursed as he stood on the battlement, stared at the new construction beginning in Comyn's encampment. Two blasted days had passed and during that time they'd received more supplies. He'd expected them to build another trebuchet, but nae so soon. With each sunrise, he'd prayed to see signs of the Templar Knights riding with the Bruce's men, hope that with each sunset faded.

Against the first rays of light, he glanced toward his father. "This time they are building four siege engines."

The duke frowned. "Aye, one for each side of Dair Castle. After you and Donnchadh torched their first trebuchet they will nae be foolish enough to leave their war machines unprotected."

On a rough swallow, Thomas met his brother's frustrated gaze before facing his father. "Regardless, we must try to destroy them."

"If I thought a chance existed, I would send you and your brother out this night." The duke glared at the encampment. "Since their last attack, their numbers have doubled, and they have tripled the amount of men guarding their supplies and siege engines. With our surprise factor lost, any attempt to infiltrate their camp will fail."

However much Thomas wanted to argue, he agreed. Nor was that their only concern. "Though Comyn's men have kept out of arrow range, throughout the morning they have begun to surround the castle."

"You think they are going to attack?" Alesone asked as she joined them.

Thomas damned the nerves in her voice. "Nae until they have finished the war machines."

"Their few failed attempts have assured them that without proper weaponry any attempt would end in further defeat," Donnchadh said. "For now they are laying siege."

"Which tells me," Thomas said, "they are confident we willna be receiving any reinforcement."

Fear slid into her eyes. "You think Sir John didna make it past my father's forces?"

His gut churned at the thought. Thomas shrugged. "We canna be sure."

The scowl on his father's face deepened. "Neither can we sit here and do naught. The day I give up without a fight is the day my bones are buried deep in the earth." He eyed his sons. "We will send a second runner to the Bruce."

"I shall go," Thomas said. "I am well enough to travel, and my men are there as well. I can answer any questions and make plans during our return."

After a moment's hesitation, his father nodded. "I will pen a writ for you to give the king." He left.

"I can ride along as well," Donnchadh said.

"'Tis best if I go alone. And," he said, glancing toward Alesone, "I ask that you watch over her."

"I think," she said, her voice cool, "that I have more than proven that I am able to take care of myself."

Pride filled Thomas. "You have, neither do I question your ability. 'Tis what any man would ensure for the woman who has become important to his life."

The irritation in her eyes faded to tenderness. "Oh," she whispered.

Donnchadh cleared his throat. "I will see you before you leave, Thomas."

He nodded.

The crunch of snow beneath the earl's boots faded as he departed.

Emotion storming Thomas, he met Alesone's worried gaze. "I must gather a few necessities. Walk with me." Inside the stables, snow whirled in the whip of wind as he secured a *sgian dubh* at his ankle, and another dagger at his hip. "I will borrow a horse from the monastery. From there, 'twill take two days at most to reach the Bruce's camp, unless I meet his contingent he sent en route."

"You believe John is still alive?"

He clung to the hope in her voice. "Sir John and I fought together in the Holy Land. I know him, his instincts, and the creative methods he has utilized in the past against overwhelming odds." He swallowed hard, and prayed he was right. "If he saw Comyn's men, he would have evaded them and then delivered the writ to King Robert. I wanted to say as much to my father except…"

"You are unsure?"

Heaviness weighed on him. "We canna risk my being wrong."

"Here." She placed a pouch of herbs in his hand. "'Tis ground white willow bark to help with any pain. I know you have recovered, but I will feel better knowing you have it with you."

"I thank you. The travel willna do more than cause a few aches and pains." As long as he was able to slip away without being seen, he refused to add. He glanced down the stalls for a sign of his father.

Naught.

Thankful, he led her inside where they kept gear for the horses, and pushed the door until 'twas almost closed. His body humming with need, he drew Alesone into his arms. "I willna be gone long."

"Swear it. Nay," she said, her face pale. "I know you canna, I am being foolish."

"Shhhh." At the desperation in her voice, he stroked his fingers across her cheek. "I will return to you. Trust me."

"I-I do, 'tis with my father and the size of his force that troubles me."

"I—"

The firm echo of boots had him looking into the main stable.

His father appeared at the end of the corridor.

However much he wanted to believe he would return, with the number of seasoned warriors surrounding the castle, the odds were slim at best.

Neither could he forget the siege engines the enemy was constructing. How long before they finished? A day? Two? Once their weapons were ready, however they'd prepared, his father and his knights could keep Dair Castle safe for only so long. God help them if Comyn successfully destroyed a portion of the curtain wall before he returned.

His father drew near.

On a mumbled curse, wishing for more time, Thomas claimed Alesone's mouth in a rough kiss. Her body softened against his, and she gave, demanded, and his hands trembled from wanting her. Needing more, on an unsteady breath, he broke away.

"I love you," she rasped.

"And I—"

"Thomas?" the duke called.

The words twisted in his throat, ached to come out. "I must go." With a hard kiss, he strode toward his father, damning every step that took him farther away from the woman he loved.

* * *

A day later, wisps of dawn smeared the sky as the duke yelled above the chaos, "They are attacking again!"

Her every muscle screaming, Alesone nocked another arrow, aimed at the closest warrior as he climbed up the rungs of the ladder, released.

The invader screamed as he tumbled to the earth.

She loaded the next arrow and scanned the distant trees looking for any sign of the Bruce's knights.

Naught.

A boom sounded to her left.

Beneath her the wall walk shook. She whirled.

Shattered stone tumbled to the ground, and a gaping hole lay at the top of the curtain wall.

Oh God, they'd moved the fourth trebuchet into position!

The duke shouted orders for reinforcement where his men had been injured or killed.

Sickened, Alesone focused on the next target, praying for Thomas to arrive.

Hurled stone slammed nearby.

She stumbled back.

"Move to the right," the duke yelled. "The curtain wall is—"

An explosion of rock shattered paces away. Shards bit into her skin, driving Alesone to her knees. The mill of bodies around her blurred.

Donnchadh's strong arms caught her, hauled her back.

Beneath the next volley, the wall walk where she'd been standing collapsed.

A tremor rolled through her. "Y-you saved my life."

Donnchadh's eyes dark with concern narrowed as he released her. "Are you hurt?"

Hurt? She gasped for breath, then another. She'd almost died.

Another round shook the castle wall to her right.

She jumped. "Oh God, all four siege engines are in place!"

The earl ran over, caught her arm. "Come. For your safety we must reach the keep."

Furious, she jerked free. Snow whipped past, the icy shards driving against her skin as Alesone met the duke's gaze. "I will fight, teach the bastard that he canna always have what he wants."

As she started to nock her bow, Comyn's command to halt rang out.

She glanced east, searched for signs of Thomas. The euphoria pouring through her faded as naught but her father's men surrounding the castle came into view.

"Westwyck," her father yelled.

The duke glared at his enemy. "Aye."

"Send my daughter out, and I willna destroy Dair Castle."

The bloody bastard, the duke hissed. "Rot in Hades!"

Comyn's face darkened with fury. "If I order my men to attack, 'twill be your bones buried in the earth."

Given the odds, the truth. Helplessness merged with outrage. Bedamned her father, his greed, and the devastation he'd caused so many. Nor could this standoff continue. "Your Grace. The castle canna take much more. A shot, mayhap three if we are fortunate, then they will have smashed a hole in the curtain wall to the east."

The noble scowled at where gaps fissured down the interior wall. "By God, Comyn willna take you."

Nor did she want to go with the scoundrel, except without reinforcements little hope remained. Sickened at the thought, aching that she'd never see Thomas again, the time had come to make the hardest decision in her life.

"Enough people have died because me," she whispered. "Let me go to him; save yourself, your son, and your home."

Outrage glittered in the duke's eyes. "What we fight for today is more than the loss of the lives of my men, my family, or my home. If your father seals the pact with King Philip, Scotland's freedom will be lost."

Humbled, she nodded. "Aye, let us fight!"

The stench of blood, soot, and fear filled the air as the hours dragged by, the loss of life on both sides leaving Alesone overwhelmed. Charred edges scarred buildings they'd been able to extinguish wove in a horrific mix with smoldering ashes where they hadna.

A boom resonated on the western side of the castle.

Screams of men melded with the slam of rock. Fractures in the castle walls by earlier attacks deepened, and several chunks toppled to the body-littered earth.

"Donnchadh," the duke yelled, "send more knights to ensure the enemy doesna breach the western wall."

"Aye!" The earl shouted orders, and several warriors ran toward the gaping hole.

Another volley from a siege engine slammed against the wall walk paces from Alesone. She clung to the trembling rock, kept her balance, barely.

"Lass, are you—"

"I am fine, Your Grace." Her fingers raw, she reloaded her bow, fought to smother the building fear. Ever since her father's men had completed the fourth siege engine, they'd assaulted Dair Castle with merciless intent.

Though the duke refused to admit defeat, with many of his warriors lying dead or dying, 'twas clear that the time to cede was drawing near.

Her hand shaking, she knocked another arrow, aimed, and released. Numb, Alesone scanned the line of trees. She willed Thomas and the reinforcements to appear. And as the hours before, naught but falling snow smeared with blood, bodies, and the roar of the enemy greeted her.

Where was he? Had he reached the king? Were he and Bruce's forces en route? Or was he lying somewhere injured, dying, or dead?

A sob built in her throat, and she shoved it aside. Thomas had promised that he would return. They only needed to buy time. She didna care how panicked she sounded, or if her rational was skewed.

A blast shook the wall to her left.

Alesone crashed against the wall walk, and rolled toward the edge.

Donnchadh caught her hand. "Hang on!"

Another blast tore into a large gap; shards toppled to the baily with a violent clatter. Three more volleys simultaneously slammed the castle.

"Comyn's men are breeching the curtain wall to the east!" the duke yelled.

"Bedamned!" Donnchadh helped her to her feet.

"Tell everyone to withdraw to the keep," his father ordered. "I will take Mistress Alesone to the secret tunnel."

"Aye." Donnchadh bolted toward their warriors.

The duke waved her forward. "Hurry!"

Heart pounding, she followed him down the turret, prayed they'd make it in time. Then what? With their forces devastated, they couldna hold the enemy off for long. Or with the men pouring into the castle, would they even reach the escape route?

Sickened, she entered the keep, the roar of battle in her wake. Comyn had proven that he would do whatever he must to achieve his goal.

"Seal the door!" the duke roared after his son and the remaining knights ran inside.

Barricades slammed into place as women rushed their children deep into the castle.

Booms rocked the exterior door below, and the duke's face paled. "Mistress Alesone, follow me."

As they reached the great hall, the entry shuddered against another volley.

Weapons raised, knights stood a safe distance from the entry awaiting the inevitable charge.

A frenzy of explosions sounded outside, mixed with the screams of men.

"Hurry!" The duke led her down a corridor, then waved her into a small chamber. He shoved aside a sturdy table, lifted a tapestry, and then wedged his fingers against a small, nondescript crevice.

He pushed.

A soft scrape echoed.

The stone panel shifted. Errant spider webs hung inside a tunnel fading to blackness musty with the scent of time. The duke nodded. "Go."

Another blast echoed against the entry door, this time louder.

"Your Grace, we must wait for Donnchadh."

His face paled. "Nay."

"Let me take—"

An explosion of wood melded with screams. The scrape of blades sounded.

"Oh God," she gasped, "they have breached the entry!"

The duke shoved a torch from a nearby sconce into her hand. "At the end of the tunnel you will hit a dirt wall. There isna much, but 'tis only for a layer of safety. Once you dig through, you will come up inside of a rotting trunk. From there travel west."

An ached burned in her chest, despising this moment, hating Comyn even more. She withdrew her *sgian dubh* from its sheath. "I willna run, Your Grace."

The echoes of screams and blades rose to a fevered pitch. The sound of boots slammed down the entry.

"God in heaven," he rasped, "'tis too late!"

Chapter Twenty

Halfway across the bailey, feet braced, sweat, soot, and blood streaked Thomas's face. He rammed his blade against an attacking warrior, slashed his throat with a dagger, then shoved him back. He whirled to face the next assailant. With a curse, Thomas angled his weapon, and drove deep. The enemy crumpled, joining the bodies scattered around him.

A distance away, wood crunched as Comyn's men, working in unison, slammed a massive log into the door of the keep.

"They are using a battering ram to gain entry!" Aiden MacConnell, his close friend and fellow Templar Knight, yelled.

A command rang out for another round, and Comyn's knights again slammed into the honed wood.

Splinters flew.

Ragged shards hung above the gaping hole exposing the great room.

Thomas cursed. He must reach Alesone! "Rónán, Cailin, and Aiden, gather the others knight we trained en route. Tell them we are forming a shield wall."

His men's yells rang out. The slap of crafted iron and wood clattered amidst the scream of swords as the men overlapped their shields against the other.

"Forward!" Thomas ordered. With deadly efficiency, they shoved ahead.

A hand reached over the sturdy defense.

Thomas slashed his dirk across the attacker's wrist. Blood spilled to the frozen ground, and he pushed the warrior back. Wind-whipped snow battered his face as the crack of blades vibrated against smithed iron.

Inch by inch he and his knights edged closer, the clash of swords in their wake diminishing as King Robert's troops continued to surge into the baily and overwhelm the enemy.

"Halt," Thomas called as they neared the steps. "Aiden and Cailin, when I give the order to lower the shields, use your bows to take out the men holding the battering ram."

"Aye," his knights replied.

Thomas nodded. "Now!"

The melee swam into view. Arrows hissed past.

Men's screams rang out.

"Another volley," Thomas yelled.

Arrows whooshed into the snow-laden sky.

Screams sounded, and the men holding the battering ram toppled, the thick log crashing atop their unmoving bodies.

Thomas cursed as at least twenty of Comyn's knights bolted inside. "Follow me!" He shoved his sword into an attacker ahead of him, withdrew his blade, then jumped over the man's falling body and bolted inside.

With a roar, three of Comyn's men charged.

Thomas slashed the first man's throat, drove his dagger into the next, and kicked the third man back before a slash ended his assault.

A scream rang out from down the corridor.

His blood iced. Alesone! "Follow me!" Damning each second lost, with each swing, each scrape of steel, Thomas carved his way through the chamber, the Templars fighting by his side.

Men's yells filled the chamber in his wake.

Thomas whirled.

A fresh wave of knights poured into the chamber, all wearing Bruce's colors.

Confident they'd seized Dair Castle and naught but a handful of resistance remained, he drove his blade into the aggressor who stood between him and the woman he loved.

"Release her!" Thomas's father ordered from an open doorway.

Heart pounding, Thomas shoved the man aside, and ran down the corridor. Through the open doorway, he saw a knight jerk Alesone against him with a harsh pull.

"Dinna move," Comyn's man warned Thomas's father, who stood paces away.

The duke's face paled.

Eyes hard, the warrior pressed his blade against her throat. "Sheath your blade or die."

Her eyes widened.

The grating of blades and screams of pain blended in a lethal backdrop as Thomas waved his men to halt.

Torchlight glinted across the duke's sword as his gaze flickered on him, returned to the enemy.

At his father's covert acknowledgment, Thomas narrowed his eyes on the intruder.

The noble scowled. "Let the lass go and you shall be allowed to live."

"You dare much to threaten me, Your Grace," the man scoffed, "when 'tis *you* who are now my prisoner." With the knife still flush against her throat, the aggressor jerked her captured arms higher up her back.

Pain darkened Alesone's eyes.

"Drop the blade, Your Grace!"

His sword half raised, the duke angled a step toward the back of the chamber, forcing the man to turn away from Thomas to keep the noble in his sight.

Thomas withdrew his bow, nocked an arrow.

Sadistic pleasure rode the warrior's expression as the duke lowered his weapon, then he lowered the dagger. "Now I will—"

Without warning, Alesone dropped her full weight. Free of her captor's hold, she withdrew her *sgian dubh*, twisted to her feet and slashed his throat.

Shock widening the warrior's eyes, he stumbled back. Blood streamed through his fingers as he clenched his throat then collapsed.

On a rough breath, Thomas lowered his bow. "Remind me to never upset you."

Alesone whirled, her fingers still clenching her blade. Eyes wide with disbelief softened, and she sheathed her dagger. "Thomas!"

He stepped forward, and he crushed her against him. Love for her swamped him, and he pressed his face against her hair. "Thank God you are okay."

"I w-wasna sure if you had made it out," she whispered, "or if you would return in time."

His chest aching, he brushed a lock of hair from her dirt smeared face. "Naught would stop me from reaching you." Movement at the entry had him glancing toward his men. However much he wished to remain, the stronghold must be secured. "The castle's status?"

"Bruce's knights have squelched the last of the resistance," Aiden replied.

With a nod, Thomas faced his father. "Are you hurt?"

The duke scoffed. "Naught that willna heal. Did you see your broth—"

"Halt," a Knight Templar at the door warned as he raised his blade.

"Thomas, tell your knight to bloody move," Donnchadh roared from outside, "or by God I will move him!"

A smile touched Thomas's mouth at his brother's threat to his warrior. The Templar could disarm Donnchadh before he realized his intent. "Make way, Cailin, 'tis my brother."

His face smeared with blood and sweat and worry, Donnchadh strode inside. He glanced from Alesone to his father, then his body relaxed. "Thank God you are both alive." He met Thomas's gaze. "What of Comyn?"

"When he saw his forces were routed," he replied with disgust, "he and a sizable contingent fled on horseback. I have sent men to follow them and, if nae capture them, ensure they have left."

His brother nodded. "Excellent."

"And the Bruce?" his father asked?

"He remained in camp," Thomas replied. "Though weak, he has begun to recover and is making plans for an upcoming attack. Information I will share once all is secure."

His father glanced at Donnchadh, Alesone, and then back to Thomas. "We can rebuild the castle. That you are all safe is what matters."

Donnchadh scowled at the dead men. "I thank you, Father, for keeping her safe."

Pride shone in the duke's gaze. "The lass defended herself."

Warmth filled Alesone at the pride in the duke's voice as he explained to his son how she'd killed the assailant.

"I commend you, Mistress Alesone," Donnchadh said. "You are an extraordinary woman."

Humbled by his compliment, heat stole up her cheeks. "I did naught but what was necessary."

"Necessary," the duke scoffed. "The lass is a fierce warrior."

"She is," Thomas agreed.

"A fact that I can attest to," said a new voice echoing from the entryway. Alesone's gaze cut to the tall, well-muscled knight with green eyes and raven-black hair. He smiled at her and arched a brow. "'Tis intriguing to know your skills extend beyond that of the bow."

Heat stole up her face as the warrior referenced their first meeting near Bruce's camp weeks before.

Additional knights filled the hallway behind him.

"Alesone," Thomas said, as the trio entered the room, "you remember Sir Aiden MacConnell, Sir Cailin MacHugh, and Sir Rónán O'Connor."

"Aye, a pleasure to see each of you again." Alesone doubted any woman would forget meeting such intimidating men.

His father nodded. "I need to take account of the castle."

Donnchadh stepped beside him. "I will accompany you."

"My men—" Admiration shone in Thomas's eyes. "Alesone and I will go with you as well."

Pleased to be recognized as his equal, she cleaned and stowed her blade, then followed the group as they began to take stock of the damage.

Hours later, a soft knock sounded at the door.

Through the thick haze of sleep Alesone lifted her lids. She glanced toward the window, frowned at the blackness coating the sky. After her bath, exhausted, she'd fallen asleep. How long had she slept?

"Alesone," Thomas whispered. "Open the door."

Worried someone might hear him, she slid from the bed, rushed over, and jerked open the entry.

Like an indomitable force, Thomas stood framed within torchlight from nearby sconces.

Her hand clenched on the hewn wood, and she braced herself for the worst. "Has my father returned?"

Tenderness touched his face. "Nay. My men sent word a short while ago that the enemy has left."

She sagged against the frame. "Thank God."

He took her hand. "Come with me."

Shaking off the last of the haze, she tugged her hand free, noted his hair was still damp from a recent bath. "I canna go out dressed in my chemise."

Eyes hot with desire skimmed over her thinly clad body, and he drew her against him. "Aye—" He backed her up against the wooden entry until his body pressed flush against hers, then caught her mouth in a heated kiss until her every thought frayed. "—you should stay in your chamber, with me. Alone. Except"—he scraped his teeth along her throat, lingered—"what I must tell you is of the utmost importance." On a groan he stepped back. "Don something warm. I will explain once we reach our destination."

On shaky legs, she tossed on a warm gown and cape, wanting to remain, to take him to her bed, and fulfill her every fantasy.

At the end of the corridor, Thomas started up the turret.

She frowned. "Why are we going to the wall walk?"

In the sheen of torchlight, a tender smile curved his mouth. "You will see."

Nerves flickered through her as she climbed the next step. "Naught is amiss?"

"Dair Castle is secure, or," he said with frustration, "heavily guarded until the damage to the curtain walls is repaired."

Confused by their nocturnal outing, she slowed. "This canna wait until morning? We could go to my chamber and—"

He drew in an unsteady breath. "Ah, lass, dinna tempt me." He opened the door. Moonbeams cut through the darkness, streamed through the openings in the battlements like whispers of hope. As he halted before a squared tower of hewn stone, Thomas drew her to his side. "What do you see?"

Alesone tugged her cape tighter, then scoured the moonlit land beyond the crenel. "A loch and bens."

He gave a frustrated sigh. "Is that all?"

Confused, she searched the stars filling the cloudless sky. "'Tis night."

He turned and cradled her within his embrace. "Ask me what I see?"

The soft seduction in his voice shot tremors of heat through her. "What," she whispered, "do you see?"

Thomas pressed a kiss upon her lips. "I see shimmers of stars against the midnight sky like a promise." He nipped the soft flesh of her throat. "The harsh cut of the Highlands against the night as if a banner of loyalty, and"—he skimmed his hands along her curves—"the loch dusted with snow as if tossed with wishes cast."

As his fingers caressed her, she melted inside. Never had a man spoken to her with such care or taken the time to show her how much she mattered. Neither had she expected to find someone like Thomas. But she had, and Alesone damned the fact that he was planning to leave.

She swallowed hard, wishing this night was but the first of the rest of their lives together, although she knew that given their country's strife, and with her father his enemy, never could it be.

Thomas straightened, then lifted her face to his.

Beneath the shimmer of moonlight, she caught the seriousness of his gaze.

Panic flooded her. He was leaving. 'Twas nae seduction, he was struggling to say good-bye. "You canna go!"

His brows lowered in confusion. "Go?"

Lost to her grief, she caught his shoulders, wanting to shake him, to convince him to remain. "You are leaving on the morrow with your men, are you nae?" she rushed out as tears burned her throat. "Blast it, just tell me!"

With care he cupped her hands and shook his head. "I am trying to woo you," he said with a half-smile. "Obviously I failed. Miserably."

Hope ignited and she stared at him, prayed she'd heard correctly. "You are nae leaving?" she whispered.

"Nay."

"And you are trying to woo me?" she repeated, trying to wrap her mind around his claim.

His smile widened. "Aye."

"Oh."

He pressed a kiss on her knuckle. "I will try this one more time."

A gust of wind shuddered within the air. Flutters of snow spiraled within the moonlight as if magic cast. "Never did I believe I would meet a woman who intrigues me, who makes me laugh, or one who would steal my heart. Then," he said with reverence, "I met you." Thomas entwined his fingers within hers and knelt. Alesone Elyne MacNiven, I canna live without you. I love you with all of my heart, and want you in my life forever." Beneath the shimmer of stars, he lifted a band engraved with delicate gold scrollwork embracing an emerald. "Marry me. I want to raise our children and grow old together, and spend a thousand sunrises with you in my arms."

Happiness exploded inside, and her breath left her in a rush. "You...love me?" 'Reality tore through her euphoria, and chills ripped through her heart.

His hand tightened on hers. "Alesone?"

A gust laden with snow slapped against her face, the pinpricks minimal against the ache building in her chest. She struggled to breath against her dreams being torn apart. "I love you, want you forever, but my father is a threat."

"Nor will that change. 'Tis you that matters, us, our life ahead." Within the sheen of moonlight, his gaze held hers. "Marry me, Alesone, I canna live without you."

Heart aching she hesitated. Mayhap 'twas wrong to love a man so much, or selfish to accept what he offered, but she couldna lose him now. Tears of joy rolled down her cheeks. "Aye!"

On a shout, Thomas swept her into his arms, crushed his mouth against hers in a fierce kiss and whirled her as snow danced upon the soft breeze. The kiss deepened, and she took, gave until her entire body trembled with wanting him.

On a rough breath, he lifted his head, his eyes hot with desire. "I want you."

Her entire body trembled. "I want you as well. Make love to me Thomas, I love you and canna wait any longer."

On a groan, he strode toward the turret.

* * *

In his chamber, shimmers of golden candlelight caressed Alesone's skin as Thomas loosened the final tie, pulled. Whisper soft, her gown puddled to the floor, and she stood naked before him.

His body pulsed with yearning, demanded he take, but with their vows of love given this night, this time, their first time would be naught but magic. "I love you, Alesone."

Hands trembling, she undid his garb until he stood as naked as she, then her eyes dark with emotion met his. "I love you, Thomas."

He swallowed hard, humbled by this woman who would soon be his wife. He wished the words were exchanged, that she held his name, but 'twould be a vow soon done.

Another burst of anticipation slid through him, smothered every thought except her. Her taste, the feel of her skin against his, the slick warmth that awaited his touch. His pulse racing, he claimed her mouth.

On a moan, she took, demanded.

His body on fire, he cupped her face and plundered, then skimmed his mouth against the curve of her jaw, along the silken column of her throat, her scent driving him wild. Thomas moved lower, caressed the fullness of her breast as he suckled on the hardened tip.

She gasped. "Thomas I—"

"Say you want me," he whispered.

"I-I want you."

Flickers of flame caressed her body as he knelt, held her gaze as he kissed her sweet essence, her slick heat driving him mad.

Her mouth parted, and her head lolled back softly as his name spilled from her lips.

Thomas slid his tongue deep, savoring her gasps, her cries as he drove her higher. Her body began to quake.

With a growl, he swept her in his arms. Relishing how she trembled against him, he laid her upon the bed and pressed his body flush against hers. "I need you."

Eyes shimmering with satisfaction and nerves lifted to his. "I need you as well." With slow, sultry movements, her mouth teased his, and he took, gave as he fought the urge to slide deep into her heat.

Alesone edged lower, and Thomas caught her hand. "What are you doing?"

"As I please," she said on a husky whisper. Her mouth teased him as her hands skimmed lower, and he groaned as she cupped his hard length, sliding closer to what he'd only dreamed.

The tip of her tongue teased him, and his body threatened to explode. He caught her shoulders, struggled beneath pleasurable assault. "A-Alesone," he gasped. "Dinna do—"

Moist lips slid over his shaft and suckled; his mind hazed.

His blood pounding hot, he buried his hands in her hair, clenched, savored her tongue's slow, wonderfully torturous journey. Through sheer will, he lifted her head.

"You dinna care for that?" she teased, her lips gleaming in the firelight. "I overheard women talking in hushed tones to one another," she all but purred in a smoky voice that drove him wild, "'tis what a man enjoys, they said."

Enjoyed, wanted, desired. "Aye," he forced out, amazed he managed to shove out a word. He cleared his throat. "But I am too close to losing control."

"Nor did you allow me to make conditions when you took me a moment ago." A satisfied smile touched her mouth. "Nae that I am complaining."

She had a point. "Still—"

Alesone's tongue again ran over his hard length.

He shuddered.

"I have found you a fair man. I canna believe you would deny me what you yourself have done."

"'Tisna the same."

"I think 'tis." She drew him into her mouth, and his entire body tightened as her mouth tasted, teased until his every shred of control threatened to break. But he held, struggled to honor her request nae to deny her as she touched him.

Sweat beaded his brow as she lingered, her hands working with gentle strokes as her tongue offered sweet torture. Bloody hell, 'twas only so much a man could take.

Alesone's eyes widened with surprise as he flipped her beneath him, pressed his tip against her moistness. "I thought 'twas my turn."

"You will have many opportunities in the future," he said between clenched teeth. "Now, I canna wait any longer." He claimed her mouth, the spicy taste of their lovemaking warm on her tongue, and he savored, teasing her until her body grew restless against his. Damning the inevitable, Thomas lifted his head. "'Twill hurt, for that I am sorry."

Her expression grew tender. "I am a healer. I well understand."

"I know but…"

"Love me, Thomas. You are all that I want, all that I will ever need." Before he could move, she arched against him, until his length pressed against her thin barrier.

Need stormed him, threatened to unravel his hard won control. She began to rock against him, and his last fragile hold shattered. He plunged deep.

Alesone cried out.

He drew her against him. "Never did I wish to hurt you."

"'Tis nature, and the pain has all but faded," she whispered, a smile in her voice. "You feel wonderful."

Aching at the rightness of this moment, he caught her mouth in a tender kiss, teased her until she moved restlessly against his, and then he began move in slow, steady strokes. When Alesone's body tightened around him, he drove deep and took her over the edge, and followed.

Happier than he'd ever believed possible, Thomas drew Alesone against him. "I love you."

Lavender eyes held his, the warmth within leaving him humbled. "I love you as well."

Hours later, in the flickering firelight, Thomas slid a damp tendril of hair from Alesone's cheek as she watched him, her face glowing after making love. Never had she looked more beautiful. He pressed a kiss upon her brow. "Wait here."

She frowned as he sat. "What are you doing?"

Thomas set another log onto the fire before moving to his chest. Anticipation filled him as he withdrew a pouch and walked over.

Naked, she sat.

Lauding his ability to nae take her again, he walked over and handed her the velvet sack embroidered with the king's seal.

She arched a brow, opened the luxurious bag, and withdrew the item bound in silk. With care, she loosened the ties.

Cradled within the luxurious bed lay a ruby ring embraced by a gold filigree carving of a lion.

Surprise widened her eyes, and then she frowned. "'Tis the ring King Robert gave Grisel."

"Aye. The Bruce wanted you to have this. He said if ever you needed his aid, you are to bring this to him."

Tears filled her eyes. "I-I canna believe he would remember me or offer such."

"You are an incredible woman, one a man doesna forget." Thomas lifted the crafted circle, secured it on the chain around her neck, and then laid her back. "One who I am proud will be my wife."

Heat swept Alesone's eyes as she sat on the dais next to Thomas while they broke their fast. The hours they'd made love throughout the night left her yearning for when she could touch him again.

"You arena hungry?" the duke asked.

Embarrassed to be caught lost in thought about her night's forbidden sensual excursion, heat swept her cheeks. "Excuse me?"

The duke frowned. "You havena touched your porridge."

She forced herself eat, but caught Thomas's sated smile as he devoured his last few bites. Smug with himself he was, but memories of how he'd trembled as she'd loved him assured her that once they were alone, his satisfaction would crumble to ecstasy beneath her touch, a time she looked forward to.

The keep door opened, and Sir Nicholai entered, looking harried.

Alesone's stomach dropped. God help us, what had happened?

Thomas, the duke, and his brother stood, and she followed suit as the Brother rushed forward.

"What is wrong?" Thomas asked as his friend halted paces away.

"Your Grace," Nicholai said, and then faced Thomas. "I bear news of great import. I must speak with you and"—his gaze shifted to her—"Mistress Alesone in private."

Thomas slid his arm around her in a protective manner. "We will go into the solar." Nerves jangling, Alesone followed the men inside. Sunlight filled the room as she stepped inside, and a fire blazed in the hearth, but neither eased the chill deep inside.

The monk shut the door.

"Tell me," she stated.

The brother nodded. "'Tis Burunild MacCheine."

Confused, she frowned. "My mother's personal maid?"

"Aye, she is dying and has been trying to find you."

Alesone glanced at Thomas, then met Nicholai's gaze. "Why would she look for me? I havena seen her since I was seven."

The Brother's mouth tightened. "'Tis her place to explain."

"Where is she?" Alesone asked.

"Waiting for you at the monastery."

She nodded. "Then let us go."

* * *

Hours later tears burned Alesone's eyes as she stared at the elder who'd been her mother's personal maid, a woman who'd dared visit her at Grisel's and had brought treats to make her smile. To see her now, her face sunken with illness, and fighting for every breath broke Alesone's heart.

"Sit, child," the elder wheezed.

Thomas held her hand as she sat; Brother Nicholai remained discreetly by the door.

Grief darkened the woman's gaze as aged fingers lay atop Alesone's. "I am deeply shamed that I never told you, but I was—" She began to cough, and waved Alesone away when she made to help. "I must finish." She dragged in a fragile breath. "I was afraid. If you could find it in y-your heart, I beg your forgiveness."

The slide of unease rolled through her. "I forgive you."

"I pray you will feel the same when I am finished" Bony fingers tightened on Alesone's hand. "He made me swear never to tell you," she whispered, "threatened to kill me and my family if I did." The elder tsked. "A coward I was. I didna do what was right, a sin I carried all these years. With my husband dead, and my sons died in battle, and my own life f-fading, there is naught left for me to lose."

Bile rose in Alesone's throat. "Who threatened you?"

A tear slid down her wrinkled cheek. "Lord Comyn."

That made little sense. "Why would my father threaten you?"

"Because," she said on a fragile breath, "he isna your father."

Chapter Twenty-One

Betrayal and fury hazing her mind, the chair scraped as Alesone shoved to her feet. "What!"

"Please—" Coughs wracked the elderly maid's body as she struggled for a breath.

Nicholai stepped over and laid his hand on Alesone's shoulder. "Let her finish. Please."

Outrage blurred Alesone's mind at the falsehood she'd believed her entire life, at the shame she'd endured for having been branded as a bastard when the entire time it had been a lie. She gave a curt nod, wanting to scream at the injustice.

Through broken whispers and several fits of coughing, the elder explained how Alesone's mother had become pregnant shortly before her husband had departed for a crusade, and so he'd never known."

"My father never knew I was his child?" Alesone whispered.

The elder shook her head. "Nay. You are of noble birth. At the time, Lord Comyn had worried over your father's growing influence and the respect he held among the nobles. Fearful of his growing power, Comyn wanted to destroy him. Aware your father was a man of pride, one who loved his wife deeply, Comyn devised a plan to shame your mother and destroy their marriage, and in the end, your father."

Stunned, Alesone listened, thankful as Thomas gave her hand a gentle squeeze. "After you were born, your mother had a tragic accident, fell, and died. Because you were born late, more than nine months after your father departed, Comyn caused vicious rumors to spread that in secret he and your mother had become lovers, and ashamed of her infidelity, she'd committed suicide."

"'Tis all a lie," Alesone whispered, embracing the words as joy poured through her, cleansing her soul.

"Aye," the maid whispered. "I wanted to tell you, but terrified of the threat to my family I remained silent. When your father returned three years later to find his wife dead, he was told that you had been born too late for him to have been your father. Hearing rumors of your mother's unfaithfulness with a man he'd once considered a friend, he confronted Comyn. A bitter row ensued. No one knew what exact words were passed, but furious, your father cursed Comyn as he strode from his keep, took his belongings, and left."

Left believing his daughter was a bastard. Alesone swallowed hard. All these years, weighted beneath the shame of her mother's actions, she'd learned naught of her birthright except the pittance that her father was a noble. Now to discover that she was legitimate, she yearned to know more about her father. Had he remarried? Did she have half brothers or sisters out there?

Alesone braced herself. "Who is he?"

Sadness weighted the elder's gaze. "Petrus Buchan, Earl of Kinlock."

"Nae Alesone MacNiven, but Buchan." Warmth filled her as the name sifted through her mind, and then she gasped.

"What is wrong?" Thomas asked.

"The noble with the Bruce the night he called us to his tent was the Earl of Kinlock." Except her father didna know the truth. When he learned his wife had remained faithful, would he want Alesone? Unsure of anything, she swallowed hard. "Where is he?"

"Hopefully en route," the elder replied. "With Brother Nicholai's help, I have sent him a missive explaining everything, including where you are. I canna tell you how each day I regretted you nae knowing, despised myself for how you were shunned."

"Which is why you visited me often during my youth."

"Aye, and because I loved you." Tenderness warmed her face. "You have the look of your mother, and the spirit of your father. I know when he meets you, he will be so proud of you. I—" Her body began to tremble, and she again began to cough.

Alesone caught the elder's hand.

"Forgive me," the elder whispered, "please."

Tears rolled down Alesone's cheeks. "I do."

Relief sifted in the woman's eyes, and she smiled, slowly, until her entire face settled into a wash of peace. "I thank you." Her eyes turned toward the cross on the wall, and she gave one last exhale.

A sob tore through Alesone, and Thomas drew her against his chest.

With quiet steps, Nicholai walked over and closed the elder's eyes. "I will ensure she receives a proper burial."

Emotions storming her, Alesone met his gaze. "I want to be there. She deserves to be honored. Burunild was as tormented by Comyn's treachery as I."

The monk nodded. "Word will be sent when all is prepared."

Outside the chamber, Alesone shook her head. "All this time 'twas naught but a lie." She stilled. "God in heaven!"

"What?" Thomas asked.

A weight lifted off her soul as joy swept through her. "With her confession, I am free. Lord Comyn canna use me to barter with France's king, and," she said with satisfaction, "willna King Philip be furious when he learns the truth?"

Thomas grinned. "Bruce will *ensure* the news reaches France's sovereign."

"And," she said, her voice rough, "I have a father, one of whom I can be proud."

"Once the Earl of Kinlock reads the missive, he will come." Thomas drew her to him. "I was wanting to marry you posthaste. Now we will wait until your father arrives and can give his beautiful daughter away."

* * *

"And do you, Thomas MacKelloch, Earl of Kincaid, take Alesone Elyne Buchan to be your lawful wedded wife?" Nicholai asked.

Love filled Thomas as he looked at the woman whom he loved with all his heart. "I do." Cheers rose within the great hall as he sealed his vow with a kiss. Amidst the roar of approval, he and Alesone turned toward the crowd and drew.

"May I present my wife, Lady Alesone MacKelloch," Thomas announced.

Yells of approval again filled the chamber, and well-wishers rushed forward to offer their congratulations.

The Earl of Kinlock stepped before his daughter. "The eve I saw you at the Bruce's encampment, you looked so familiar. Now I understand why." A tender smile touched his mouth. "You resemble your beautiful mother. King Robert said you were an extraordinary woman, and I am anxious to learn more. There is so much to discuss, so much time to make up, but nae on your wedding day."

Alesone sniffed. "I look forward to getting to know you as well. My humble thanks for being here to give me away."

"I wouldna have missed this day, and I wish you every happiness." Her father's assessing gaze cut to Thomas. "Our king speaks of you with high praise, a fact that bodes well in my eyes. But, if you make my daughter unhappy, 'twill be me you answer to."

"I swear that I will cherish her always." Nor would he mention that Alesone needed little aid holding her own. "You are always welcome within our home."

Satisfaction glinted in his eyes as the earl stepped back, and the crowd of well-wishers rushed forward with congratulations.

* * *

A short while later, Thomas stood with his Templar warriors, still stunned by his father's gift of his mother's book of drawings and stories. He would cherish it always. He downed the last of his wine.

"I am happy for you, Thomas," Aiden MacConnell said. "Alesone is a beautiful lass, but a woman and a family are nae my desire. I prefer the life of a warrior."

Cailin scoffed. "One day, Aiden, you may meet a lass who will turn your head."

"After the battles I have fought," Aiden scoffed, "I doubt one simple lass will ever present a challenge."

A smile touched Stephan MacQuistan's eyes as he glanced at Thomas.

Thomas returned his friend's grin, remembering how months ago when they'd fled France he'd believed the same. Then he, as Stephan, had found love. His gazed shifted to Alesone, and warmth filled him. Aye he'd enjoyed celebrating with friends, but hours had passed since he'd made love to his beautiful wife, and he'd wait nay longer. "I will see you in the morn."

"As if you will get any sleep," Aiden teased.

Thomas winked. "I didna say that I had planned to rest."

His men laughed, but Thomas ignored them and focused on the woman he loved, the woman who would forever hold his heart. He wove through the throng, and pulled her against him. "Come away with me," he whispered in her ear. "I want to run my tongue over every naked inch of you."

A wicked sensual light shimmered in her eyes. "I think turnaround is fair play," she replied, her voice low, "except this time when I take you in my mouth, I willna show mercy."

The air left him in a rush as his body went up in flames. He tugged her with him and hurried toward the turret. "I am counting on it."

With a laugh, she bolted up the steps. Thomas followed, thankful for this woman in his life, one he adored, and one he would love forever.

Keep reading for a sneak peek at
FORBIDDEN VOW
The next in the Forbidden Series
Coming soon from
Diana Cosby
and
Lyrical Books

Chapter One

Scotland, August 1308

A hawk screeched overhead as Sir Aiden MacConnell wiped the sweat from his brow. He noted his men's positions, then scoured the uneven ground, smothered with summer dried grass and rocks, to the edge of the forest.

Blast it! Where was the enemy warrior bearing Lord Comyn's colors?

How had he missed the knight's approach a short while before? He'd double-checked the clearing, had heard naught but the rustle of wind tossed leaves—except when he and his men had slipped from the shield of trees, Comyn's man had ridden into view.

As he'd spotted them, eyes wide with terror, the rider had whirled his mount and fled.

Aiden had noted the blood smearing the man's chest, and how, as he'd galloped into the woods, his body had slumped over the steed's neck.

By God they must find the warrior before he could warn Comyn of their presence. With Latharn Castle's treacherous cliff-side location, the details he and his men could learn of the fortress were crucial in the Bruce's preparations for the upcoming attack.

If they could find a way inside…Nay doubt he could discover the enemy's weakness, perhaps strength of numbers, and more that would aid his king. If only he could find the injured knight.

A cool breeze rich with the scent of rain buffeted him. Aiden glanced north. He scowled at the rain-thickened clouds smothering the roll of hills. They had to find the man before a downpour washed away his tracks.

He scoured the rough slide of land tattered with clumps of brush for any sign of the knight, convinced the warrior who'd galloped away didna travel alone. With Scotland at war only a fool rode without an escort.

Near several large boulders, the land cut away, but he stared at the swath of red staining the edge of one of the rocks.

Blood.

Aiden waved his two friends over, pointed to where clumps of rock disappeared from view. "He must be hiding down the brae. Rónán, circle around to the right. Cailin, you come in from the left. Once in place await my command."

His men nodded, then slipped into the dense foliage.

Dagger in his hand, Aiden crept through the brush. Below, through the break in the rocks, a bay munched on sun bleached grass, his reins dragging on the ground.

A moan sounded further down the embankment.

Aiden motioned for his knights to hold. Weapon readied, he edged around the shield of stone. As the bank began a steep decline, he squatted, his gaze narrowing on the prone form.

Through the summer-burnt shafts swaying in the breeze lay the armored knight. Blood smeared his mail, and one of his legs lay twisted in an awkward shape.

After another thorough search of his surroundings, confident the warrior was alone, Aiden stood and stepped closer. The dying man looked familiar, but Aiden had left the Highlands too many years ago to remember his name.

He scanned the bastard's mail bearing Comyn's colors.

Eyes dark with pain focused on him, grew wary. "To whom do you swear your loyalty?" the man rasped.

His gut tightened. "'Tis to Comyn," Aiden replied. With the man's obvious loyalty and this deep within enemy territory, he'd be a fool to state otherwise.

"Thank God. W-When I saw you, I thought you were with Robert the Bruce." The stranger gave a rough cough and then sagged back. "Early this morning, my co-contingent was attacked by his forces."

"God's sword, are they near?" he asked, needing the noble to believe him nae a threat.

"I think I lost them, but I canna be sure." Wracking coughs shook his body, and a drizzle of blood slid from his mouth.

Aiden knelt beside him, took in the deep sword slashes along his neck. 'Twas incredible he still lived.

Face ashen, the stranger grabbed Aiden's arm. "Y-You must swear to help me."

Help him? With the man's loyalty to Comyn, Aiden would rather drive a dirk into his heart and end his miserable life. Aiden took in his finely crafted armor, stilled. Few could afford mail of such quality. Whoever he was, the man wasna a simple knight. Mayhap the warrior held sensitive information valuable to the Bruce? "What can I do?"

Hand trembling, the man withdrew a sealed writ, set the missive into Aiden's hands. "D-Deliver this to Lady Gwendolyn Murphy of Latharn Castle. Warn her that the enemy is near." Grief-stricken eyes held his. "We were to marry. Tell her…Tell her that I am sorry to have failed her."

Aiden's throat tightened as he glanced at the rolled parchment, the enormity of the man's disclosure pounding in his chest. Latharn Castle; his and his men's destination. He refocused on the wounded knight. "I would need your name to tell your betrothed."

"Bróccín MacRaith, Earl of Balfour," the man whispered.

Aiden's throat constricted. "Of Gilcrest Castle?"

"Aye."

Memories rolled through Aiden of the numerous occasions in his youth of how they'd sparred and hunted along with the first time they'd tasted mead. Except their friendship was long ago, and everything had changed.

Nay longer was he an innocent lad with dreams of war and victory in his head. Over the years with in his service to the Knights Templar, he'd seen enough bloodshed, and had witnessed too many of his friend's die.

"I will have your name," Bróccín demanded.

"Aiden MacConnell, Earl of Lennox." He swallowed hard. The truth mattered little now.

Recognition flared in the man's eyes, replaced by sadness. "After the terrible tragedy of your family, I-I never thought to see you again."

Ice slid through his veins at the mention of his family. He shoved the unwanted thought aside. "Nor I you." Aiden nodded to the writ. "I give you my word, I will deliver the missive to Lady Gwendolyn."

"I thank you. 'Twas a blessing that you found me." Another shudder raked his body. "After all of these years, I canna believe 'tis you. We-We had so many dreams, did we nay?"

Aiden forced a smile. "Aye, foolish ones. Dreams of lads."

"They were." Bróccín coughed.

His face twisted in pain, the knight settled back, and Aiden helped him take a sip of water. "I will tend to you as best—"

"Dinna. My fate is sealed."

However much he wished to assure the man otherwise, neither would Aiden lie. "More water?"

"Nay." More blood bubbled from the man's mouth. "In truth," he forced out, "I have never met my betrothed, but 'tis rumored the lass is a beauty. With the stories I have heard—" He coughed and blood slid down to his chin. "I was anxious to bed her."

Cold seeped through Aiden at thought of any woman weakening him to where he'd think of little else but her. His life was dedicated to God and war, nae the luxuries of the flesh. He laid his hand on Bróccín's shoulder. "I will tell her what a fine man you were."

"I thank you." The noble shuddered again, and then gasped. His eyes grew fixed.

With the flickering images of his youth fading, Aiden closed his lids. Mouth set, he stood, found his men approaching.

"Is he dead?" Cailin asked.

Aiden nodded. "His name was Bróccín MacRaith, Earl of Balfour. Incredibly, long ago we were friends. Now, unknown to him, 'twould seem we are enemies."

"A Comyn supporter," Rónán said with a grimace. "A bloody shame."

"'Tis the way of war." Aiden shoved his sadness behind his carefully built wall, having lost too many friends throughout the years to allow the hurt to burrow deeper. "Yet, he has presented us an unexpected opportunity. Twould seem the earl was betrothed to Lady Gwendolyn Murphy and was en route to marry her."

Cailin arched a curious brow. "What has a wedding to do with our gaining information for the king's upcoming attack on Latharn Castle?"

"The lady in question," Aiden replied with a wry smile, "is the stronghold's mistress."

Rónán frowned. "'Tis a most unusual coincidence, but that knowledge does nay much to aid us."

"It wouldna," Aiden agreed, "except before he died, the noble admitted that he hadna meet the lass before."

Cailin's eyes widened. "God's blade, you are nae thinking of taking his place?"

The thrill of the unknown filled him, and Aiden clung to the danger, a way of life he thrived upon. "I am," he replied. "I swore to deliver this betrothal writ, a promise I shall keep. Except as the lass has never met Bróccín MacRaith, 'twill be a simple task to play the part of her suitor for a few days. Once we have the information we need, we will slip away and share with King Robert all we have learned."

"We?" Rónán asked.

"Aye," Aiden said with flourish, enjoying crafting the story. "The Earl of Balfour and two of his stalwart knights escaped the ruthless attack of King Robert's men."

A frown deepened in Rónán's brow. "A brilliant plan, except your memories of the earl were those of a lad. You didna know the man, or if his betrothed was accepting of the betrothal, nae to mention if anyone at the castle might have known him."

Aiden shrugged. "I have heard that the earl is a warrior to fear, and that knowledge will suffice for the meager time we will remain at the stronghold. Other concerns are nothing against the information we can glean of the castle's defenses. Details that against an otherwise impenetrable fortress, will assure our king a swift victory."

"And what of the lass?" Cailin asked. "With her anticipating marriage, she will expect a courtship."

"A task that will be naught but a minor distraction," Aiden said. "Before Bróccín died, he confessed that the lass is fair to look upon."

Rónán chuckled. "Wooing her might be a pleasant diversion."

Far from amused at the jest, Aiden lowered his hands to his side. "My intent is to gain information for our king, naught more," Aiden snapped. "Though the Knights Templar are secretly dissolved, my allegiance remains with the Brotherhood."

The humor in his men's eyes fled. "Never will I forgive King Philip's treachery," Cailin said.

Rónán gave a curt nod. "Nor I."

The French king's duplicity burned in Aiden's gut. The bastard had betrayed the Templars. The knights had guarded him over the years, loyalty he'd rewarded with deceit. Almost a year had passed since Aiden and the other Templars had sailed from La Rochelle, yet each time he thought of the French sovereign's treachery, fury blackened his soul.

He glanced at the muscled knights at his side, men who he'd fought alongside in many a battle, Templars who he would give his life to protect. "We will map the layout of the castle grounds, take stock of stores, the number of guards, and other details imperative to plan a successful attack."

"Mayhap," Cailin said, "we can discover a secret entry."

The twisting in Aiden's gut eased. "Aye. I find it hard to believe that a hidden tunnel doesna exist, and I am convinced my *betrothed* would know of it."

"What will happen to the lass once our king seizes her stronghold?" Rónán asked.

Aiden shrugged. "If she is as beautiful as Bróccín claimed, 'twill be a simple task for King Robert to find a nobleman willing to wed her.

"Mayhap the lass will have an admirable spirit that will catch the king's notice," Cailin said with a smile, "and like Stephan and Thomas, our sovereign will guide you down a wedding path."

"With the demands on the king's time," Aiden said, his voice cool, "I doubt he will meet Lady Gwendolyn much longer than to learn her name and decide upon an appropriate match." Refusing to entertain the topic further, he stowed the writ, then glanced to his dead friend. "We bury Bróccín, then ride to Latharn Castle."

* * *

Wind thick with the scent of the sea whipped against Lady Gwendolyn Murphy. She aimed her dagger, threw.

Thunk.

A deep chuckle sounded to her right. "I dinna think your betrothed would be praising your skill, my lady."

"As if I care what he thinks." She glanced at the well-armed knight leaning against a nearby rock. At the humor in her friend's eyes, she took in the rough charcoal outline of a man on the nearby sun-bleached limb, her blade lodged in the center of the crudely shaded heart.

"I know you are upset with Lord Comyn's dictate to marry," Sir Pieres continued, "but with the Earl of Balfour occupied with the upkeep of his numerous holdings, as well as his strategic meetings along with combat for your liege lord, 'tis said he is often away."

Scowling Gwendolyn walked over and jerked her blade free. "If I didna need Comyn's guard, I would keep the gates barred and deny the earl entry."

"If you wish, that could be arranged."

The lazy teasing in her friend's voice prodded a smile. "You would do that for me, would you nae?"

Pieres's expression grew serious. "My lady, I would give my life to protect you."

Humbled, she shook her head. "Nor would I ask such."

Eyes dark with concern, he walked over. "'Tis said your betrothed is a hard man, one feared by many, but those beneath his command give him their respect."

She smothered the roll of nerves. "And you tell me this because?"

"You need truth, nay wisps of fancy. That the Earl of Balfour earns respect from his men indicates however strict his rule, he is fair and his dictates given with reason. His success in battle along with the praise earned from Lord Comyn reflects his cunning as a warrior."

She gave a curt nod.

"My lady, Lord Balfour is a man of war and willna tolerate defiance on any level." Expression grim, he paused. "With your headstrong ways, I ask that you tread with care. You could do far worse."

"A warning?" Furious he'd feel the situation warranted such, or that the time had come in her life where she'd need such advice, she stalked to where she'd drawn a line in the sand; turned; threw. A chunk of the charcoal stained heart tore free as the dagger sank deep. "I am nae a fool."

"Nay. You are a woman whom any man would be blessed to have as their wife, but sadly, many nobles dinna want anything from a woman beyond an heir."

She again jerked her weapon free. "I willna be cast aside in my own castle, treated as if I were naught but a scullery maid fit only for the bedding. I need no husband."

Sir Pieres remained silent, the worry in his gaze easy to read.

Frustrated, she sheathed her dagger, turned toward the waves sliding up the shore to toss about stones and shells within the tangled rush. Water sloshed against her boots as if laying siege, like the intruder whom she would pledge her life.

Bedamn this entire situation! "If only I could think of a way to convince him to nae wed."

Firm steps crunched on the sand. Pieres paused at her side. "There isna."

The exasperation in his voice matched her own. "I know." She wanted to scream at the injustice of losing her home to a stranger. In the weeks since the writ had arrived announcing her betrothal, she had tried to think of a way, often with Pieres's aid, of negating the union, and at every turn, had failed.

With her heart in her throat, Gwendolyn picked up a fragment of shell abandoned by the sea. She weighed the fragile piece in her hand as the damnable frustrations all but smothered her. "Over the years my father would bring me here and tell me of his dreams, or talk about mine. He never laughed at what I shared, but encouraged me to achieve any goal that I could envision."

"He was an extraordinary man."

"Aye, he was." Emotion welled in her throat, and she fought the swell of grief. "W-When my mother died during my youth," she breathed, "'twas here that my father consoled me, and years later, where he asked me to marry Lord Purcell to strengthen our bonds with our neighboring clan."

Pieres's mouth tightened. "Your father was wrong to have forced you into a marriage, more so to a man who was a fool to nae notice what an incredible woman you are."

The soft fury in his voice left her humbled. Her fingers curled against the memories of how she pushed away his tender advances since their childhood. However much she'd wished otherwise, never had she felt more than friendship, nor would she dishonor him by offering him false hope. She prayed one day he would find a woman who could give him the love he deserved.

"And 'twas on this stretch of sand," Pieres continued, drawing her from her musings, "that you learned of your husband's death but a month after you had wed."

She grimaced. "I was foolish enough to believe that I would never again have to marry a man for duty. With my father's blessing, I believed that I could live the life I wished." Anger twisted inside, and Gwendolyn gave a cold laugh. "Yet with my father's death, I have once again become naught but chattel."

"I am sorry."

Mouth tight, Gwendolyn cast the fragment into the incoming wave. The battered shell that'd once held life tumbled beneath the current and was swept out to sea. Like the shell, she was merely a pawn to those who held power.

"I will do my duty and wed Lord Balfour," she said, "for my people's protection along with that of my home, but I willna tolerate being treated as a half-wit." She started toward the castle. "'Tis time I checked on Kellan."

Pieres said as he fell in alongside. "With her girth, I would have thought she would have foaled by now?"

"As I. This morning I found her pacing in her stall. I expect the colt will come this day."

Warmth touched her as she started toward the cave accessible only during low tide, remembering when the coal-black mare was born, and of how her father had gifted her with the steed. Now Kellan would have a babe of her own.

"I want to be with her when her foal is born," she said. "I wish my father was alive. I—"

She stumbled, and Pieres caught her, turned her toward him. "I am here."

"I know," she said with a rough whisper, thankful for his friendship. "I still struggle with his death even though half a year has passed."

"A horrible day," her friend said, his words quiet, "but he died a warrior's death fighting for—"

A horse's neigh sounded in the distance.

The slide of steel upon leather hissed as Sir Pieres withdrew his sword. "Hurry inside the secret tunnel."

Gwendolyn removed her dagger, far from convinced. "If there was danger, we would have heard warning shouts from the castle guards." She scanned the lull of land and rock above that led to the castle's entrance.

Three riders came into sight.

Relief flooded Gwendolyn. A larger force would ride beneath the Earl of Balfour's standard.

The trio of riders halted before the gate.

Even from this distance, she noted the lead warrior. Broad shoulders. Confident. A shiver of unease rippled through her.

"Do you think 'tis your betrothed?"

She shook her head. "The writ stated the earl would arrive with a sizable contingent of men. I suspect 'tis but knights traveling through."

A faint echo of a man's voice reached her.

A guard's voice rang out. A clank sounded, then the slow rattle of the portcullis.

Gwendolyn relaxed. Whatever the traveler had shared with her guard, they werena a threat.

A frown tightened on her lips as she rushed toward the secret tunnel. With King Robert's determination to unite Scotland, how many years would pass before their country found peace? She damned the war, the struggle for power that claimed too many innocent lives.

She inhaled to settle her nerves, then focused on the upcoming birth of her prize mare. "I wish the groom was here was here. 'Tis Kellan's first foal, and 'twould ease me to know she is in Edmund's competent hands."

Inside the cave, Pieres lit a candle. Golden light cut through the blackness, the walls slick with moisture drenched moss, and the sandy path scattered with wave-smoothed pebbles.

He raised the taper, started down the tunnel. "MacDuf has observed Edmund many times as he helped to ease a mare's birthing process."

"He has. But a few months studying beneath Edmund's skilled guidance hardly gives MacDuf the expertise he needs."

A short while later the smell of hay and horse filled the air as Gwendolyn stepped into the stable.

Pieres slid the hidden entry shut behind them, nodded. "I will check on who has arrived."

"I thank you." Afternoon sunlight flickered over her friend's shoulders as he entered the baily.

A snort sounded from the corner stall.

Warmth spilled through her at thoughts of the newborn foal, and she hurried over. "How fares Kellan?"

"She has begun birthing," MacDuf replied.

At the worry in the stable hand's voice, her chest tightened. She slipped inside the stall.

Heavy with foal, the mare trudged around the stall, her laden steps cushioned beneath the bed of straw. She nickered, half collapsed to her side, rolled, then shoved back to her feet and once more paced.

"Easy girl," Gwendolyn soothed as she stroked the coal-black beauty's velvety muzzle. "How long has she been acting like this?"

MacDuf rubbed the back of his neck. "A short while after you left."

The mare tossed her head and half reared. As her feet hit the floor, her entire body shook. On a whinny, she again dropped to her knees, fell to one side, and then rolled.

"There should be some sign that the foal is coming by now," MacDuf said, his voice raw with worry. "I…I fear the foal is turned around inside her."

Ice slid through Gwendolyn's veins. She fisted her hands against the horrific stories of a mare's screams as she suffered during a difficult foaling, of the loss of blood, trauma that could leave the mother and foal dead.

Male voices echoed from the stable entry, but she ignored them and damned her lack of knowledge, a fact she would remedy after this day. "Surely Edmund has attended such difficult births in the past?" she forced out.

A ruddy hue swept the man's face. "Aye," the stable hand agreed, "but none after he began instructing me."

There had to be a way to help her! Anger at her helplessness nearly strangled Gwendolyn as she knelt beside the horse. Hand trembling, she stroked her sweat slicked neck. *Please God, dinna let her die.*

The mare snorted, kicked.

Gwendolyn ducked the slash of hooves, terrified as the mare again began to squeal in distress. "Fetch the healer. Delivering a foal canna be any more different than a babe."

"Aye, my lady." Steps slapped as MacDuf bolted toward the keep.

On a tormented scream, the horse tried to struggle to her feet, collapsed. Froth slid from her ebony coat.

Tears burned Gwendolyn's eyes at her each snort, her whinny of distress.

The hooves of the horse again slashed, missing her by a hand.

An ache built in her chest as she reached over to try and relax the mare. "The healer will be here—"

Behind her the gate scraped open. "Get away from her," a deep voice ordered.

Stunned at the harsh command, Gwendolyn glanced up.

A hulking man with raven black hair towered above her. His green eyes riveted on her with unyielding authority. "Move!"

She slammed her brows together. "I willna—"

With a muttered curse, the stranger hauled her up, and shoved her aside. "Cailin, Rónán, help me get the mare on her feet!"

Shaking with outrage, Gwendolyn elbowed her way past the two burly knights and glared up at the beast. "How dare you—"

"We are trying to save her life," he growled in fierce warning as he shifted to the horse's chest. The warrior's muscled arms bulged as he and his men worked in unison to shove the mare to her feet. Inhaling, he glared at Gwendolyn. "If you want to be useful, lass, go stand by her head and talk to her while I deliver the foal."

Shaking with anger at the braggart, she straightened her shoulders, her fists curling at her sides, then stilled at the deftness of his actions, and his quick decisions. Whoever he was, he knew what he was about.

"I have the foal's foot," he called a moment later.

Kellan screamed a strangled nicker then shifted.

The formidable stranger's mouth tightened. "Keep the mare still!"

Hooves scraped across the bed of straw. On a strangled whinny, Kellan started to step back.

"God's sword, hold her!" the fierce warrior roared.

Muscles flexed as his men complied.

Distant footsteps slapped upon the dirt.

Gwendolyn glanced out the entry to see the healer and MacDuf running across the baily toward them.

"'Tis done," the stranger called out. "Let her go."

She turned as he laid the newborn on the hay.

His men stepped away.

On a soft nicker, the mare nuzzled her foal. Coal black like his mother, and the proud lines of his sire. On spindly legs the colt shoved to his feet.

Tenderness filled her as the mare nickered at her son, nudged him to suckle. Tears burned her eyes at the miracle before her, of how within but moments she'd witnessed life. She swallowed hard. "He shall be called Faolán," she whispered as MacDuf halted beside her.

"Wolf, aye," the stable hand said, head nodding in eager agreement, "'tis a fine name."

The healer stopped at the stall's entry, her face flushed and her breaths coming fast. As her gaze landed on the foal, aged eyes wrinkled with pleasure. "It looks like you dinna need me to rush over and help after all."

Her words a stark reminder of the strangers, Gwendolen shook her head. "Nay, but I thank you for hurrying."

As the elder departed, Gwendolyn studied the imposing man who had dared to take charge. Under ordinary circumstance, he would receive a tongue lashing for his bold manner. Except he'd saved the foal, and possibly the mother's life.

Her fingers trembled as she handed him a nearby cloth. "It seems," she said, "that I owe you my thanks."

A scowl marred the muscled knight's handsome face as he wiped his hands. "Why was she unattended when she was clearly in distress?"

His two knights moved to the man's side.

Refusing to be intimidated, she glared at the daunting stranger. Of all the audacity! 'Twas her castle they stood in. She refused to justify anything to this arrogant man. "I owe you nay explanations."

He tossed then stained cloth aside. "Aye. That you can give to the mistress of the castle."

Indeed. She angled her chin at the towering dolt. "Then," she said with cold authority, more than ready to take him down a well-deserved notch, "as mistress of Latharn Castle, I give you permission to speak."

Stunned disbelief flickered in the knight's eyes before he shuttered his expression. He gave a formal bow. "'Tis my pleasure to meet you, Lady Gwendolyn."

That she doubted. "And you are?" she prodded, ready to toss the boil brained lout out on his ear.

His fierce gaze leveled on her. "The Earl of Balfour, your betrothed."

A retired Navy Chief, AGC (AW), Diana Cosby is an international bestselling author of Scottish medieval romantic suspense. Diana has spoken at the Library of Congress, appeared at Lady Jane's Salon NYC, in *Woman's Day,* on *Texoma Living! Magazine, USA Today*'s romance blog, "Happily Ever After," and MSN.com.

After retiring from the navy, Diana dove into her passion—writing romance novels. With thirty-four moves behind her, she was anxious to create characters who reflected the amazing cultures and people she's met throughout the world. Diana looks forward to the years ahead of writing and meeting the amazing people who will share this journey.

Diana Cosby, International Bestselling Author

www.dianacosby.com

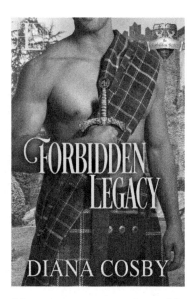

A betrothal neither wants . . . a passion neither can resist.

When the English murder Lady Katherine Calbraith's family, she refuses their demands to wed an English noble to retain her home. Avalon Castle is her birthright, one she's determined to keep. After Katherine's daring escape, she's stunned when Scotland's king agrees to allow her to return to Avalon, but under the protection of Sir Stephan MacQuistan . . . as the knight's wife. To reclaim her heritage, Katherine agrees. She accepts her married fate, certain that regardless of the caliber of the man, Stephan may earn her trust, but he'll never win her love.

One of the Knights Templar, Stephan desires no bride, only vengeance for a family lost and a legacy stolen. A profound twist of fate tears apart the Brotherhood he loves, but offers him an opportunity to reclaim his legacy—Avalon Castle. Except to procure his childhood home along with a place to store Templar treasures, he must wed the unsuspecting daughter of the man who killed his family. To settle old scores, Stephan agrees, aware Katherine is merely a means to an end.

The passion that arises between them is as dangerous as it is unexpected. When mortal enemies find themselves locked in love's embrace, Stephan and Katherine must reconsider their mission and everything they once thought to be true . . .

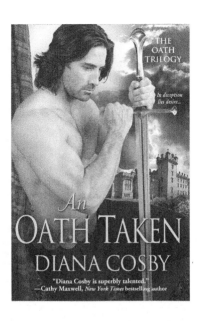

As the new castellan, Sir Nicholas Beringar has the daunting task of rebuilding Ravenmoor Castle on the Scottish border and gaining the trust of the locals—one of whom wastes no time in trying to rob him. Instead of punishing the boy, Nicholas decides to make him his squire. Little does he know the thieving young lad is really . . . a lady.

Lady Elizabet Armstrong had donned a disguise in an attempt to free her brother from Ravenmoor's dungeons. Although intimidated by the confident Englishman with his well-honed muscles and beguiling eyes, she cannot refuse his offer.

Nicholas senses that his new squire is not what he seems. His gentle attempts to break through the boy's defenses leave Elizabet powerless to stem the desire that engulfs her. And when the truth is exposed, she'll have to trust in Nicholas's honor to help her people—and to surrender to his touch . . .

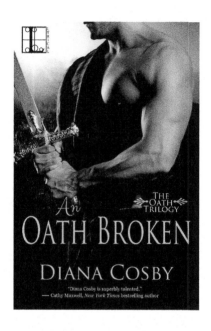

THE
OATH
TRILOGY

An
OATH BROKEN

DIANA COSBY

"Diana Cosby is superbly talented."
— Cathy Maxwell, *New York Times* bestselling author

Lady Sarra Bellacote would sooner marry a boar than a countryman of the bloodthirsty brutes who killed her parents. And yet, despite—or perhaps because of—her valuable holdings, she is being dragged to Scotland to be wed against her will. To complicate the desperate situation, the knight hired to do the dragging is dark, wild, irresistible. And he, too, is intolerably *Scottish.*

Giric Armstrong, Earl of Terrick, takes no pleasure in escorting a feisty English lass to her betrothed. But he needs the coin to rebuild his castle, and his tenants need to eat. Yet the trip will not be the simple matter he imagined. For Lady Sarra isn't the only one determined to see her engagement fail. Men with darker motives want to stop the wedding— even if they must kill the bride in the process.

Now, in close quarters with this beautiful English heiress, Terrick must fight his mounting desire, and somehow keep Sarra alive long enough to lose her forever to another man . . .

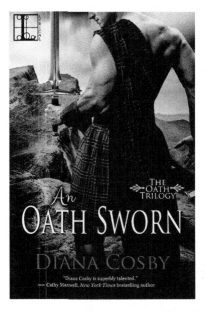

THE
OATH
TRILOGY

An
OATH SWORN

DIANA COSBY

"Diana Cosby is superbly talented."
— Cathy Maxwell, *New York Times* bestselling author

The bastard daughter of the French king, Marie Alesia Serouge has just one chance at freedom when she escapes her captor in the Scottish highlands. A mere pawn in a scheme to destroy relations between France and Scotland, Marie must reach her father and reveal the Englishman's treacherous plot. But she can't abandon the wounded warrior she stumbles upon—and she can't deny that his fierce masculinity, Scottish or not, stirs something wild inside her.

Colyne MacKerran is on a mission for his king, and he's well aware that spies are lying in wait for him everywhere. Wounded *en route*, he escapes his attackers and is aided by an alluring Frenchwoman...whose explanation for her presence in the Highlands rings false. Even if she saved his life, he cannot trust her with his secrets. But he won't leave her to the mercy of brigands, either—and as they race for the coast, he can't help but wonder if her kiss is as passionate as she is.

With nothing in common but their honor, Colyne and Marie face a dangerous journey to safety through the untamed Scottish landscape—and their own reckless hearts . . .

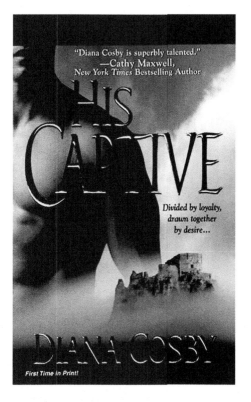

HIS CAPTIVE

Divided by loyalty,
drawn together
by desire...

DIANA COSBY

First Time in Print!

With a wastrel brother and a treacherous former fiancé, Lady Nichola Westcott hardly expects the dangerously seductive Scot who kidnaps her to be a man of his word. Though Sir Alexander MacGruder promises not to hurt her, Nichola's only value is as a pawn to be ransomed.

Alexander's goal is to avenge his father's murder, not to become entangled with the enemy. But his desire to keep Nichola with him, in his home—in his bed—unwittingly makes her a target for those who have no qualms about shedding English blood.

Now Nichola is trapped—by her powerful attraction to a man whose touch shakes her to the core. Unwilling and unable to resist each other, can Nichola and Alexander save a love that has enslaved them both?

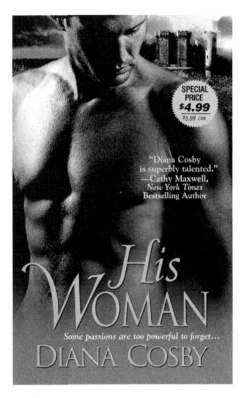

"Diana Cosby
is superbly talented."
—Cathy Maxwell,
New York Times
Bestselling Author

His
WOMAN

Some passions are too powerful to forget...

DIANA COSBY

Lady Isabel Adair is the last woman Sir Duncan MacGruder wants to see again, much less be obliged to save. Three years ago, Isabel broke their engagement to become the Earl of Frasyer's mistress, shattering Duncan's heart and hopes in one painful blow. But Duncan's promise to Isabel's dying brother compels him to rescue her from those determined to bring down Scottish rebel Sir William Wallace.

Betraying the man she loved was the only way for Isabel to save her father, but every moment she spends with Duncan reminds her just how much she sacrificed. No one could blame him for despising her, yet Duncan's misgivings cannot withstand a desire that has grown wilder with time. Now, on a perilous journey through Scotland, two wary lovers must confront both the enemies who will stop at nothing to hunt them down, and the secret legacy that threatens their passion and their lives . . .

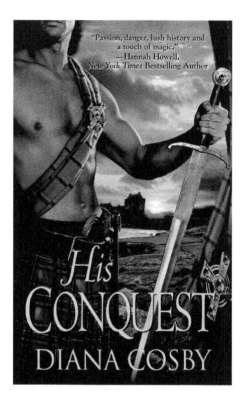

His
CONQUEST
DIANA COSBY

Linet Dancort will not be sold. But that's essentially what her brother
intends to do—to trade her like so much chattel to widen his already
vast scope of influence. Linet will seize any opportunity to escape her
fate—and opportunity comes in the form of a rebel prisoner locked in
her brother's dungeon, predatory and fearsome, and sentenced to hang
in the morning.

Seathan MacGruder, Earl of Grey, is not unused to cheating death.
But even this legendary Scottish warrior is surprised when a beautiful
Englishwoman creeps to his cell and offers him his freedom. What Linet
wants in exchange, though—safe passage to the Highlands—is a steep
price to pay. For the only thing more dangerous than the journey through
embattled Scotland is the desire that smolders between these two fugitives
the first time they touch . . .

DIANA COSBY

His **DESTINY**

"Medieval Scotland roars to life in this fabulous series."
—Pam Palmer, *New York Times* Bestselling Author

As one of England's most capable mercenaries, Emma Astyn can charm an enemy and brandish a knife with unmatched finesse. Assigned to befriend Dubh Duer, an infamous Scottish rebel, she assumes the guise of innocent damsel Christina Moffat to intercept the writ he's carrying to a traitorous bishop. But as she gains the dark hero's confidence and realizes they share a tattered past, compassion—and passion—distract her from the task at hand . . .

His legendary slaying of English knights has won him the name Dubh Duer, but Sir Patrik Cleary MacGruder is driven by duty and honor, not heroics. Rescuing Christina from the clutches of four such knights is a matter of obligation for the Scot. But there's something alluring about her fiery spirit, even if he has misgivings about her tragic history. Together, they'll endure a perilous journey of love and betrayal, and a harrowing fight for their lives . . .

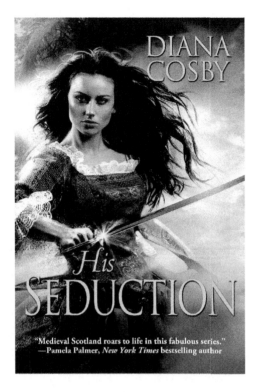

Lady Rois Drummond is fiercely devoted to her widowed father, the respected Scottish Earl of Brom. So when she believes he is about to be exposed as a traitor to England, she must think quickly. Desperate, Rois makes a shocking claim against the suspected accuser, Sir Griffin Westcott. But her impetuous lie leaves her in an outrageous circumstance: hastily married to the enemy. Yet Griffin is far from the man Rois thinks he is—and much closer to the man of her dreams . . .

Griffin may be an Englishman, but in truth he leads a clandestine life as a spy for Scotland. Refusing to endanger any woman, he has endured the loneliness of his mission. But Rois's absurd charge has suddenly changed all that. Now, with his cover in jeopardy, Griffin must find a way to keep his secret while keeping his distance from his spirited and tempting new wife—a task that proves more difficult than he ever imagined . . .

"Medieval Scotland roars to life in this fabulous series."
—Pamela Palmer, *New York Times* Bestselling Author

His ENCHANTMENT
The MacGruder Brothers

Lady Catarine MacLaren is a fairy princess, duty-bound to eschew the human world. But the line between the two realms is beginning to blur. English knights have launched an assault on the MacLarens, just as the families of Comyn have captured the Scottish king and queen. Now, Catarine is torn between loyalty to her people and helping the handsome, rust-haired Lord Trálin rescue the Scottish king . . .

As guard to King Alexander, Lord Trálin MacGruder will stop at nothing to defend the Scottish crown against the Comyns. And he finds a sympathetic, and gorgeous, ally in the enigmatic Princess Catarine. As they plot to rescue the kidnapped king and queen, Trálin and Catarine will discover a love made all but impossible by her obligations to the Otherworld. But a passion this extraordinary may be worth the irreversible sacrifices it demands . . .

Printed in Great Britain
by Amazon